SUSAN BRINKMANN

LIONESS LOST

A *CHRONICLES OF ARIELLA* NOVEL

FEMININE GENIUS

www.femininegenius.org

This is a work of fiction. Any names or characters, businesses or places,
events or incidents, are fictitious. Any resemblance to actual persons,
living or dead, or actual events is purely coincidental.

Design by Todd Detering

ISBN: 978-1-63582-561-9 (hardcover)
ISBN: 978-1-63582-557-2 (softcover)
ISBN: 978-1-63582-558-9 (eBook)

10   9   8   7   6   5   4   3   2   1

Printed in the United States of America

TABLE OF CONTENTS

AUTHOR'S NOTE

AS ENGAGING AS THIS STORY MAY BE, it's important for the reader to understand that it is not entirely fictional. Only the characters, locations, and plot are imagined. Everything else is true and based on fact. The New Age and occult activity described in these novels is based upon the documented testimony of Catholic exorcists and experts in the various disciplines associated with the study of New Age alternatives. The diverse tactics of the devil, manifestations of demonic entities, and the Satanic rituals used by the gang members is also based on real events. Although it might make for a thrilling read, this information is the result of two decades of serious research, first while serving as a reporter at the *Catholic Standard and Times* newspaper of the Archdiocese of Philadelphia, and then in my work under the leadership of Johnnette Williams of Women of Grace, the great early pioneer in the field of New Age research.

In addition, the history of the Church that is presented in the various novellas of Ariella's ancestors is also based upon real history as documented by historians such as Warren Carroll, Jay P. Dolan, and Eusebius, to name a few. The different eras in Church history that are represented in this series were carefully chosen to correlate to current issues in the Church today—the priest abuse scandal, the seemingly out-of-touch responses to social issues, bishops who cave to politics rather than defend the teachings of Christ, the ongoing problem of poor catechesis, and the impact of persecution upon the Suffering Church.

Also to be regarded as factual are the descriptions of the various types of prayer Ari experiences in the chapel. The anointings, infused states, and use of Scripture are all part of the Catholic mystical tradition as taught by the Carmelite doctors of the Church, St. Teresa of Avila, and St. John of the Cross.

Ari's discovery of these truths very much mirrors my own experience when reverting to Catholicism many years ago. Like her, I looked to the New Age and its Universal Mind for the kind of spiritual highs I could never seem to find in the Mass. And like her, I thought I knew what the Church taught, even though I never read a single encyclical or page of the Catechism. The only Scripture I knew was what I cherry-picked to fit my own narrative. By the time I found the courage to put aside my biases and self-imposed bigotry and really study Church teaching, I was already badly beaten and broken by a world that I thought had all the answers.

When this series ends, Ari will have discovered exactly what I did when I finally summoned up the courage to face what I had so long refused to accept: there is such a thing as objective truth, and we dismiss it at our peril.

ONE

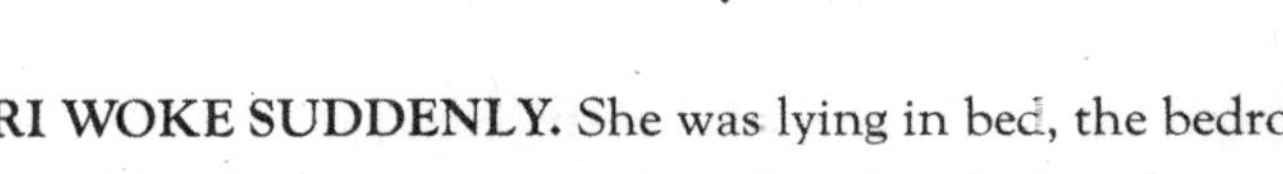

ARI WOKE SUDDENLY. She was lying in bed, the bedroom lights on and her laptop open on the pillow beside her. It was 4:02 a.m. The last thing she remembered was writing an article about a local car theft for the morning edition, but she was so tired she must have dozed off and slept almost through the night.

It was too early to get up. She yawned, rolled over, and closed her eyes. Images of yesterday fluttered across her sleepy brain: the interviews, the traffic jams, eating a Chick-fil-A sandwich while barreling down the turnpike, her editor's face peering through the window of her office at the *Pennsylvania Tribune*.

It all began to run together, the people, the places, the faces, until she felt herself drifting into what appeared to be a sterile white hospital room. It was familiar. She recognized the table. It was stainless steel and ought to be cold to the touch, but she couldn't feel it because she wasn't lying on it. She was hovering just a few inches above it.

Am I dreaming?

She was on her back, looking up at a circle of people in green scrubs. Their hands were moving amidst intermittent flashes of silver instruments. Lights were blinking and monitors were beeping while a man hovered directly above her, bobbing up and down as if he was pushing on her chest.

Who are these people? What are they doing?

They were leaning so close she could smell their breath and feel the hot wind of their words on her face. "Ari! Ari! Don't go. Please don't go!" a woman sobbed from what seemed like very far away.

Gram? Is that you?

No one answered. She tried to talk but no sound came out. It was such a strange, frightening feeling to be invisible and yet in plain view. Why could she see them, but they couldn't see her?

Am I dead?

The thought terrified her, made her struggle even harder to move, to speak, to do anything that might make the people realize she was trying to communicate with them.

Just then, a doctor's commanding voice ordered, "Little girl! Wake up!"

There was a loud swishing sound that turned into a roaring whir, startling her awake.

Her eyes popped open, and she found herself sitting up in bed, staring into the familiar darkness of her bedroom, sweating profusely.

The dream. Again.

She sank backward in relief. It had been years since she'd had this particular dream, which was more of a flashback to the diabetic coma she'd fallen into at the age of sixteen. They said she died that day, but she didn't remember. Only when she had the dream. Then she remembered it all. The doctors in their scrubs and masks, monitors beeping and blinking, nurses rushing around the table, Gram crying and squeezing her hand.

Her life was never the same again. From that day forward, she changed from being just Ariella Joan Dalton into Ariella Joan Dalton, Type 1 diabetic.

She looked at the clock. It was 5:45 a.m., which meant she could sleep for another forty-five minutes, but that would never happen now. It usually took two hours to calm down after "the dream."

Instead, she flipped on the police scanner by her bedside. There was a loud crackle just before a female voice spoke in a calm monotone. "Calling more units. St. Peter Damian's Catholic Church, 5th Street, Monmouth."

"St. Peter Damian's Church. . ." a man repeated. Ari recognized the voice. It was Chief Calvin O'Rourke of the Monmouth Police Department. "We've got a DB," he said. "187."

DB was code for dead body. A 187 meant homicide.

At the church?

Ari bolted out of bed, grabbed a pair of jeans and a sweater, and tripped over her boots on the way into the bathroom.

Dear God! What could be going on at the church? This was her grandmother's church. It was where her daughter attended faith formation classes.

A dead body? Whose?

She washed her face and ran a brush through her long, black hair, which everyone thought was so beautiful, but she found to be impossibly thick. It took half a day to dry.

"Wake up Annette," she texted her boss at the *Trib* as she headed down the hall. "Homicide at St. Damian's. On my way."

"Take your camera!" Annette texted back right away. What was she doing up this early? "Morning edition?"

"I'll try." It would be tough to make the morning online edition, but Ari would give it a try. She was a good reporter with more than a decade of experience and a long list of credible sources in law enforcement. If anyone could get the story fast, she could.

She peeked into her daughter's room. Chloe was sound asleep, her arms and legs wrapped around the giant stuffed unicorn she'd won at the carnival last summer.

"Ari? Is that you?" her grandmother called out as she padded past her room.

She cringed. The last thing she wanted to do was tell Gram there was a dead body at St. Peter's. Until she knew exactly what was going on, there was no point in frightening her.

"Yes. There's a story breaking," was all she said and hurried past her room. There was no point in frightening Gram prematurely. "Get Chloe on the bus?"

Of course she would. She always did. Ari's grandmother was utterly dedicated to Ari and Chloe even though she was an esteemed genealogist with two doctorates in history and anthropology who had more than enough to do in her professional life. Whatever scant downtime she found was devoted to writing historical fiction novels, all of which were critically acclaimed due to her unique style of combining compelling historical fact with lively storytelling. But in spite of her fame and success, Jacqui Dalton's faith and family came first. It kept her grounded.

Ari stopped in the kitchen to check her blood sugar. It usually dropped during the night, but her glucose monitor flashed a good number today. 120. This ritual used to be so tedious but now she had an infusion set in her abdomen and an insulin pump that was all connected by Bluetooth to an app on her phone. If her sugar was too high or too low, the monitor would beep, and she could administer insulin to herself whenever she needed it.

It beat pricking her finger ten times a day.

Just in case, she stuffed a baggie full of gummy bears in her back pocket, grabbed a hard-boiled egg, and shoved the whole thing in her mouth as she headed out the door.

The route to St. Damian's was familiar. Although she didn't consider herself to be a Catholic, this was her parish, and Chloe was being raised in the Church. It was the least she could do for her grandmother, who had taken them in years ago when Chloe's father abandoned them. Ari had barely been out of college and nearly died in childbirth due to complications from diabetes when her live-in lover, Jack Frielen, freaked out.

"Look, I just can't. . .I mean, I'm just not into all this right now, Ari. . .the baby, you being so sick. . .I'm only twenty-three. . ."

She could still see him sitting there on the edge of the bed, running his hands through his dark red hair and giving her that look, that pleading, petulant, little boy look that never failed to remind her that she was romantically involved with an eternal adolescent.

"What are you saying, Jack?"

"I've got to go. I can't handle this. . ."

"Seriously?"

Seriously.

There she was, barely out of college with a newborn and an apartment she couldn't afford without his paycheck. Because her relationship with her own parents had always been strained, she turned to the one rock she had in life—her grandmother.

They'd lived together ever since.

It was still dark outside. A light drizzling rain carried the scent of wet dirt and earthworms and chilled her to the bone. The heater in the car barely warmed up before she traveled the ten blocks to the church.

St. Peter Damian's was located in an older part of town where most of the buildings were at least one-hundred years old. Monmouth had been settled by millworkers in the late 1700's and had quite a few original buildings still standing in this part of town. Largely a bedroom community of about 50,000 residents, it was one of the more crowded and affluent of Philadelphia's suburbs.

As soon as she made a left turn onto Fifth Street, she saw the bright flash of emergency lights up ahead. Red, blue, and white lights reflected off the wet surfaces of the road, the buildings, the cars. Police tape prevented her from getting close enough to the scene, so she turned left again, headed down an alleyway between two blocks of stone rowhouses, and went the rest of the way on foot.

The church itself was a sprawling brick structure with a steeply pitched roof and 1970's-style stained glass windows that formed a very tall and impressive triangle in front of the building. It looked much too modern for the otherwise century-old buildings that surrounded it, but the church was nicely positioned at the back of a wide expanse of green lawn speckled with small grottos of statuary and now-fading flower beds. It was a tranquil, almost park-like setting.

But not today. The towering glass and brick walls were garishly slashed with the flare of lights from dozens of police and emergency vehicles. News vans were already on the scene and reporters leaned over the yellow police tape waving at whoever looked official enough to give them a statement.

The whole scene was chaotic. The police were still struggling to keep people out to prevent destruction of evidence and get the scene under control. At least a dozen officers were moving around the property with their flashlights, searching every corner of the building, calling out to one another while their radios crackled and chattered.

Ari slipped out of the alley and perched on the steps of one of the rowhomes. From there, she could fix her camera on a large group of police and EMTs who were gathered around something that was lying on the walkway at the side of the building, near the entrance to the sacristy.

It was obviously a body, crumpled and unmoving.

Residents were coming out of their houses now, most of them in jackets tossed over their robes, to watch from their porches.

A group of elderly women rushed up the street toward the church and stood a few feet away from her.

"Stay back!" an officer shouted at them.

"We're here for the 7:00 a.m. Mass!" one of the women shouted back at him.

"Just stay behind the tape," he said gruffly.

"That was rude," she whispered loud enough for everyone to hear, including the policeman.

"Oh, don't be so sensitive, Helen," the tallest woman in the group scoffed. "This is an emergency."

"I can see that, Alice!" Helen snapped, obviously offended.

"Then you have better eyes than me because I can't see anything. It's too dark," the tall woman, Alice, retorted. Her short, white hair was cut in a bob that was being crushed under a dark woolen cap. A pair of round glasses dominated her face. "It looks like there's something on the sidewalk. . .where all the police are gathered."

"It looks like a body to me," the third person, a tiny woman in a knee-length black puffer coat told them. Her silver hair was perfectly coifed beneath an accordion-pleated rain bonnet, the likes of which Ari hadn't seen since she was in kindergarten.

"You always think the worst, Betty," Alice said dryly. "Maybe there was some structural damage or. . ."

"Look!" Helen cried and pointed at a spot away from the police. "They cut off Mary's head!"

Ari immediately shifted her camera to where the woman was pointing. Sure enough, as the first shards of daylight began to brighten the scene, she could see the outline of a headless statue.

"What? Where?" Alice demanded.

"Over there!" Helen grabbed Alice by the arm and pulled her a foot to the right. She pointed again. "See it?"

"God have mercy," Alice breathed as she squinted at the scene.

"The church was vandalized!" Helen gasped. "But who. . ?"

"It could be anybody," Betty speculated. "This world has gone mad. Everyone hates each other."

"I think something very serious has happened here," Alice said in a solemn voice, and the other two shorter women looked up at her almost reverently.

They suddenly reminded Ari of the Golden Girls.

Quite a crowd of residents were gathered behind the police tape on Fifth Street now. She scanned the crowd with her camera and noticed a Black man walking down the street toward the scene. He was tall and had a bushy afro that was only getting bigger in the mist. He was pushing a stroller with what looked like a toddler sprawled within it.

How odd. What father brings out a child in this weather so early in the morning?

"Isn't that Father Luke?" Betty was asking.

Once again, Ari shifted her camera to where Betty was pointing and watched the familiar sight of Fr. Lucas "Luke" Bednarczyk, the pastor of the parish, come out the sacristy door and say something to the police who were huddled around the crumpled form on the sidewalk. They all stepped aside as Fr. Luke knelt beside the body.

"Oh God!" Alice said again. "He's praying over someone."

"Is he dead?" Helen asked, clearly horrified.

"We don't know if he's dead, or even if it's a 'he,'" Alice said sensibly.

"Well, if there are all these ambulances here and nobody is rushing the person to the hospital, whoever it is, is probably dead," Betty deduced.

"She's right, Alice." Helen was starting to panic. "Someone got killed here!"

"Just calm down. . .we need to pray."

The three of them fumbled in their purses, pulled out their rosary beads, and started to pray. "In the name of the Father, and of the Son, and of the Holy Spirit. . ."

Now that the police had stepped back from the body, Ari made her move. She hopped off the stone steps and started walking down the sidewalk, able to see more and more of the scene as the sky began to brighten.

With the light better now, she started snapping pictures.

The Blessed Mother statue had been defaced. The head was knocked off and lay in several pieces on the ground at the foot of the statue. Someone had used dark spray paint to make lewd markings on her body along with the words, "God's whore." The statue of St. Peter Damian was knocked over and lay on its side on the ground. There were strange markings on the wall of the church. They looked like symbols of some kind.

This was a hate crime.

"Cal!" she called when she spied the police chief walking across the lawn toward his car.

He turned, waving her closer like he usually did. The two of them had worked together with the FBI on the Jack Flint corruption case, which had been a big break in her career as an investigative reporter.

She'd always had a soft spot in her heart for avenging victims, perhaps because of her own life story, which motivated her to uncover crime whether it involved corrupt politicians, greedy CEOs, or gang leaders. Thankfully, her investigative work on the Flint case had made an arrest possible, and Cal's whole police force looked like heroes. Cal had never forgotten it and always gave her a statement on new cases. But their relationship was professional, and she had to get each statement cleared through the Public Information Officer, also known as the PIO, just like everyone else. Cal didn't play favorites.

"This is bad news, Ari," he said now in a very serious tone. He was middle-aged, his blue eyes just beginning to look tired as the first lines of wrinkles began to etch their way down the side of his nose. A shock of blond hair stuck out of the back of his cap.

"Here's what you can print. 'St. Peter Damian's Catholic Church was vandalized this morning around 5:00 a.m. The culprit, or culprits, were surprised by the sacristan who unfortunately lost his life in the incident. . .'"

"Marty Mason?" she interrupted.

"You knew him? I'm sorry. Next of kin has just been notified. She lives right over there," he said and pointed to one of the rowhomes. Police officers were moving in and out of the house, and the Golden Girls were huddled together on the steps, holding each other and crying as they watched for any sign of Marty's wife, Rose.

"This is horrible," Ari said, genuinely sorry.

Marty Mason was a sweet, old man. He was short, very thin, perhaps seventy years old with a ring of white hair around his otherwise bald head. She never saw him in anything other than perfectly pressed slacks and button-down shirt. The children called him "Mr. M&Ms" because he always had a bag of M&Ms in his pocket and gave out the candies to anyone who asked.

Ari had. Once. Her sugar dropped so low she almost went into convulsions. Jacqui and Marty had led her to a bench outside the church and fed her M&Ms until she recovered herself.

"You can release his name," Cal was saying. "Because of the nature of the vandalism, we suspect this to be a hate crime. We'll be referring this case to the FBI. If anyone has any information, please contact the Monmouth Police Department."

He stopped, looked over her head, and waved at someone.

"Speaking of the FBI. . .here they are now. That was fast." He waved at them again. "Yo! Over here!"

"Do you have any suspects at all?" Ari asked.

"None at this time."

"Any evidence, fingerprints?"

"We're going to leave that to the FBI's Evidence Response Team. They'll be scouring the premises in a matter of minutes and sending everything to their labs in Quantico."

"What about surveillance video from the church? Or maybe some of these houses have cameras?"

Cal looked back at her and smiled the way he did when they were working together and he was impressed by something she said or did.

"Of course we're looking into that. We'll be interviewing the residents and parishioners to see if anyone heard or saw something suspicious this morning. Ask around and see if you can find anything out."

"Of course."

"Make sure the PIO gives you approval on that statement," Cal reminded her.

They were interrupted just then by two men in dark jackets with "FBI" written in bold yellow letters across the back.

"Special Agent Jesse Sandoval," one of them said in a deep voice that had just a whisper of a Spanish accent. He was very tall with long, black hair that had been combed away from his face and now curled around the collar of this jacket. The lines of his face were very broad and strong and masculine. He shook Cal's hand and introduced the other agent, a Black man named Mackenzie Jones who was equally tall and good looking.

"This is Ari Dalton," Cal was saying. "You might have heard of her. She's the investigative reporter who helped crack the Jack Flint case."

Jesse looked directly at her, one eyebrow raised in surprise over a set of warm, brown eyes that were unexpectedly warm and friendly for such a masculine face.

"My pleasure," he said politely. "You worked with Special Agent Tony D'Angelo?"

"I did. It's nice to meet you." she said and had to force herself to look away from those soulful eyes of his. They were the kind a woman wanted to drown in. "I hope I can help in some way," she said quickly. "This is my family's parish."

"Tragic," Jesse said, still looking at her very directly, which she found vaguely disarming, in a flattering kind of way.

Who is this guy?

"Ari will do some checking around. She always manages to find something," Cal was saying.

"In that case," Jesse said, pulling a wallet out of his back pocket. Ari caught a glimpse of a copper FBI badge just before he pulled out a card and jotted a number on the back. "Text me if you uncover anything interesting."

The two agents feigned tipping a hat at her, then headed across the lawn to the place where the sacristan lay bleeding onto the sidewalk.

Her first thought was to let Annette know the story was coming and then to call Jacqui with the news before someone else did. She hurried back to her car and her laptop.

"Gram? Is Chloe around?"

"She's getting dressed."

"I've got bad news. It's about the church."

"What about the church?"

"It was vandalized."

She heard Jacqui's breath catch.

"That's not the worst of it." She took a deep breath. "Marty surprised them, and he was killed."

"Wait. What did you say?"

"I'm so sorry, Gram. Marty was killed. Do you need me to come home?"

There was no answer.

"Gram?"

"Who would do something like this?"

"No one knows anything yet. I'm going to try to get something from Fr. Luke. Will you text him for me, see if he'll talk to me?"

"Yes, yes, of course!"

"Are you alright, Gram?"

"I think so, dear. I'm just shocked. . .poor Rose. . ."

"She's been notified."

"This is awful. Evil."

"I know, Gram. Listen, if you want to spend time with your friends from church today, don't worry about Chloe. I'll make sure I'm home in time to get her off the bus."

"I think we should tell her together, don't you? It's going to frighten her."

"I know. And she has PREP tonight too. I'm sure it's cancelled."

"Yes, certainly it's cancelled. I can't image what Fr. Luke is going through. Let me text him and see if he can see you. We'll talk later, dear."

Ari hung up, put in a call to the PIO and the FBI press office for a statement, flipped open her laptop, and started writing the story.

TWO

"HE NEVER KNEW WHAT HIT HIM. The medics said the force was brutal. Probably broke his skull. There will be an autopsy, of course."

"Did anyone see anything, Father?"

"No. Adam Thiel, our intern sacristan, found Marty when he got here at 5:15 a.m. We don't know if it was one perp or many."

Fr. Luke shut the door to his office and sat down behind his desk. Ari thought he looked drained. He was a younger man, but he seemed much older that day. The stress, the sorrow, made his face look stiff and hard, almost ready to crack.

Except for his eyes. They were the gentlest eyes, so clear and pale gray, almost silver. If it wasn't for his rapidly receding hairline, Ari would have guessed he was thirty-five years old, even though he was closer to fifty.

"Did the police find any evidence on the grounds?"

"Yes, but I can't disclose that. All I can say is those two FBI agents are sharp as tacks."

"What about the drawings on the building?"

He sat back in his chair, put his arms behind his head and let out a very heavy sigh. "Satanic. That's another reason why the FBI are here. Those agents are specially trained in these kinds of cases. Cal called them as soon as he saw the drawings and the blasphemies painted on the statue of Our Lady. It's a hate crime.

A Satanic hate crime."

How he could report these horrific details in such a quiet voice was beyond her, but Fr. Luke always spoke like this. Very soft, very deliberate. He was an incredibly intelligent man who worked as a clinical psychologist before entering the priesthood and earning a doctorate in theology.

"But why target this church? There are six other Catholic churches within ten miles of here. Why this one?"

"Good question! That's the one we're all asking. . ."

"Any sex abuse issues at this parish?"

"You're good, Ari, smart as a tack, just like your grandmother."

"Well?"

"None that I know of. Nothing in recent years. Before the sex abuse scandal broke in 2002, these problems were handled differently from diocese to diocese. Some just transferred the priest to another parish. Others quietly removed them and gave them a desk job somewhere. The FBI are going to look into it. They're probably already in touch with the Archdiocese."

"What other reason could there be?"

"There needn't be any reason other than that we're Catholic. Christianity is the most hated denomination in the world. . .and Catholics bear the brunt of it."

Although she dared not say so aloud, she was hardly surprised. The Church stood against modernity. It condemned everything—birth control, abortion, euthanasia, same-sex relations, gender identity. Its strict and backward dogma accomplished nothing but to make everyone feel bad about themselves for being human. In her opinion, there was no future in this church, at least none that would serve in the interest of progress.

For this reason, she'd left the church a long time ago, at least in her heart, and only attended special functions for Chloe's sake and because she owed it to Gram who was as Catholic as they came. The fact that she didn't pressure Ari to return was truly remarkable and one of the many reasons why she so deeply admired her grandmother. The woman was an all-around class act.

Fr. Luke was looking at her very closely. She was reminded of his psychology background. He was probably reading her body language right now.

"How do you plan to take the parish forward?" she hurried on.

"We're going to forgive who did this and pray for him or her," he said at once. "No one else should ever have to suffer the loss we suffered today, not here in the United States where we're supposed to tolerate our cultural and religious differences—although that's really just a bunch of happy talk, as we all know. Why do you look so shocked?"

"Because they killed Marty! Don't you want justice?"

He sighed again, put his elbows on the desk and rubbed at his eyes for a moment. "I've worked with people who got involved in Satanism and I can say that they are often young adults from dysfunctional backgrounds who were recruited in high school because they were loners."

"Recruited?"

"Yes. Serious Satanists like to hang around high school bus stops and popular teen gathering places to spot the kids who don't have a lot of friends. They make conversation with them, befriend them, invite them to their 'club' or a party, and ever so slowly begin to introduce them to the dark arts. For the most part, these kids have no clue what they're getting into. They think it's like their video games or the books they read. It never even occurs to them that this stuff is real. And once they figure it out, it's too late. There's no getting out, at least not without some kind of violence either to themselves, their loved ones, or their pets." He stopped. "Sorry, I didn't mean to frighten you."

"It's just so. . .so ghoulish."

He half-laughed, if that reaction was possible on such a dark day. "This is nothing compared to what those two FBI agents have seen, some real hard-core stuff like ritual murders that tend to be particularly heinous crimes. Most of it is gang-related these days, MS-13 and the like. But my point is that the people who commit these crimes are often deeply disturbed because they're deeply wounded. They almost always come from a dysfunctional home where there was neglect or drug, alcohol, or sexual abuse. Without the healthy affirmation of a mother and a father in their early development, their emotional growth is stunted. Most of them grow up without ever really knowing what it feels like to be loved."

You mean like me?

"Yes, but that doesn't make someone a murderer. . ." she argued.

"No, but it certainly can. For most, these wounded souls just encounter someone who makes them feel loved, even though it's not real love, and are easily led into one bad relationship after another. It's a vicious cycle."

Tell me about it.

Except for the Satanism part, Fr. Luke had just described her own childhood and the damage that found her falling for all the wrong men in a never-ending search for the love she never received from either parent. The end result was a mixed bag of self-hatred and an almost terrifying sense of insecurity.

She suddenly felt uncomfortable with this conversation, the way she always felt when she looked too closely at herself. Why dwell on the past? There was nothing she could do about it. She couldn't make her mother or father love her or even care about her. It only made her feel responsible and guilty and ultimately hateful toward herself.

Instead, she forced herself to focus on Marty, on the pain his family was feeling right now, rather than her own. After all, this could be one of the biggest stories of her career.

"Ari?"

Fr. Luke looked at her in a way that suggested he knew where her thoughts had wandered just then. She shook them off and hurried on. "What will you tell the children, father? I'm not sure how to handle Chloe tonight."

"I'll tell them what I told you. The people who did this need our prayers. They've gone astray. They took the life of Marty, they defaced our buildings and destroyed our statues, but they can't destroy our faith. Evil will never win this battle. This war has already been won, and we are the victors. The power is on our side, and we will use it to pray for those who have come under the sway of the Enemy so that we can loosen his hold on this world and make it a better place for all of us."

She wanted to admire his enthusiasm, but not when he talked about the devil. That was just so "Middle Ages."

"You're right," she lied, and he probably knew it. "I'll do my best with her."

"Chloe is fortunate to have you and Jacqui to raise her. She'll be fine. Maybe a little shaken at first, but she's very level-headed."

"Like Gram."

"And you. Remember, we're all wounded people, Ari. It doesn't make us less capable. We learn to adapt."

What did he mean by that? The way he said it made it sound like Gram might have told him some things about her childhood.

"Us? We? You don't seem too wounded to me," she evaded.

He grinned and his eyes sparkled again, the way they usually did. "I've got my share of wounds. And I'm a shrink, remember?"

She laughed shortly.

I kind of like this guy.

"Well, I've taken enough of your time." She stood up and so did he. "I'd like to write a follow-up on Marty and his life. Can I interview some parishioners, those who are willing to speak about it?"

"That would be good of you. Why don't you come to the funeral? The whole parish will be here that day."

The phone rang and he reached for it.

"You'll have to excuse me. I sent Joan home. I sent everyone home; it's just me here today. May God bless you, Ari." He made the sign of the cross in the air, winked at her, and picked up the phone.

THREE

THE APARTMENT WAS EMPTY when she got home. Chloe wasn't due for another hour, and Jacqui was probably with friends from church.

Ari loved it when the home was quiet.

They lived on the top-floor condominium of a five-story building on the outskirts of Monmouth. It was spacious and open, from the kitchen through the living room and into Jacqui's small office niche with its tall bookshelves and huge mahogany desk that was always piled with papers, open books, an iMac, and a laptop. Floor to ceiling windows spilled light onto the walls, painted in pale shades of blue gray. An overstuffed, crème-colored sectional sofa with piles of colorful pillows dominated the main living area. It was the perfect place to hang out at night to watch television, play games, or just talk.

Beep. Beep. Beep. A warning sounded from Ari's glucose meter. Her sugar was too high. This was the third time the monitor had gone off today. Yesterday was four. Maybe she should lay off the gummy bears. She gave herself a dose of insulin and headed down the hall to the quiet of her bedroom.

"What a day!" She whipped off her boots and flopped on her back in the middle of the bed. Seven hours had gone by since she'd left, and in that time, she'd written two articles on the church murder, two lifestyle pieces, and updated the online community calendar.

"Ari, you work like a madwoman," Annette had said with a

grateful smile on her face. "You do more work in a day than three reporters."

"Just call me an overachiever," Ari joked, but it felt good to be appreciated.

Annette LeBarre was a joy to work for. She was a very accomplished journalist who'd won her coveted Editor position at one of the country's top four newspapers through hard work and diligent reporting. Annette was not a player. She was a worker, which is why she and Ari hit it off from Ari's very first day on the job. They both worked hard, weren't afraid to get their hands dirty, and insisted on maintaining high journalistic standards. No anonymous sources. No uncorroborated details. No spin. Just facts.

"You look as tired as me," Annette had said as Ari was shrugging into her vest to go home for the day. "And wear something warmer tomorrow. It's winter."

"Yes, Mom."

Annette laughed and her dark brown bob bounced around her face. She was an attractive woman in her early sixties. Despite the gray streaks in her hair and the pretty blue eyes that were slowly disappearing into folds of creped skin, she had the look and vitality of a much younger woman.

For a few minutes, Ari lay very still on the bed and let the insulin seep into her bloodstream until that vague ache in her head began to fade away. Feeling much better, she got up and filled her diffuser with a cocktail of essential oils. Blue Tansy, orange, a little tangerine, and patchouli. She grabbed one of her crystals—an amethyst—and started to fondle the stone as she lay back down on the bed. Amethyst was known to resonate with the nervous system and to help bring about inner calm and strength. She felt the peace begin to roll over her as she rubbed the stone and inhaled the sweet, honeyed scents that were slowly seeping into the very cells of her body.

Calm settled over her spirit, and she began to recite a new mantra to clear her mind.

"Ad Guray Namay, Ad Guray Namay. . ."

I bow to the Primal Wisdom.

"Ad Guray Namay, Ad Guray Namay. . ."

I bow to the Primal Wisdom.

Random thoughts danced across the lobes of her brain. Cal's hair blowing in the wind. The Golden Girls. An FBI badge flashing in the pale morning light. Running up the stairs to the office.

She felt herself sinking into the void, the blackness, the peace of no thought, just as Fr. Luke's voice rose out of her memory. *"We're all wounded people, Ari. It doesn't make us less capable. We learn to adapt."*

She sat up, her peace gone in an instant.

Why had he said that?

It must be her sugar levels. They were off. Something was off.

A half hour later, Chloe was jumping off the bus with her two best friends, Missy Maure and Emma Worthington. They were all dressed alike in leggings, Uggs, and brightly colored puffer coats. Chloe was the tallest of the three, and Ari noticed how she was beginning to walk with her shoulders hunched forward a bit, the way girls did when they felt like they were too tall. She'd done the same thing at her age. Although Chloe had not yet reached her mother's five-foot-ten height, she was well on her way for a ten-year-old girl.

"Mommy!" she called when she saw Ari. With her usual dramatic flair, she ran toward her at breakneck speed, her backpack flapping, and her long auburn hair flying every which way. No matter how neatly they fixed her hair each morning, Chloe always came home from school looking like a wreck.

They hugged tightly. She smelled like Twizzlers.

"Come on. Let's make something for Gram," Ari said, leading them back inside.

"Leftover turkey and stuffing sandwiches!" Chloe cried.

"Aren't you sick of them yet?"

"It's the best thing about Thanksgiving. . .leftover turkey, stuffing, and cranberry sauce sandwiches."

"You're the only person I know who puts cranberry sauce on a sandwich. Yuck!"

Chloe giggled and hopped onto one of the kitchen island chairs to watch her mother arrange a dozen frozen meatballs on a cookie sheet.

"Who's driving us to PREP tonight?" she asked, and Ari's heart fell. She would have to tell her soon.

"I think it's been cancelled," she deflected. "Let's see what Gram says when she gets home."

"I hope it's cancelled. It's so boring." Chloe had no filter. She always said exactly what she was thinking.

"I know, honey."

"I mean, I like God and everything, but I don't like PREP."

"There are a lot of things in life that we don't like to do but we have to do anyway," Ari said, "like taking tests, making our beds, and not passing wind in public even when it hurts to hold it in. . ."

Chloe collapsed to the countertop in a fit of giggles. "Potty talk! Potty talk!"

"Who me?" Ari joked, putting on a pot of water and opening a jar of Ragu spaghetti sauce. "You know what happens to me when I eat spaghetti sauce. . ."

Chloe held her nose and they both laughed.

How she loved this little girl! Jack had wanted her to have an abortion, but she couldn't bring herself to do it. She always thought of herself as being a pro-choice feminist, but when it came to acting upon the holy grail of feminism, she just couldn't do it. Maybe that made her less of a feminist, but she didn't really care. Her identity was nothing but a blur anyway.

Now she looked at the auburn-haired girl slouching over the Carrara marble countertop, absently twirling a strand of hair around her finger while gazing at her cell phone and couldn't imagine life without her. As Chloe approached womanhood, they were developing a new closeness. It wasn't just teasing and cuddling anymore. Now there were more serious conversations about boys, friendships, the future. Chloe was at the age where her body was about to change, and she was very self-conscious about herself. Tall and thin like her mother, Gram referred to her as being "all legs, like a chicken."

But her heart-shaped face was already very pretty, her skin pale and clear. She had her father's brown eyes, large and round and heavy lidded. Perpetual dark circles, which she'd had since the day she was born, gave her an almost waif-like appearance.

"Mommy, I have to tell you something," Chloe said in that suddenly serious tone of voice she always used when she was about to reveal something that was supposed to be kept secret. She leaned across the island, lowered her voice, and whispered excitedly, "Gram has a boyfriend!"

"Who?"

"Eric!" she said.

"Whitby?"

"Yes!"

"Why do you say that? And why are you whispering? No one's here but us."

"So the neighbors won't hear," Chloe said pointedly.

"They can't hear us!"

She rose off her stool, leaned closer, and whispered even more insistently, "He walked her to the door!"

"So what? That doesn't mean anything."

"Your boyfriends always walk you to the door."

"I don't have boyfriends, Chloe. Just dates."

"Well. . ." Chloe shrugged, "Eric is her date!"

"I think you're reading too much into it," Ari said gently and giggled at the girl who suddenly deflated back into her seat. "Besides, Eric is a doofus. Gram would never like him. She's a professor with two doctorates!"

"What's a doofus?"

Uh-oh. Knowing Chloe as well as she did, Ari knew she would repeat this term to Eric the next time she saw him, which was not the way to stay on their building manager's good side.

"I didn't say doofus," Ari quickly lied.

"Yes, you did, Mommy! I heard you!"

"No, I didn't! I said oo-puss. . ."

"What does that mean?"

"Gentleman."

"Oh."

I totally made that up.

The key sounded in the door. "Hello girls!" Jacqui called more brightly than she looked and stepped into the kitchen. "Smells good in here."

She looked like she might have been crying, although Ari had only seen her cry once before, when they brought her back to life in the hospital the day she died. But those had been tears of joy, not sorrow. Now she sat in her usual place at the head of the table, the sides of her silver bob pushed behind her ears, her blue eyes looking unnaturally large behind her thick, rimless glasses.

They decided to wait until after dinner to tell Chloe about what happened at the church and kept the girl occupied with talk about her Christmas list.

"Do you think I'm old enough for a kitten yet?" Chloe looked between them.

"It depends on the kind of commitment you're willing to make for the animal, my love," Jacqui said.

"I'll take care of it."

"Every day for eighteen years? Because that's how long indoor cats live."

"Eighteen years?" Chloe looked intimidated by that number.

"Yes, and by then you'll be off to college. What then?"

"I'll take it with me!"

"They don't allow cats in dorm rooms," Ari chimed in.

"Then I'll go to school around here!"

Ari and Jacqui exchanged knowing looks. They had already decided that this would be the year they allowed her to have the kitten she'd been asking for since she was eight years old.

"We'll see," Ari said dismissively. She wanted it to be a surprise.

"Gram, Mommy called Eric Whitby an 'oopus' today. Do you know what that means?"

"No. I've never heard that word before."

"It means gentleman!" Chloe said smartly.

"I never heard of it. . .must be slang. . ."

Phew!

"Emma said her mom has a head cold, so who's driving to PREP tonight?" Chloe asked. She was done eating. It was time.

"There is no PREP tonight, love," Jacqui said sadly and tossed the conversation to Ari.

"Something very bad happened at the church today, baby."

Chloe's attention was caught. "What?"

"Bad people attacked the church. They broke the statues, wrote hateful things on the walls of the building, and they hurt Mr. M&Ms."

"They did?" She looked suddenly stricken. "Is he okay?"

Ari's heart nearly broke as she whispered softly. "No. He's not okay."

"Did he die?"

Ari nodded.

Chloe's eyes filled with tears as they shifted between Jacqui and Ari. "But why?"

"We don't know. The police are looking into it and—"

Chloe pushed back her chair, rushed over to Ari, and collapsed on her lap in a fit of tears.

"Sweetie, it's okay. . ."

"I'm afraid, Mommy!"

"Of what?" Ari whispered into her hair.

"Of the bad people! What if they come here?"

"The police are looking. Even the FBI are looking."

Her head popped up. "The FBI? Like on TV?"

"Yes! Everyone is looking for whoever did this."

* * * * *

Jacqui watched the two of them huddling together at the table, with a much-too-tall Chloe sitting on her mother's lap the way she used to do as a little girl. The way they clung to each other tugged at her heart.

They were so alone. So abandoned.

What had been done to her beloved Ariella by Jacqui's narcissistic son and his equally self-absorbed wife was one of the greatest sorrows of her life. Although they never laid a hand on her, the injuries Ari suffered by their indifference and neglect were as serious as any broken bone, probably more so. She had often heard them speak to Ari with disdain or impatience or just plain indifference, paying as little attention to her as they could while they pursued their own lives. Ari was an imposition, and this is how she was treated.

As a result, she was raised with little or no positive affirmation or emotional support and suffered all the injuries inherent with this kind of neglect, such as insecurity, low self-esteem, self-criticism, self-loathing. Broken bones could heal, but the kind of emotional wounds Ari suffered may well last a lifetime.

As if her childhood wasn't hard enough, Ari had only made matters worse by getting involved with Jack Frielen. He was just like her father. Spoiled and selfish and incapable of loving anyone but himself. But Ari insisted he was the one, that they would get married soon enough. It never happened. She got pregnant three months after they moved in together and, a year later, he was gone.

Good riddance! Jacqui could still see him sitting stone-faced and disinterested in the hospital room the day Chloe was born while the doctors scrambled to get Ari's sugar under control. She was going in and out of shock, and all Jacqui could think of was that horrible night when she'd developed diabetic ketoacidosis at the age of sixteen.

She had actually died on the table but, by a miracle of God, the doctors were able to bring her back. And it was all due to the negligence of her parents who weren't helping her to learn how to monitor her diabetes. They just couldn't be bothered. And Ari knew it. She always knew that her parents didn't want her and just put up with her because they had to. She once described herself as being like the puppy everyone wanted for Christmas, but no one wanted when it grew up.

Ari had no one else but Chloe, so Jacqui was determined to be there for her as well. It was Jacqui who held her hand while she lay in a coma, Jacqui who cried and prayed and begged God to spare the life of this beautiful young woman whose whole life read like a study in the art of abandonment.

And yet no one would ever know it looking at her. She was an outgoing, friendly person, very responsible and mature, without even a hint of conceit about one of her most outstanding traits—her rare beauty.

When Ariella Dalton walked into a room, every head turned. A tall, patrician beauty, she wore her dark hair long, reaching to the middle of her back where it hung in luxurious black waves. She had her mother's full pink mouth that always hinted at a smile. But her most striking feature was by far her spectacular blue eyes—the color of aquamarine—so vibrant that at first sight they were almost startling.

Ari could easily win any beauty contest she entered, but it was the last thing she would ever do. Thanks to her parents, she hadn't an ounce of self-confidence.

Her healing would be nothing short of an act of God.

"There's a rosary tonight at Rose's place," Jacqui suddenly told the girls.

"How is she doing?" Ari looked up from Chloe's buried head.

"So strong! I'm amazed. We all are. She keeps saying that Marty would want her to go on, for all of us to go on, and that he had always loved God above all else and. . ." Jacqui's voice cracked just then, which was unusual. She was always so stoic and reserved.

"I think you should go, Gram. It'll be good for you, too."

* * * * *

An hour later, Ari and Chloe were laying on the bed. Ari was propped up against the headboard with her laptop, while Chloe lounged at the foot of the bed texting Missy and Emma. Ari flipped through the images on her camera until she came to the shot of the strange symbols that were spray painted on the outer wall of the church. She had never seen anything like them before and began to root around the internet for sites devoted to analyzing symbols.

"Mommy, can I sleep in here with you tonight?"

"Of course, baby."

"Thanks. Can I have some ice cream?"

"Sure. Get me some too. Cookie dough."

She gave herself a small dose of insulin just in case.

Page after page of symbols came up. Malachim, celestial writing, runic.

Her cell phone chimed, and she read a text from Mary Kate, aka "MK," her best friend since the fourth grade.

"Wanna get a stone massage? I've got a discount coupon for two."

"Can't. Something bad happened today, and I'm home with Chloe tonight."

"What happened?"

"Vandals attacked the church and killed the sacristan."

"Are you kidding?"

"No. It was bad."

"Did you see the body?"

"No." MK always wanted the gruesome details.

"Are you alright?"

"I think so. I couldn't get close enough to see anything that would scar me for life."

"Yoga this week?"

"Not sure. Call you when I get free."

She went back to the internet and stumbled across an alphabet known as the Theban alphabet. The symbols were a perfect match.

She sat up and started to decipher the letters. In a matter of minutes, two words formed that made the hair on her arms stand up.

"K-I-L-L G-O-D."

FOUR

YURI SAT CROSS-LEGGED on the floor in the front of the small, cramped living room, a picture of the sigil of Baphomet hanging on the wall above him. The symbol, believed by Satanists to contain magical power, was used to invoke Lucifer. While his priestess, Rena, carefully placed a black candle on the floor in front of him and lit it, Yuri closed his eyes and began to chant under his breath, "Hail Satan! Hail Satan!"

Ever so gradually, his voice rose, his breathing became more rapid. A fine layer of sweat formed on his bald head and began to trickle down the sides of his face.

"Hail! Hail!" he cried, his voice becoming deep and raspy. His chest heaved, his head tilted from side to side, then finally fell backward as his eyes rolled back in his head.

Rena gasped, bowed to Yuri, then backed out of the room and disappeared into the kitchen of her small apartment.

Kyle watched the spectacle with a mixture of fear and disgust. An unofficial member of the gang known as Hades Hood, he had little patience for the Satan-worshiping aspect of the group. For most, it was just a front, an excuse to commit a variety of sick, heinous crimes. Although he had given up on the whole God thing a long time ago, he wasn't comfortable with going this far in the other direction. It was just too dark, too cold, too evil. But at this point, he was in too deep and would never be able to get out. At least, not alive.

Out of the corner of his eye, he watched Jamahl, the only other person in the room. A tall, lanky Black man, Jamahl stared at Yuri with unmasked contempt. The two hated each other. It was only a matter of time before one of them killed the other, Kyle mused.

When the ritual ended, Yuri came back to himself and stood up. He was a short, stocky man of about five foot five who wore a black sweater over black jeans and a pair of black-and-red Air Jordans.

"The Beast is satisfied with our offering," Yuri told them.

"Why did you kill him, Yuri? Who said anything about human sacrifice?" Kyle demanded angrily. "This was supposed to scare them, not—"

"If the Beast wants blood, he gets blood," Yuri cut him off sharply, looking at him with eyes that were cold and hard and black. Kyle could feel the evil from across the room. "That's how we roll in the Hood. When you gonna figure that out?"

"The Beast is shrewder than that, Yuri," Jamahl argued in a passionless, almost bored tone of voice. "Killing that old man just got the feds involved. Now we've got the FBI after us."

"So what?" Yuri asked flippantly.

Jamahl sauntered across the room and stood over him in an obvious attempt to intimidate him. "They called the Aztec right away. He's on the case, man! Him and Jones. Those two crack every case they get. They decimated the Hood in Minneapolis."

"That's who I want! The Aztec! The Beast will reward me big for that prize. . ."

"You won't get near him, not with Her watching over him."

"No? Well, she's going to watch me offer him up to my lord one day," Yuri said, looking past them now and into some dark world of his own imagining. "I dream of it sometimes. . .getting him on the altar, cutting him, listening to him scream, cutting out his heart while it's still beating and showing it to him. . .seeing the shock in his eyes just before he snuffs out."

"You're one sick dude," Jamahl said with unmasked revulsion.

"You're just scared of him." Yuri taunted.

"I told you. I don't want to get sent up again. I just got out."

Yuri scoffed at them both. "You two need some smack. It'll make you feel better."

"What did you call us here for?" Jamahl asked.

"The Beast wants more."

"No way," Kyle said.

Yuri glared at him. "There's no getting out, Kyle, except in a body bag, so shut up and take notes." He turned his attention to Jamahl. "I've got my eye on another church. Sacristan comes in early. It would be an easy hit, scare the hell out of the community."

"How do you want to do it?" Jamahl was interested now.

"Same as this one. Send the vandals in first to take out the cameras, desecrate the premises, make sure no one's around so I can come in, do the hit, then get out."

"We ought to use the same Hooders for it. They did a good job," Jamahl suggested.

"They did. Tell them I said so. They'll be rewarded. Anytime they do a job and leave no evidence behind, they get rewarded. Feds didn't get anything from the scene."

"How do you know?" Jamahl scoffed. "Those guys got all kinds of equipment."

"Yeah, their forensics and their human assets. You catch any finks, I'll do them myself." Yuri was obsessed with the idea of FBI informants in the Hood. He had already killed several people on the basis of nothing but suspicion.

"When do you want to do it?"

"I'll tell you when it's time."

Kyle and Jamahl were both only too happy to leave. They walked out of the room and said nothing as they followed each other down a narrow staircase and through a door that led straight out into a dark alley. It was lined with dumpsters from the various eating establishments that fronted the street, the gravel path littered with used napkins and bits of pizza crust from the overflowing receptacle outside Tony's Pizzeria.

Jamahl kicked at a pile of dirty litter. "Yuri's sick, you know. He's a homicidal maniac, always has been."

"Yeah. He's insane alright."

"But he's the high priest. At least until someone kills him."

"What are you waiting for, Jamahl?"

"The right time."

"But he's going to keep on killing. This isn't what we talked about."

"I warned you about him, man," Jamahl sighed. "Yuri lets himself be possessed at will. You saw it tonight. You've seen it at the rituals. Yuri's the real deal, which means the only person who can control him is the Beast. What happens now is out of our hands."

Jamahl turned away, strode up the alley and disappeared on the street, leaving Kyle alone with his second thoughts.

FIVE

ARI WALKED INTO CAL'S OFFICE and tuned out the noise of the bustling precinct behind her. "Can you go on the record with anything more on the church case?"

Cal pushed aside his paperwork and gave her his full attention.

"Here's what I can tell you. We were able to acquire some trace evidence on the scene. It appears that Mr. Mason may have tried to defend himself against his attacker, then turned to get away when he was struck from behind. This evidence is being analyzed by FBI forensics in Quantico."

"DNA?"

"Could be. We can only hope they find something we could run through the database."

"Do you have any leads, suspects? Anything yet?"

Cal shook his head and sighed. "None. All I can say is that there's a lot of occult activity in this area now—ever since Hades Hood moved into town."

"Who?"

"Another gang, but this one is different. It's run by hard-core Satanists. And I mean so hard-core I won't even tell you the stuff they do. Suffice to say, they're dark characters who strike fear in the hearts of even the most streetwise MS-13 leaders. MS-13 leadership also claims to worship *La Bestia*, otherwise known as The Beast, but even they run in fear from the Hood because these guys don't mess around. They kill for no other reason than because they believe Satan told them to do it."

"Do you think they had something to do with the attack on St. Peter's?"

Cal looked at her squarely. "I do. The symbols drawn on the walls were odd. I've never seen them before. That's why I called the Bureau. Besides, it's a hate crime, which means it's a civil rights violation. The feds handle those cases. You saw what they wrote on the Virgin's body."

"I did. And the writing on the wall was from the Theban alphabet."

"You figured that out already?" he grinned proudly, as if he was personally responsible for her investigative abilities. "Jesse picked that up right away."

"It spelled, 'Kill God.'"

"Yeah. Apparently, it's an alphabet used primarily by occultists."

"Can I put that in the follow up article?"

"Yes, but nothing about the Hood because that's just conjecture. And if it is true, we don't want to tip them off. . ."

"Got it."

"The rest is okay. Everyone knows this occult stuff is going on around here. God only knows how much. But it's no wonder. This stuff is in kids' books nowadays."

She sat back in her chair and looked at him for a long moment while an idea danced around in her mind.

"I see those wheels spinning, Ari. What are you thinking?" He looked so boyish without his hat on. His blond hair was too curly, his eyes too blue, and his cheeks a bit too plump.

She decided to just think out loud. "Well, I might be able to find out a few things about the extent of these activities around here.

What if I were to do a series about the rise of New Age and occult interest among millennials? You know, what they call 'progressive occultism.' I could interview the owners of New Age head shops and botanicas. Maybe someone will know about occult operatives in the area or at least give us an idea of how vast a network is out there."

Cal's face lit with interest. "I like it. And it just might help. Give us a few places to look."

"Great! Let me run it by Annette." Ari was already on her feet.

"Ari."

She stopped with her hand on the doorknob.

"Keep us informed of where you're going and who you're seeing. Just in case. And keep your cell phone on at all times so we can track you if we have to."

"You're giving me the willies, Cal," she tried to joke.

"I'm serious. Most of the people involved in this stuff are stupid kids or kooky tree huggers, but like I said, some of them are very, very dangerous. And they could care less who they kill. The meaner the better, and I'm talking about some really merciless torture like skinning people alive, burning them in their cars, cutting out their hearts. . ."

Ari looked at him, horrified.

"I'm sorry, but you have to know what we could be dealing with here, Ari. This isn't like a corruption case. These are mean perps too, but not like this. This is. . .this is inhuman stuff. So, if anything seems strange to you, run it by me or Jesse. He gave you his card, right?"

"He did."

"Trust me, he only gave it to you because of your work with the FBI on the Flint case. Otherwise, you'd never get anywhere near Sandoval's squad."

"Why do you say that? He seemed like a nice enough guy." *Besides being the most handsome man on the planet.*

"Oh, he is, but he supervises a very elite squad. They're experts on gangs and, in particular, gangs that are associated with Satanism, such as MS-13. He spent some time in South America working with law enforcement on some of the meanest streets in Honduras, El Salvador, and Mexico. Now he's supervising a whole squad, and I don't think the man is even forty years old. He's got the instincts, they say, but he's not like Tony DeAngelo, who was all business."

"Yeah, he was a really stiff guy. Tough to get along with."

"Sandoval's the exact opposite. Laid back, cracks jokes, does a lot of his own field work—a real humble guy—but he's brilliant and he runs a tight ship. His team reveres him. They call him '*El Jefe*' which means 'The Boss.' If you got his card, use it. He'll tell you himself that some of these people are ugly, so don't try to go it alone. Keep us abreast of what you're doing. Stay safe."

Ari let all this information wash over her before nodding. "Got it."

Twenty minutes later, she was back at the office, pitching her idea to Annette.

"I love it. Get on it as soon as you can," Annette said, whipping off her glasses and pushing her laptop aside. "Give it a catchy title. . .Mystical Marvels, or something like that."

"I like it!"

"But stay on the hate crime story. You know how the media chiefs are. They like articles like this because it keeps the priest abuse story in the news and makes the Church look bad. They're always eager to disparage Christianity. Typical 'woke' crowd, always crowing about how tolerant they are while being intolerant of anyone who disagrees with them." She rolled her eyes at the ceiling. "Sure do miss the good old days when the media let the news make itself instead of manufacturing it to suit an agenda.”

“That kind of reporting is ancient history, Annette. They don’t even teach it in college anymore.”

“Tragic. The Fourth Estate is here to stay. So, what about the murder? Did Cal have anything else for you?”

“They found some trace evidence. Marty might have tried to fight them off, which means there could be some DNA under his finger-nails. The evidence is at Quantico.”

“Damn FBI,” Annette cursed under her breath. “I wish they weren’t involved. You’ll never get anything out of them. They never talk to reporters.”

“I got a card from one of them! Some guy named Sandoval. Cal was going on and on about him and how great he is.”

“Maybe so, but we both know he won’t let you print anything unless you get it from their press spokesman.” She suddenly stopped and cracked a half-smile. “Unless you put those baby blues to work.”

They winked at each other. “I’ll see what I can do, boss.” The thought of flirting with a drop-dead gorgeous FBI agent like Jesse Sandoval was enough to make Ari feel giddy as she headed out of the office and back into her cubby.

The go-ahead to write a new series always lit a fire in her gut and made her anxious to begin. She decided to write this series the way she wrote everything else, fact-based and with various points-of-view equally represented. Because she was so intimately involved in this kind of spirituality, she looked forward to learning more about the various practices she had been enjoying for years.

Why not get started today? She decided to visit her psychic on the way home to ply her for possible contacts, then whipped out her phone and texted her.

"I knew you were going to call today, Ari," Priscilla texted back right away. "Come at 4:30. I'll be waiting."

SIX

PRISCILLA TOMLINSON WAS UNIQUE in that she didn't look like a typical psychic, and her home was unlike those run-down ranchers with the half-lit neon sign in the window shouting, "Psychic Readings Here!" Hers was just a normal-looking home on a nice tree-lined suburban street.

Priscilla was a heavy-set woman in her late fifties who managed to pull off a nice balance between accentuating her curves while keeping hidden what she wanted hidden. Her clothes were plain, usually dark stretch pants and a flowing blouse that was always clean and pressed. Her hair had been bleached to the point of destruction, but she did an admirable job of styling it around her face in a way that flattered her nearly wrinkle-free complexion.

"Sit here, Ari," she said in her usual dreamy, stargazer kind of voice. "I've been thinking about you."

"Anything good?"

"It's always good where you're concerned. Your energy is intoxicating."

Priscilla always made Ari feel good about herself, which is why she'd been coming here almost monthly for the last ten years.

They settled at a small dining table in the corner of a neatly furnished living room that smelled of patchouli with a hint of lavender. Priscilla reached across the table and took both of Ari's hands in her own. Her hands were warm and soft and soothing.

"How have you been, Ari?"

"Okay."

"Just okay? There's a sadness about you. Was the holiday difficult?"

"No. Thanksgiving is not bad because Mom and Dad don't come for that. Christmas is the one I hate."

"I sense a darkness. . ."

"Someone was murdered at Gram's church this week."

"Ah. . .that explains it."

The psychic closed her eyes, took a deep sigh, and fell silent for a long moment. Suddenly, her brows crinkled, and her eyes shot open. "This is dangerous. The murder. . .there is real darkness involved here."

Ari immediately thought of the Hood. "The police suspect it was the work of Satanists."

"Yes, yes, they're right. Pure evil is at work here."

Ari's interest piqued. "Is there a lot of Satanism around here, Priscilla?"

"Yes, quite a bit."

"Do you know any of the people involved in it?"

"Not well. I just know of them. The real Satanists keep to themselves. Most of the ones I know don't really worship Satan. They just see him as a pre-Christian life principal worth emulating. You know the type, the 'indulgence instead of abstinence' and 'vengeance instead of turning the other cheek' crowd."

She stopped, and a deep frown furrowed her carefully plucked brows. "But this isn't the type I'm sensing here. I'm sensing the real Satan worshipers. Some might even be possessed by him. . ."

"You don't think the devil's real, do you?"

"Does it matter? Whatever it is, it commits acts of evil and you could be in danger, Ari, but. . .but. . ." Priscilla fell silent for a minute too long.

"But what?" Ari prompted.

"Someone is protecting you. Someone very powerful. A man. Someone you barely know now, but you will, maybe even. . ." she stopped again, slowly squeezed her hands.

These pauses were brutal. The suspense had Ari on the edge of her seat. But she knew better than to interrupt. Whenever Priscilla acted this way, she was onto something big.

"I think. . .I think we need to look at your chart, Ari."

She got up, opened a drawer in an old file cabinet in the next room and returned with Ari's natal chart. After glancing at it for several moments, she asked, "Have you been seeing any Angel signs lately, repeating numbers like 111 or 444?"

"No."

"From what your chart is showing, Saturn is about to transition into Capricorn, which always triggers some kind of earth-shattering, life-changing moment. Something is going on and it has to do with the murder."

"You started to say something about the person who is protecting me?"

"Yes." Priscilla shut the file and looked directly into Ari's eyes as she said, "It's a love interest. Someone is coming into your life."

Ari's face fell. The last time she'd told her this, it resulted in another date-from-hell.

"No, not this time," Priscilla read her mind. "This is for real. Ari, hold my hands for a moment. I need to keep reading your energy."

They held hands as Priscilla seemed to slip into a deep trance. She began talking then, in a strangely low-pitched voice, much lower than her usual tone.

"You are a chosen soul, Ariella. You have a very special heritage that goes back to ancient times. . .maybe even a past life. It's all about to culminate into something. . .something that has to do with the murder, the man." She stopped again, squeezed her hands very tightly and said in a more normal tone of voice. "You are a woman of destiny, destined to do great things for this world. You were created for this work, and you will accomplish it."

She opened her eyes, blinked a few times, then said, "It's all about to begin."

"What? What will begin?"

"The work that is your destiny."

"Wow," was all Ari could say. "That was. . .incredible."

Ari let go of her hands and sat back in her chair. This was the most intense reading she had ever received. It poked at that place deep inside where she always wondered about who she was, where she came from, where she was going, what was real, and what wasn't. These mostly unspoken questions were part of the reason why she was so interested in the spiritual realm, in what lay beyond human sight and comprehension.

"Yeah," Priscilla said. "Really incredible. I'm glad you came by. This explains why I've been thinking of you." She shook herself, as if trying to shake off the last traces of the trance. "How about a drink? A little wine?"

"Just the usual."

Water. Although Type 1 diabetics could drink, Ari's sugar levels didn't tolerate alcohol very well, so she mostly avoided it.

They talked about other things for a few minutes, then Ari told her about her new story idea.

"Alleluia!" Priscilla said. "We love good publicity and stories that take us seriously."

"Is there any kind of network in this area, like a network of psychics, tarot readers, and wiccans? How do you all communicate with each other?"

"Well, remember, many of us are competitors, but we psychics get together now and again and go out to dinner just to 'talk shop' so to speak." She stopped to think for a moment, then offered, "But there are a few people in this trade whom I would consider to be local leaders. Why don't I give you their contact information? I'm sure they'll talk to you if I vouch for you."

"That would be great. And what about some of those Satanists you mentioned?"

"I don't know them very well, Ari, and I wouldn't want to send you to someone who could be a danger to you. Let me ask around first to see what I can find out."

"Good enough. I would appreciate it. And trust me, this is not going to be a series of hit pieces. I respect what you all do and want to present it in a positive light to the public."

"Gotcha! I'll talk to them for you," Priscilla said with a wink.

SEVEN

MARTY MASON'S FUNERAL WAS PACKED. The crowd filled the side aisles and spilled into the vestibule with people standing two rows deep across the back wall of the church. Men, women, and children of all ages came to pay their respects to the humble sacristan who everyone believed had been a living saint.

"What most people don't know about Marty is that he was an orphan," Fr. Luke said as he began his homily. Robed in a brilliant white chasuble with gold embroidery, his head turned as he slowly scanned the crowd and then opened his arms wide. "Look at this crowd! For an orphan!"

The congregation broke into applause as women wept, men cheered, children giggled, and babies wailed. It was like a wave of joy washing over a thousand grieving hearts. Two pews ahead of Ari sat the Golden Girls, with Alice in the middle and Helen and Betty on either side. They looked at each other and smiled, dabbing at their tears and looking around at the crowd.

When the room settled, Father continued.

"Marty was abandoned by both parents at the age of eight. He had no siblings. They just drove him to the orphanage one day and left him there. Imagine how frightening this must have been for an eight-year-old boy to be taken to this strange new place full of people he didn't know.

"Although the good sisters did what they could on their meager budget, Marty had a difficult time there. He was shy. He didn't fit in well and never made a lot of friends. His life was filled with desperate loneliness until one day at Mass, he heard a verse from the prophet Jeremiah, 'I have loved you with an everlasting love,' and it struck a chord deep in his heart, as if God Himself was speaking those words to his soul at that very moment.

"He could barely imagine love, let alone an everlasting love, because the only love he'd ever known was fleeting, unreliable, and eventually abandoned him. But in that moment, he said he felt a peace, a solace, that seemed to rush over his heart like a warm bath on a cold winter's night. He never felt anything like it before, but the experience touched him so deeply that on the days when he was feeling the most sad and alone, he would go into the chapel and sit in the exact same spot where he heard those words and he would relive the experience.

"God touched him in those moments again and again until he finally realized what was happening to him. He was having an encounter with the Living God. God was real. He was alive. And he became Marty's only friend.

"Slowly but surely, that everlasting love began to heal Marty, and he blossomed into a fine young man who excelled in sports and school and eventually his job as a postal clerk. He wore his uniform proudly and quite handsomely, I hear from the woman who captured his heart, the woman he referred to as his 'Irish Rose'—Rose MacMurray—the love of his life."

Everyone craned their necks to see Rose, who was sitting in the front row on the Blessed Mother's side, dressed in all black and flanked by the couple's two sons. The only thing Ari could see of Rose was her fisted hand raising a crumbled Kleenex to her face.

"It was Rose who showed Marty that not all love leads to

abandonment and heartbreak. Like the love of her Creator, Rose's love was faithful and true for more than fifty years.

"Marty served the post office for four decades and served just as long as sacristan in our churches, until we were blessed to welcome him to our staff more than twenty years ago. He wanted to remain close to his 'only friend' and would come here to open the church at 5:00 a.m., serve the 7:00 a.m. Mass, then go to work. Did it every day, fiercely loyal up to the last day when the church alarm went off at 5:00 a.m. on the morning of November 29th.

"Of course, he didn't hesitate to get up, get dressed, and rush across the street to investigate, and there came upon the perpetrators of this shocking crime. Marty's earthly life ended that morning and, as sad and heartbroken as we are, who among us does not rejoice that Marty is now with his 'only friend' forever? Now, he is enjoying the promise of everlasting love made to that little orphan boy so many years ago." Father's voice cracked ever so slightly, and it was only then that Ari noticed how mesmerized the whole congregation was by this story, including herself.

He cleared his throat. "Marty Mason's life was a triumph of love, it was a natural and supernatural love story, a testament to the triumph of love over abandonment, faithlessness, woundedness, and despair. Through Marty, God taught us what a higher love can do. . .if we let it."

It was one of the most moving stories she had ever heard. There were actually tears puddled in her eyes. How poignantly she related to what that little orphan boy must have felt the day he realized his parents no longer wanted him. Only someone who had been in the same place could know the kind of terror that rattled through a child when this realization was made.

"You're the one who wanted a baby!" her father's voice shouted from her memory.

"I thought it would bring us closer together," her mother shouted back.

"Well, it didn't. Neither of us want her and now we're stuck with her."

"*We're* stuck with her? You dump her on me all the time." Her mother's voice was getting shrill, the way it always did when she was angry.

Her father scoffed. "What am I supposed to do with an eight-year-old girl?"

"Give her to your mother!"

"Are you crazy? We can't do that! She'd never stand for it!"

"Just tell her the truth! We made a mistake. Ari will be better off with her than us."

"No! I'm not doing it!"

"We can't keep her! She's tearing us apart."

It had been years since the memory of that night flashed so vividly in Ari's mind. The fear, the panic, came back so poignantly it was startling and left her feeling oddly shaken by how ferocious those feelings returned as she sat in the pew next to Jacqui. How could these memories be so fresh, so clear, after all this time? With all her might, she struggled to cram them back into the deep black hole inside her where she stored these and other ugly recollections from her childhood. She tried to look away, to think of something else, to do anything that might help her ignore the gut-wrenching, almost nauseating, sorrow that flooded over her heart the same way it did on that night so long ago.

Get a grip!

She started fumbling around in her purse, silently scolding herself for having looked at those memories. Anytime they tried to rear their ugly heads, she would push them away, but she couldn't today for some strange reason. Instead, she sat here, steeped in the same smothering desperation she felt that night. It was as if she was left permanently traumatized by that single conversation, forever waiting for the day when they would take her away and never bring her home again.

Just like Marty.

An hour later, she and Jacqui were on their way back from the cemetery and headed down into a church hall that smelled like coffee and hot roast beef. Children, pent up from the confines of a church service, were releasing their energy by sliding across the glossy waxed floors and chasing each other through the crowd. Everyone was talking at once and the din became louder and louder as more people piled into the room and lined up at the food tables.

She was just about to get in line when someone tugged on her arm. "Excuse me, aren't you Ari Dalton?"

It was one of the Golden Girls.

"Hello, Helen," she said to the same petite woman she'd seen on the morning of the murder. The woman's short white hair was just as perfectly coifed, but now Ari could see into a pair of pretty green eyes that were sunken into the folds of crinkled, pink skin. Her rouged cheeks were jowly, and her lips were painted a rather startling shade of coral.

"How do you know me?" Helen asked in surprise.

"I was standing near you on the morning of the crime. You probably didn't see me."

"Oh! Well, I'm Helen Babbitt. And you're Jacqui Dalton's granddaughter!"

"I am."

Helen looked around herself, then grabbed Ari's arm and steered her closer to the cinder block walls of the hall. "I need to tell you something. It's about the article you wrote. Something in it was inaccurate."

"It was?"

"Well, you said that there was no history of abuse in this parish. That's debatable."

"It is? Why do you say that?"

Helen lowered her voice to a whisper. "There was a priest here about thirty years ago. He was here one day and gone the next. No one ever said where he went or why."

"Do you suspect something?"

She completely ignored the question and went on. "He wasn't the pastor, just the parochial vicar, but I know someone whose son was, well. . .hurt by him."

"Hurt? Do you mean molested?"

"Shhh! Hardly anyone knows this. Not even Fr. Luke," Helen said, unaware of how hard she was squeezing Ari's arm. "His mother told me about it once."

"Can you give me her name?"

"No! At least not yet. I'd have to talk to her first."

"Can this go on the record?"

"Good heavens, no!" She looked ready to faint. "It's just something for you to look into."

"But I'm working with law enforcement, the police, the FBI. If there's some information that will help this case, I would have to tell them."

"I know that, and she may agree to it, but I have to talk to her first."

"Of course!" Ari was intrigued enough to give Helen her card. "Call me when you talk to her and let her know that nothing goes on the record unless she permits it."

"I'll do that." Helen smiled a bit smugly, tucked the card into her handbag, and walked away.

Ari made her way back toward the food line. Her sugar was low, and she was starting to feel shaky. As slyly as possible, she reached into her bag, found the gummy bears, and shoved a fistful into her mouth when no one was looking—except, of course, Gram.

"Let me get you some juice," Jacqui said knowingly and came back with one of the children's juice boxes.

It did the trick.

"Do you see Adam Thiel anywhere?"

"Yes, he's right over there." Jacqui pointed at a tall, thin young man with a crop of shaggy brown hair and a long, pointed face.

"I'll be right back."

Ari approached and waited for him to stop speaking with a parishioner.

"Adam Thiel?"

"Yes, ma'am."

"Ari Dalton of the *Pennsylvania Tribune*. Do you have a minute?"

"I guess." His small, narrow-set brown eyes lighted upon her just briefly, almost shyly.

"I'm writing a follow-up story on Marty and this hate crime. How close were you two?"

"We were sort of close," he shrugged, obviously not the sort to offer much information. She was going to have to drag it out of him.

"I'm sure you spoke to the police."

He laughed shortly. "Yeah, lots of times. The FBI too."

"It must have been very traumatic for you."

"Yeah. I was scared. Real scared."

"And you didn't see anything at all?"

He suddenly looked nervous, his eyes darting around the room, everywhere but on her face. "No, ma'am. Nothing. He was on the pavement when I got here."

"Did you hear anything? Any noises like people running away?"

"Nope," he said a bit too quickly. "It was quiet like it always is at that hour."

This line of questioning was obviously making him nervous, which made her instantly suspicious.

"What is it like to have to carry on without him?"

"He taught me real well," he said. Ari clocked his half-answer.

"If there was one thing you could say to him right now, what would it be?"

He shifted in his shoes, shoved his hands in his pocket, and then said rather sadly, "Wish I could have helped you."

She patted his arm. "I'm sure you do. Thank you for your time."

Hours later, a follow-up story about "Monmouth's Saint in the Making" was online, and Ari went home to spend a quiet evening helping Chloe do homework. She tried to meditate but her thoughts kept floating back to that sermon, that story, the connection that was made between Marty's wounded heart and her own.

". . .the only love he'd ever known was fleeting, unreliable, and eventually abandoned him," Fr. Luke had said. "But in that moment, he said he felt a peace, a solace, that seemed to rush over his heart like a warm bath on a cool winter's night. God touched him in those moments again and again until he finally realized what was happening to him. He was having an encounter with the Living God."

What did that mean? Who was the Living God? Was it an energy of some kind? A spirit guide? An astrological force? What power could touch a child as wounded as Marty and not only leave him healed, but change the whole course of his life? Was it possible that a human could make such a personal connection with a Being from another realm?

If so, could it happen to her?

The question barely registered in her mind when a counter suggestion quickly smothered it.

This can never happen to you. You're too broken. There's no hope. You're going to live the rest of your life like this, with this ache in your soul, slowly tearing you apart, until one day you just decide to end it all.

At first, she passed off these thoughts as coming from her usual vast pool of self-loathing, but there was something about them that seemed different. There was a power in them, like they were coming from somewhere other than herself. She shivered, hugged herself, and looked around the room, half suspecting someone to be there.

Just then, another thought sped across her mind about the quarry on Swamp Road and how easy it would be to drive off the road and through the wire fencing that protected people and animals from falling into the quarter-mile-deep chasm. It would only be terrifying for a few seconds during the drop, but once the car hit bottom, she would die instantly.

What the hell?

She sat up and shook herself. Hard.

Why am I thinking like this?

It had been a long time since she'd thought of suicide, and even then, she never thought about how to do it, just that it would at least make the pain, the self-hatred, the shame, finally stop.

But that was before Chloe. Once her daughter was born, there was no way she would ever kill herself. Chloe suffered enough from her negligent father. The last thing Ari would ever do is abandon her too.

She laid back down, tried to focus on the new series, on how intrigued she was by the spiritual, the supernatural. Behind her closed eyes, she recalled pictures of Marty Mason, a slight little man with a shock of white hair and a happy-go-lucky smile whose lifetime was on display in two giant photo collages that were set up in the vestibule of the church. She wanted to remember him as he appeared in those photos, not the way she last saw him, crumpled on the sidewalk outside the sacristy of St. Peter Damian's Church.

She couldn't shake the feeling that something very evil was afoot. And it seemed to be very near her.

I can almost feel it.

EIGHT

"WHAT'S WRONG, ARI? You're not yourself."

Ari and MK were on their yoga mats, their brows to the floor as they relaxed into the child's pose.

"I'm sorry to be such a drag."

"You're not a drag, I just know you too well. You can't get away with anything with me."

It was true. No one knew her like MK. They had been best friends since the age of ten, had gone to the same schools and the same college. Mary Katherine Paige was always the brightest—and the brashest—kid in the class, famous for her quick wit and penchant for hyperboles.

"It's the murder. . .and the homily at the Mass," Ari admitted.

"The homily? What were you doing at Mass?"

"Fr. Luke let me come to interview people."

"Oh, that's right. I read your piece. It was nice."

The instructor led them through a stretching sequence which usually relaxed Ari, but tonight, she just couldn't loosen up.

"What about the homily?"

"Marty was an orphan. His parents abandoned him at an orphanage."

"Who does stuff like that?" MK snarled into the mat.

"Parents like mine," Ari said dryly. "Only his actually did what I was always terrified my parents would do to me, just leave me somewhere one day."

Their eyes met and she saw the sorrow flit through MK's pretty brown eyes. They were soft eyes, doe-ish, and expressive. At times such as this, she felt as if she was seeing her own soul mirrored in the eyes of this long-time faithful friend.

"I'm sorry. I know how you hate to be reminded of it."

Ari sighed and rolled over. "It came back with a vengeance at the funeral like I haven't remembered it in years. I don't know why it still bothers me so much."

"Because you drop out of counseling before anyone can get anywhere with you. That's why you never heal."

"All they want to do is talk about it! I just want to forget it and move on!"

"Shhh!" the man next to her hissed at them.

MK rolled her eyes and whispered, "Old grumpy pants strikes again."

When the class was over, they rolled up their mats and headed for the door.

"I know what you need, girlfriend."

"What?"

"Your energy's out of whack. Let's go see Kim and Susie and get ourselves a good massage. They're open 'til eight. No appointment necessary."

Twenty minutes later, they were laying on two tables side-by-side in the main room of K&S BodyWorks. Susie was working Ari hard, pressing and pushing at the muscles in her back until she was sighing with delight.

"This feels great. . ."

"You are a tense woman," Susie said.

"I told you," MK muffled into her towel as Kim quietly plied the muscles of her shoulders. "Her energy's all out of whack."

"Maybe you need a Reiki massage instead," Susie suggested.

"I'll try anything," Ari offered.

Susie switched from a Swedish massage to a hands-off technique that Ari had only experienced once before. But the masseuse at the time was a bit curt and Ari couldn't make a connection with her. Their personalities didn't meld the way hers and Susie's did.

"Whatever you're doing feels really good," Ari breathed.

MK turned her head to look at her and grin, smug with herself for having come up with just the right idea. The expression made her look even more girlish than she already did with her short, curly blonde hair and petite little frame. Jacqui called them "Laurel and Hardy" because they were polar opposites in appearance. Ari was tall and dark; MK was short and blonde.

"What are you grinning at?"

"You! And you wanted to go straight home."

"No, I didn't," Ari scoffed and changed the subject. "And what are you doing to your hair? Are you letting your roots grow out again?"

"Yes. So what?"

"The blonde is better."

"I've been wearing my hair like this since I was ten."

"Okay, so you want a change. Just let it grow longer."

"It's too thin and breaks off when it gets to my shoulders."

"Get some hot oil treatments. Try to strengthen it."

"It's easy for you to say, Miss Universe, with your perfect hair, perfect eyes, perfect boobs, perfect butt."

"I hate you, MK."

Kim and Susie burst out laughing.

"Don't laugh at her! She's ruining it for me. I could lay here all night," Ari sighed again, rapt in the pleasure of the heat soaking into her muscles. "Why does this feel so wonderful?"

"Reiki is more of an energy therapy than a massage," Susie said sweetly. "It's based on the concept that disturbances in a person's energy field can result in feeling poorly, even causing illness. What I'm doing with my hands right now is serving as a channel for my spirit guide, who is directing the energy from the Reiki Source into every energy imbalance in your body to eliminate any obstructions and restore your balance."

"I think it's working. . ." Ari breathed. "Your spirit guide is the best."

"Watch it, she's a reporter," MK quipped. "The next thing she'll want to know is the name of your spirit guide, when you linked up with him, where he lives in the universe, and if he might be willing to make a comment."

They all laughed, including Ari, who was feeling better now than she had since Marty's funeral.

"Speaking of being a reporter, I'm starting a series for the *Trib* on all the metaphysical activities going on in this area. Maybe we could do something on Reiki and energy work and include interviews with you. It might be good for your business. How does that sound to you?"

"We'd love it!" Kim said.

"I'm in!" Susie exclaimed.

"Great! It's the least I can do after this great massage."

Before leaving, they checked into the various membership programs that would include weekly massages.

"Let's go again. How about next Saturday?" MK suggested. "We can get a massage and go Christmas shopping at that new International Mall over in Oak Terrace. I hear they have some fabulous Fair Trade stuff like you won't find anywhere else, even on the internet."

"I've done most of my shopping, but I'd love to go."

An hour later, Ari had finished up a load of laundry, cleaned the bathrooms, and helped Chloe straighten her bedroom.

"Where'd you get all this energy?" Jacqui asked as she was fixing herself a cup of tea before bed.

"I had a Reiki massage tonight and it was really great!" she said without thinking. She instantly regretted it when Gram got that look on her face, a kind of dimming of its usual brightness, the way it always did when Ari talked about anything New Age.

As usual, Jacqui never said a word. She didn't have to. Her suddenly discordant energy said it all.

"Sleep well, my love," was all she said as she headed down the hall to her room.

"You too, Gram."

Sorry I disappointed you.

Again.

NINE

ARI WENT TO BED HAPPY but woke up feeling groggy and terrible. Her sugar see-sawed all day long. It was either too much or too little and set off the glucose meter what seemed like every ten minutes.

"Maybe you should go home and relax for the rest of the day," Annette called from inside her office without looking up from what she was doing.

"I don't know what's wrong with me today," Ari muttered to her colleague, Janey, who kept glancing at her worriedly. The girl was fresh out of college and still trying to deal with the harsher realities of life beyond the dorm room with its murders, robberies, white collar crimes, and Type 1 diabetes—all within ten miles and, in some cases, within ten feet of her.

"I'll update the calendar for you, Ari. Just go."

"Yeah. I guess you're right. I felt so good last night, though."

She considered another Reiki massage, then decided a nice refreshing walk in Pennypack Park would be the best thing for her. It was a beautiful day, the sun was shining, and it wasn't too cold. She steered her pale blue Honda CRV into the closest spot she could find at the condos, ran upstairs, and changed into jeans, sneakers, and a sweatshirt, pulled her hair up into a ponytail, and was back in the car in less than twenty minutes.

The scenery in the park had lost its fiery fall foliage and was now painted in the dull grayish-brown shades of winter, except for the occasional burst of evergreen. Ari parked close to the entrance of the main path and hopped out of the car.

She saw it immediately, the minute her foot hit the ground.

One of the two wooden posts erected at the entrance of the path had a peculiar marking on it, painted in pale blue. It looked like a triangle laying on its side, but with no bottom on it. Instead, there was a line extending upward with a little box painted on the end.

It was familiar, but from where? Where had she seen this before?

"Yes! At the church, this was one of the symbols," she said out loud and looked around to be sure no one overheard.

She was quite alone. There were no other cars in the parking lot.

Bending close over the symbol, she studied it for a long moment, certain now that it was one of the symbols that had been drawn on the church. Her first thought was to text Cal, but then she thought of that FBI agent, the one who made her heart skip a beat just looking at him.

Why not?

She pulled his card out of her wallet. *Federal Bureau of Investigation. Supervisory Special Agent Jesse J. Sandoval.*

She snapped a photo of the symbol, flipped the card over, and texted it to the number scrawled on the back. "Ari Dalton here. Isn't this the same symbol that was painted on the church wall at St. Peter Damian's?" she texted and decided to sit on the bench just inside the trail to wait for a response.

Her phone beeped a few minutes later. It was Agent Sandoval.

"It is. Where did you see it?"

"On a post at the main entrance to Pennypack Park in Monmouth. I just arrived and saw it right away."

"Stay there. I'm on my way."

She was surprised at his response, then excited about the prospect of seeing him again, until reality set in. If the symbol was connected to the hate crimes, should she be sitting out here all alone? What if the person who drew that Satanic symbol on the post was still here? Maybe she should sit in the car with the doors locked.

Good idea.

The FBI field office was in center city Philadelphia, which was about twenty miles away, so it was a good thirty minutes before a big black Range Rover SUV pulled into the parking lot and slid into the spot directly alongside her car. She hopped out of the car just as the same two agents she'd met at the church last week did the same. The lighting was much better now than when she first saw them, and she was surprised at how much younger they looked. Neither man appeared much older than herself, perhaps in their mid-thirties. Dressed in jeans and navy-blue FBI jackets, their eyes hidden behind mirrored sunglasses, they were even more formidable than she remembered.

"Hello, Ari. Jesse Sandoval. We met at the church." He motioned toward the slightly taller Black man at his side. "You remember Mackenzie Jones."

"Just call me Mack," his friend offered.

"Hello, Mack."

"Miss Dalton."

"Call me Ari."

The two of them went straight to the post, flipped up their sunglasses, and squatted down to inspect it. For several minutes, they studied the scene so closely Ari dared not speak for fear of ruining their concentration.

"Same as the church," Jesse muttered.

"Same color paint," Mack added. "I want to compare it to the photos we have of the church, see how similar it is, maybe drawn by the same hand?"

They both started flipping through the pictures on their cellphones.

"Sure looks like it," Jesse said and held a picture up to the drawing.

Mack whistled through his teeth. "I'd say it's the same hand. How do you like that?"

"Get forensics out here."

"*Sí señor.*"

They each started snapping pictures with their cellphones.

Jesse stood up and looked back at Ari, the wind blowing a bit of his jet-black hair across his eyes. If MK was there right then, she'd be swooning at his feet.

"You didn't touch anything, did you?" he asked and shook the hair out of his eyes.

What?

"Of course not!" she said, offended.

"Uh-oh!" Mack looked up with a big grin on his face. "You're getting the stink eye, *amigo*."

Jesse put up his hands in mock self-defense. "No offense! I was just asking."

"And I'm just telling," she said, trying not to smile at their antics. They hadn't been there five minutes, and she was already starting to like them. But if she was going to work with the FBI on this case, they had to get a few things straight. "I know what evidence is and I don't touch it. You can trust me."

"Good to know," Jesse said and looked at her with obvious appreciation. "However. . ."

"Uh-oh, this is where he lays down the law," Mack joked.

"Nothing we say or do is on the record unless we say so," Jesse said in an unyielding tone of voice that instantly reminded Ari of everything Cal had said about him. "Agreed?"

"Agreed," she sighed.

Sorry, Annette.

She decided to change the subject. "What does this symbol mean?"

"It's a trail marker," Jesse said, his attention turning toward the path. "They're used to direct people to the location of a secret event." His voice trailed off as he looked up the path. "It's pointing up there and then directing them to the left."

"Oh! I think I know where that is!" Ari said brightly and started up the path. Now that she had two armed FBI agents at her side, what was there to fear? "There's a large clearing up here."

"Let us go first," Mack said and skirted around her. "Just in case."

That was probably a good idea.

They walked for several minutes before reaching a fork in the path and the two agents started off to the left.

"No, not that way. It's over here. It's not on the path," she said and started stepping over branches and weaving around bushes. They walked for several minutes, deeper and deeper into the woods.

"How did you ever find this place?" Jesse asked.

"My daughter. She pretends to be Pocahontas."

They both chuckled.

It was a rigorous hike, and she tripped more than once, which made both agents nervous. Mack would reach for her, and Jesse would mutter something in Spanish under his breath that sounded like "*Santa Maria.*"

They finally came to a large clearing, well-illuminated by a late afternoon sun that drenched the area in giant puddles of bright, golden light. It was beautiful there, so quiet, and smelled of fresh earth with a hint of pine. A twig cracked nearby and both agents turned toward the sound, their hands instinctively reaching for the guns under their jackets.

"It's probably just—" Ari began, but Jesse put up his hand for silence. He came to stand in front of her, his back to her as he scanned the woods in all directions. Mack took up a similar position, doing the same thing in the opposite direction. The two men were so tall she could not see around them and found herself staring at their backs until Jesse finally relaxed.

"Probably just a rabbit or something," he said and returned his attention to the clearing. "This looks wiccan to me."

He motioned at the rocks of various shapes and sizes that were arranged in a circle in the middle of the clearing. "Those rocks. . .wiccans arrange them in a circle because they believe it protects them from dark spirits. Satanists don't typically do this around their ritual sites because they don't want protection from the dark, they consort with it."

"Oh." She'd never heard that before.

"It's possible that this is a meeting place of some kind," Mack was thinking out loud. "But Wiccans claim they're not into Satan so why would they use the Theban alphabet and on a church wall?"

"I don't know," Jesse said. "But remember, these dudes are very eclectic. They're into everything. Wiccans aren't normally connected to Satanism, but there's no law saying they can't be. They do what they want."

"Yeah, but the Satanists might meet somewhere else out here. Maybe we're reading the symbol wrong," Mack suggested.

"You're right. Let's look over here." Jesse was already heading back toward the main path. For such a big man, he moved in and out of the woods with great stealth and ease, his head constantly moving as he scanned the surroundings.

They finally ended up back on the path.

"Something's going on out here, *amigo*," Mack pointed out. "It's the same hand, the same color paint. There's a connection."

"Let forensics scour the area and see what they find," Jesse pulled out his cellphone and texted someone.

"Can't hurt."

"God knows we need something." Jesse ran a hand through his hair in a gesture of frustration. "Anything."

"No leads?" Ari asked, and he looked at her as if he just remembered she was there.

"A few things, some footprints," he evaded.

She knew FBI agents were not permitted to talk to the press, but it didn't hurt to ask. "Cal said some trace evidence was sent to Quantico?"

"We got some fibers," Mack told her as they all started to make their way back down the path. "It might help down the road, but for now, we're stumped."

They walked quietly for a few minutes, each in their own thoughts.

"I talked to Adam Thiele at the funeral," Ari mentioned. "I don't know about you, but there was something about him that I thought was, well. . ."

"Suspicious?" Jesse asked.

"Yes! You too?"

They both nodded.

"He probably saw something, and they threatened him," Jesse said.

"Threatened to kill him if he said anything," Mack finished the thought. "It happens all the time. Witnesses say they saw nothing, but they really did."

"He's just a kid," Ari said. "He was probably traumatized by all this."

"He's not acting traumatized though," Jesse argued, and they all stopped to look at him. "He's acting scared. There's a difference. It's slight, but it's different. Someone who is traumatized is not all there, like they're in a mild state of shock. Someone who is scared is all there, but jumpy, shifty-eyed."

"That describes almost perfectly how he behaved with me," Ari said. "But that's not all. One of the parishioners told me something that I want to check into."

"Like what?" the men both asked at once.

"A woman named Helen Babbitt claims to know someone whose son was possibly molested by a priest at St. Peter Damian's."

They both stopped on the trail behind her.

"And?" Jesse asked.

"She won't give me any names and doesn't want to talk to anyone unless she gets permission from this person. Helen is an older woman, so I'm not sure how credible she is. I intend to talk to Fr. Luke about it."

"There's a lot of history of molestation in this diocese," Mack said, "and it's certainly a viable motive for murder."

"There's a lot of molestation everywhere," Jesse agreed. "It seems inside the Church is not a whole lot different than outside the Church. But remember, the molestation did not necessarily have to take place at St. Peter Damian's. It could be just someone out for revenge on the whole Church and any church within their reach," he opined.

"True," she said, and they all looked at one another for a long, sober moment.

Ari turned back to the trail. "But why Marty? Such a sweet

old man."

"That might have been an accident," Jesse said. "Marty spooked them, so they hit him a little too hard."

"Father said he probably died instantly."

"I'm sure he felt nothing," Jesse said.

"The whole parish is—"

Beep. Beep. Beep. Her meter sounded.

"What the. . ." Both agents froze, their hands once again reaching for the guns under their jackets.

"It's just me! My meter," she said quickly.

"Your what?"

"My, uh, continuous glucose meter."

"What is that?" Jesse asked.

"I'm a diabetic, Type 1," she said, utterly mortified now. "The meter is connected to an insulin pump." She patted a spot on her abdomen. "It's, well, this is probably too much information. I'm so sorry, but can I check my meter?"

"Sure!"

"You want to get your hands off your guns first?"

"Oh. . .sorry."

The meter said her sugar was low, which didn't surprise her. She had been feeling weak ever since they'd reached the clearing but had thought it might have been from the physical exertion.

"This meter has been going off all day," she grumbled, reaching into her back pocket, pulling out a bag of gummy bears, and tossing a handful into her mouth. "I'm so sick of gummy bears."

The two agents just stood there, as still as statues, staring at her as if they'd never seen a woman with diabetes before.

Ari munched away, looked between them, and choked on a laugh. "If you could see yourselves right now," she joked because it took their attention off her. "Like two fish who suddenly found themselves out of water."

Mack took the bait. "Fish, eh?" He playfully punched Jesse's shoulder and said, "He's the barracuda. I'm the peaceful one, like a dolphin."

Jesse scoffed. "You mean bottom feeder, right?"

She grinned, liking their easy banter. "You two are more fun than you look," she quipped, and they all laughed at each other.

But she still felt weak.

"I'm just going to sit for a few minutes. You go ahead."

"What? We're not leaving you here," Jesse said as if that was the stupidest thing he'd ever heard. He took hold of her elbow and steered her toward a fallen tree. "Sit here."

"I'll get her some water," Mack said and headed down the path for the car.

"No really! I'm okay. This happens all the time."

"Just sit here and rest," Jesse said in a tone of voice that was just commanding enough to make her realize there was no point in arguing with him.

So, she sat.

TEN

JESSE SAT NEXT TO ARI, elbows on his knees, his fingers laced together. He had the biggest hands she'd ever seen.

No wedding ring.

She took a deep breath, closed her eyes, and shoved her hands up the sleeves of her sweatshirt to hide their shaking.

"You're cold?" He immediately took off his jacket, exposing the Glock that was holstered under his left arm, then draped it over her shoulders. It smelled like him, clean and musky.

"I'm embarrassed."

"Don't be. My godmother has diabetes."

"Oh. That's too bad," she said and opened her eyes to look at him.

His eyes were as brown and luscious as melted milk chocolate, with long lashes that any woman would envy. She could almost feel his eyes as they swept over her face, from the top of her head to the bottom of her slightly pointed chin, slow enough to cause a fluttery feeling in the pit of her stomach.

Butterflies? Me?

They both looked away at the same time.

"So how did you get involved in this kind of crime?" she asked, trying not to feel unnerved.

"I was assigned to gangs right out of Quantico because I'm bilingual."

"MS-13?"

"Exactly. Some of those punks believe Satan tells them what to do, and I soon found out that he probably does."

"What do you mean?"

"One of my first assignments involved a thirteen-year-old kid who was possessed by the devil."

"Oh, come on!"

"I'm serious!" They were looking at each other again and she liked his attention, the way he looked at her, as if he appreciated what he saw.

"He stood about five foot three inches tall, weighed maybe 140 pounds," he said with great animation, as if he secretly enjoyed the danger. "He picked me up and threw me against a wall so hard, I had a hematoma on the back of my head the size of a baseball. I'm six four and weigh 220 pounds." He chuckled at her obvious astonishment. "How does that happen?"

"It can't. . .it's impossible."

"Except if you're possessed. That's one of the signs. Unnatural strength."

"You don't really believe in that, do you?"

It was his turn to look surprised. "Don't you?"

"Not really."

"If you don't mind me asking, what is your faith?"

"I'm a none."

He sat back, looked her over in obvious astonishment. "A nun?"

She burst out laughing. "Oh! Sorry! I meant none. N.O.N.E."

"Oh! I was going to say they don't make nuns the way they used to."

She giggled, and he smiled like he liked the sound of it.

"None, eh? Well, in my line of work, you need faith. When you come face to face with *el diablo*, there's only one weapon that can take him out, and you'd better have it."

He was serious now. Dead serious. It made a chill run down her spine.

He seemed to sense it. "Forget it. My line of work is not the kind of thing a lady wants to hear about."

"I can handle it," she scoffed, unaware of the fear that was still sparking in her blue eyes.

He hid a smile. "I don't doubt it. I hear you're pretty fearless when it comes to tracking down crime," he said.

"Oh? Who told you that?"

"DeAngelo. That's the only reason I'm talking to you right now, because I know you can be trusted."

They looked at each other again and she had the impression that he had just paid her a very high compliment. "Thanks. I'm feeling stronger now."

"Are you sure?"

"Yes." She got up, took a few steps. "It just takes a few minutes for the sugar to go to work."

"Okay but take my arm. I won't bite you."

She agreed and took the arm he offered as they made their way back to the path. Still slightly weak, she was glad for the support. As they walked along, she told him about the feature she was planning for the *Tribune*.

"I see its purpose as two-fold. First, it will help to educate people about the metaphysical world, and second, it might give us a few leads about local covens or cults that might be involved in Satanism, perhaps a link to the people who murdered Marty."

He was quiet for a moment, just long enough for her to look up at him and see his dark brows furrowed in thought.

"You don't like the idea?"

"I do like the idea. Of course, we are looking into this as well, but you may be able to get information out of people that they won't tell us."

"Then why do you look worried?"

"Because I'm concerned."

"About what?"

"You don't want to encounter the dudes who fool around in Satanism. They kill for kicks, and they do it brutally. If any of them get suspicious of you, they'll take you out."

The hair on her arms stood up. "You're scaring me."

"I'm trying to."

"It's working. Look, I'll be careful."

"Do you have a license to carry?"

"No."

"You should."

She stopped walking. "I don't want a gun around the house. My daughter is ten years old and she's into everything. If she found a gun, she'd probably take it to school for show-and-tell."

He threw back his head and laughed heartily. "*Santa Maria!* Is she as feisty as you?"

"You're a tease!" she accused with a laugh and pulled her arm away. Cal hadn't mentioned this quality, but she kind of liked it because it made her feel less intimidated by him.

"Hey!" Mack shouted from down the path, waving a bottle of water in his hands. "Sorry, forensics had me on the phone," he apologized. "My lady," he said and bowed playfully as he offered her the bottle.

She took it and drank a few deep draughts of water. Juice would have been better, but this would do. "Thank you, Mack. I'm sorry for all the trouble," she told them both.

"It's no trouble," Jesse brushed it off with a wave of his hand.

As they headed back down the trail, he told Mack about her planned feature. Mack had the same concerns about her safety.

"Jesse's right. This could get dangerous for you."

"I suggested she get a gun."

"Or a taser."

"I might consider a taser. Something that I could handle, nothing too heavy." She nodded toward Jesse's Glock. "Nothing like that."

She told them what Cal had said and they agreed that she should keep them all informed of where, when, and who she was meeting.

When they reached the parking lot, they stopped beside her car where she returned Jesse's jacket.

"Let us follow you home to be sure you get there alright," Mack suggested. "It'll take forensics thirty minutes to get here anyway. You live far?"

"No, I'm ten minutes from here. But I'm fine, and I have some food in the car. I'll eat on the way."

"Not good enough," Jesse said in that firm commanding tone he used earlier when laying down the terms of their working relationship. "We're following you home, but if we start stalking you, call the cops."

She laughed in spite of herself. "Okay."

True to their word, they did not part ways until she pulled into the parking lot of her condominium. Jesse gave a quick toot of the horn as the Rover sped past and disappeared down the road.

Later that evening, when Jacqui retired to her study and Chloe was busy doing her homework, Ari decided to text MK.

"You got any weed?"

"Yeah. Come on over."

She grabbed her coat and keys. "Gram? I'm going to run over to MK's for an hour. I'll be right back!"

"Okay, dear!" Gram said without looking up from her desk.

Twenty minutes later, she was sitting on the sofa in MK's townhouse, smoking a joint and holding it in until her head started to spin into a blissfully silly high. Engulfed in a cloud of smoke, they bantered, joked, choked on smoke, and munched on a bag of Oreo cookies.

"I have to tell you about this guy I met," Ari sighed. "He's an FBI agent and he's the handsomest man I've ever seen."

"I can't believe you just said that." MK looked at her as if she was an alien from another universe. "Who are you? And what have you done to Ariella?"

"I'm serious."

"Who is this guy who got Ari Dalton to notice him?"

"Will you stop it? I told you, he's an FBI agent. And he's one of those rugged, masculine types. You know what I mean, really good-looking with this great mouth and hair, and his eyes! They're big and brown and full of. . .of feeling, or something like that. When I looked into them, I actually felt kind of swoonish."

"Swoonish?" MK burst into a fit of laughter, smoke pouring out of her nose and mouth. She choked, fanned herself, gasped, "That's not even a word."

"Yes, it is! I swear! I actually got. . .what do they call them? Butterflies in my stomach when he looked at me today."

"This is historic. I've never heard you talk about a man like this."

"He has the biggest hands I've ever seen and no wedding ring!"

MK laughed so hard she rolled off the sofa and hit the floor with a bang. "You're killing me!"

"And he's got this longish black hair with a little bit of curl to it. The guy belongs on a calendar without a shirt!"

"Longish? You've got the 'ishes' tonight," MK said, and they both laughed until their sides ached.

"Uh-oh! I can't laugh anymore,' MK gasped and flew down the hall to the bathroom.

"He probably has a thousand girlfriends," Ari called after her friend. "Any guy who looks like that. . ."

"Yeah probably, but hey! Look at you, Miss Universe!"

"He was definitely checking me out," Ari grinned. "And he was telling me these stories about people possessed by the devil, how some little guy picked him up and threw him against the wall, how he's six foot four and two hundred and twenty pounds."

"Wow! That's a big man! Just the way I like them."

"Me too. But those stories were kind of scary."

The marijuana high started to dissipate, just enough for her to remember how chilled she was by the story, the same way she felt on the night of Marty's funeral when those thoughts of suicide rushed over her with a strange, compelling kind of power.

"What's the matter? Your face just fell ten stories," MK asked as she came back to the living room.

"Something bad happened after Marty's funeral."

She told MK about how the sermon dredged up memories of that awful night when her parents argued about giving her up. MK was the only person who knew about it. Not even Jacqui was aware of what she had overheard that night.

"I was lying in bed thinking about all this, and I felt like something really dark come over me. I suddenly started to think about the quarry on Swamp Road and how easy it would be to drive off the edge."

MK was shocked. "Ari! Don't say that! Don't talk like that!" She was suddenly sitting next to Ari on the sofa, clutching her arm. "Don't ever think those thoughts!"

"They were so powerful. It was like I couldn't stop them."

"Well, you have to. You're a survivor. Your parents were losers but you're not. You should have died eighteen years ago but you didn't. There's a reason why they brought you back, Ari."

"I wish I knew what it was." Ari's eyes filled with tears. "It really scared me, MK. I've never thought like that before. As bad as I feel about myself, I never thought of ending it, and I'm afraid that I might start to like the idea."

"No, you won't! It's just not you. To kill yourself would be to let your parents win. Do you really want to do that?"

"No! Never!"

"I thought not! Now put it out of your head!"

Ari nodded, blinked away her tears, and gave a small smile. "Did you finish all the cookies?"

"There's one left. Better give yourself a hit of insulin first."

She checked her sugar. "No, I'm good. Split it with me?"

ELEVEN

"**THANKS FOR YOUR TIME,** Father. I only have a few questions, and they're off the record."

Fr. Luke motioned her into the chair across from his desk. "You're never a bother, Ari."

"It's about Adam. Do you think he might have seen something that morning? When I was talking to him at the funeral, he just seemed. . .well, not entirely honest."

Father nodded his head in agreement. "I know what you mean."

"Really? What do you think?"

He looked out the door to where the parish secretary, Joan Hanscampf, was plugging away at her computer. She wasn't paying attention to anything except what she was doing.

"I think he saw something, but for the life of me, I can't figure out how to get it out of him. Cal told me to contact those FBI agents. He said Sandoval has an expertise in behavior analysis and knows how to interrogate people to make them talk. And I don't mean the kind of rough stuff you see on TV shows. They're specially trained to know how to get into a suspect's head."

"You should do it. Mack and Jesse would help you for sure."

"You know them?"

She told him about their encounter in the park the other day.

"You found a symbol at Pennypack Park?" He was surprised.

"I did, but they don't know how it might be connected. At least not yet. They want to check into it a little more."

"I knew this stuff was around here, but it's really shocking when you get hit in the face with it like we just did."

She looked at him with sincere understanding and almost hated to bring up her next question.

"But there's something else I need to run by you. It's about Helen Babbitt. She spoke with me at the funeral and claims to know someone whose son may have been molested by a priest who once served here. A priest who was 'here one day and gone the next,' as she put it."

Fr. Luke let out his breath in a long sigh and sat forward in his chair. "And?"

"She says she knows the person and is going to speak to her to see if she'll talk to me. Is this something I should take seriously?"

He leaned to the right to look out the door again to check on Joan, then said in a low whisper. "Let me put it this way. They don't call her Helen Babbles for nothing."

She laughed shortly. "So, she's not credible?"

"I didn't say that," he said quickly. "Just take what she says with a grain of salt. Helen has been in this parish her whole life. If anyone would know something, it would be her. Helen knows everybody, and she knows everybody's business."

He leaned forward again so that he could speak more softly and not be overheard by Joan, whose keyboard was still clicking away in the other room. "Here's what I know. There were two priests who were removed from ministry in this parish within the last five decades. One was removed in 1966 because he left the priesthood. The other was removed in 1991 because of illness. Now that doesn't mean they weren't involved in something that no one knows about."

"Do you mind if I pursue it?"

He cringed a little. "I'd hate to see something get into the paper and upset the parish even more than it already is."

"I would work in tandem with you."

"I appreciate that, Ari, and not because I want to cover it up. If something happened here that might have caused Marty to be killed, the people deserve to know it. But it must be presented correctly, with prudence and a lot of forethought."

"I agree," she said. "You'll be kept abreast of everything I uncover."

"I'm grateful for your understanding, Ari. No wonder Jacqui is so proud of you."

"And I'm proud of her."

Relieved, he sat back. "The Archbishop is coming this weekend to bless the grounds after the vandalism. It's all been cleaned up. The statues are being repaired. It's time for our wounds to heal. But I really want to see justice done for Marty."

"Me too. Your homily was. . .well, all I can say is that I was very touched by it. His story was incredible."

"I know a lot of priests, bishops and nuns, and many of them are very devout and holy people, but Marty Mason was the closest to a saint that I've ever known."

They looked at each other in a moment of shared sorrow.

"Can I ask you something, Father?"

"Sure."

"Remember what you said about Marty in the orphanage? How he heard that Scripture verse and felt something very powerful, and he always came back to the same place so he could feel it again?"

He nodded.

"What was it? What did he feel?"

"It's what's known as a signal grace," he said at once. "These are extraordinary communications from God that impact the intellect and the will of a soul to move it in a certain direction. They can come in the form of so-called 'coincidences' that suddenly show you the right path to take, or they can be more sensible, such as the warm feelings of love that Marty experienced. God obviously wanted Marty to know that even though his parents abandoned him, he was not alone. He had other parents, supernatural parents, and they loved him with a love that would never end. For a child who never felt real love, you can just imagine the impact this lone signal grace had on him."

She nodded but didn't dare speak because of the huge lump of emotion that was starting to collect in her throat.

Father didn't seem to notice. "He probably felt, for the first time in his life, the love and affirmation of a parent, something he never got from his parents. This is why he always described it to me as a healing—it completely changed him. Did it heal him instantly? Of course not. What he experienced *after* this initial grace, when he would go back to the same pew and relive the experience, were probably consolations. According to St. Ignatius, these are more like motivations, deep feelings of joy, peace, and love, that encourage us to continue in a certain direction. So as the days and months and years went on, God was showing this little boy that His friendship was a good thing, that He would not abandon him as his parents did. He was wooing him, if you will, proving to Marty that He could be trusted."

Is this stuff Catholic?

"It was a slow healing, I'm sure, because a child without affirmation is deeply wounded in their psyche. Even after years of work in the clinic, which was one of the best in the area, I remain convinced that only God can heal wounds that deep. No matter what I tried, it never excised the root of the damage. Especially in the case of lack of affirmation. This is truly debilitating and will impact a person for the rest of their lives. Sadly, too many parents have no clue how important it is to tell their child that he or she is loved, wanted. It makes them feel worthy, confident, sure of themselves."

This was precisely why she told Chloe every day that she loved her, that she was the light of her life, that she was the best thing that ever happened to her. That, and because it was all true; and these feelings of love for her child comforted her because they were proof that she hadn't grown up to be a narcissist like her parents.

"But how do you know it was God who did all that? Why couldn't it have been an energy force? We're all connected to the universe and our thoughts give off vibrations," she said and let the statement hang to see if he would pick it up.

He did, but not the way she thought he would. "Well, that's a good question, but it's been asked before and the answer will interest you. This energy force you speak about, universal energy, is known as putative energy. There's no evidence that it even exists."

"What? Of course it exists," she argued. "Our bodies are full of energy. Monochromatic radiation, magnetism, mechanical vibrations such as sound waves. . ."

"Yes, but that's veritable energy," he corrected politely. "Science can detect and even harness veritable energy. This is what we do with CT scans and MRIs. But this is not the same thing as the universal life force known as chi, ki, prana, yin-yang. This is what you're referring to, right?"

"Yes."

"This is part of a pantheistic belief system that believes God is a kind of energy force who supposedly permeates all of creation. And because God is in all of creation, including humans, we're all gods and just need to discover our divinity, right?"

"Exactly."

"And so, people meditate to achieve an altered state which is believed to facilitate enlightenment of their inner divinity."

She nodded. He was right on the mark.

"Well, this god, whom they believe is an energy force, has never been proven to exist. According to science, it's just not there. Neither the external energy fields nor their therapeutic effects have ever been demonstrated convincingly by any biophysical means."

"But your God has never been proven to exist either," she countered.

"That's not so. Aquinas gives us five ways that God's existence can be proven, such as how nothing exists prior to itself and therefore nothing is the efficient cause of itself. For example, you were born because of your mother, and she was born because of her mother, and her mother was born because of her mother, and so on. If you follow this all the way back, you have no choice but to come to a first efficient cause of you, and all other things as well. Such a mighty creative force is what we call God."

"You call it God. Maybe I call it the Universe."

"Do you have any proof that the Universe has such powers? At least we have proof of God through His Son who came to earth and was resurrected from the dead. We actually have more evidence of the resurrection than we do for any other ancient writer, such as Plato. And this Jesus identified God as the Father and Creator of the Universe. Do you have any proof that even comes close to this?"

She thought for a moment.

Why am I drawing a blank?

"Not off the top of my head, but I find this subject to be very interesting. The supernatural, it intrigues me."

"Me too. That's why I'm a priest. This is where I ended up after all my searching."

"You were a seeker?"

He nodded. "For many years. I just wanted the truth, whatever it was. And this is where it led me."

Knowing that he was a seeker at one time made her feel more comfortable with him, so comfortable she decided to mention the Reiki massage she had the other night. "It was glorious! I felt the warmth, the calm. It's hard to believe this energy she was channeling wasn't real, which is what you're saying."

"There are many reasons why people believe they've been healed by these energy forces, but it's never been proven in a controlled environment like a laboratory. You just can't dismiss that fact."

"Why does everything have to be proven in a laboratory?"

"It doesn't, but if it has something to do with your health, it probably should be. Consumers deserve that. Otherwise, we'd be going back to the era of the snake oil salesman who peddled all kinds of nonsense without ever having to prove that the potions worked. We have the science to prove it now. Why not use it and protect ourselves from potential fraud?"

"Good point," she said and liked how calm and intellectual he was about this kind of discussion. "Do you recommend anything I can read about this energy?"

"Check out anything written by a professor known as Dr. Victor Stenger. He was a particle physicist and philosopher at the University of Honolulu and a hard-core atheist. One of his favorite sayings was, 'Science flies you to the moon; religion flies you into buildings.'"

She laughed. "An atheist? Really? You want me to read what an atheist has to say?"

"Absolutely! Many people try to convince us away from God with this energy force, but in Stenger's case, he doesn't believe in

God either, so he has no horse in the race. He tells it like it is. If you want an honest assessment of the whole subject, that's where you'll find it. You can't go by what the purveyors of these energy practices say on their websites because they have a vested interest in getting you to buy their product." He sat up. "But you know all that. You're an investigative reporter and a good one at that. Let me know what you dig up, on all fronts."

She grinned, sincerely liking him.

"I will! And think about talking to Jesse and Mack about Adam. It can't hurt."

"You've made up my mind." He stood up, walked around the desk, and shook her hand. "Always a pleasure, Ari. Come back anytime."

TWELVE

ARI AND MK OVERSLEPT on Saturday morning, missing their Reiki massage. Ari was secretly relieved because she was in the middle of researching Reiki and discovering that most of what Fr. Luke told her was true. How would this impact the article she was going to write? If she wanted to be fair and balanced, she would have to include it. She decided to cross that bridge when she got there.

After dropping Chloe off at Missy's for the day, she picked up MK, who chattered the whole way to Oak Terrace.

"I hate my job," MK complained. "It's so boring. Why did I get into this business anyway?"

"Because you're a brainiac and a math whiz."

"That doesn't mean I have to be an accountant."

"You're not just an accountant. You're a partner in a very successful accounting firm and you just turned thirty-four. That's quite an accomplishment."

"Yeah, but it's still boring."

"Alright. Look into your heart. What is it that you really, really love to do?"

"Baking."

"Be serious."

"I am! You know I love to bake and I'm good at it too. You just can't eat pastries without shooting yourself up with insulin."

"You make me sound like a drug addict."

"Well, you *are* addicted to insulin. But seriously. I've been looking into opening my own place."

"Really?" Ari glanced over at MK, who looked pretty in a pale blue puffer vest and white turtleneck. The colors complimented her blonde curls and light skin. "You're serious."

MK shrugged. "I'm just thinking about what kind of investment would be needed and how to make my bakery stand out from all the others."

"That's easy. You could feature French pastries. You're really good at making them."

"Maybe I'll come up with a fancy French name for the place, like *Convections du Ciel*."

"What language was that?" Ari teased.

"French!" MK swatted her.

"You totally butchered it."

"I hate you. Shut up and park."

The Oak Terrace shopping center was packed. They found a spot on the far end of the lot and made their way across the large, brand new strip mall. There were several outlet stores, a pizza shop, a restaurant, and a Hobby Lobby at the far end. The mall's pillars were decorated with Christmas garland and all the store windows were adorned with sparkling Christmas lights, wreaths, and images of Santa.

"This place puts me in the Christmas spirit," Ari smiled as they headed toward the main entrance of Fair Trade City.

"Yeah," MK beamed. "You just can't get this vibe from the internet."

The store was massive, selling everything from kitchenware to linens to toiletries and even food. Ari picked up a litter box, some toys, and a carrier for Chloe's new kitten. MK had their cart half full of a variety of crocks and kitchenware, eagerly scratching items off a list she had stuffed in her pocket.

"I'm getting so much done! This place is great!"

"Let's look at the linens. Gram is always complaining about how old her sheets are."

Ari turned back into the main aisle and was looking up at the signage when something caught her eye at the far end of the store. Two very tall, very handsome, and now very familiar, men who appeared to be wandering aimlessly along the back wall of the store.

"I don't believe it," she said, grabbing MK's arm. "See those two guys down there?"

"Do I ever!" MK breathed as soon as her eyes fell upon them. "Are they gorgeous or what?"

"That's him! The guy I told you about."

"You mean *swoonish?*" She looked closer. "Oh wow! I see what you mean."

Ari lowered her voice. "They're the FBI agents on the church case."

"*Ooh la la. . .viva la difference!*"

"MK! Do *not* embarrass me."

"Just shut up and follow me," MK said with a wink. The woman was already shooting down the aisle, leaving Ari to shake her head and follow. Her best friend was notoriously bold when it came to men, which seemed to be the pitfall for why she often scared them all away.

Ari sped up, nearly running MK over with the cart in her haste to overtake her. "MK, let me introduce us first!"

MK slowed down, unapologetically staring at the agents. "They both look like Adonis reincarnated, one white and one Black."

"Will you get a grip?" Ari scolded, even as she tried to hide the flush in her own cheeks. They came up behind the two men, who were pawing at a shelf full of candles and arguing with each other.

"Why don't we just get candles?" Jesse was saying. "Everybody likes candles."

"For my dad?" Mack wasn't buying it.

"Well, not for him. Will you start picking stuff out? I don't want to be here all day."

"Well, well, well," Ari spoke up. "If it isn't the barracuda and the dolphin."

They both turned around, took one look at her, and grinned from ear to ear.

"It's the beautiful Miss Dalton," Mack exclaimed, feigning a bow. He looked at MK and one of his eyebrows shot up with interest. "And who is this lovely lass?"

"My friend, Mary Katherine." Ari turned to MK, whose eyes were sparkling prettily at Mack as he kissed her hand.

"This is Jesse Sandoval and Mack Jones. They're working on the Marty Mason case."

"The pleasure is all mine, gentlemen," MK said. "And you can call me MK. Everybody does. So, tell me, which one is the barracuda, and which one is the dolphin?"

Jesse laughed. "He calls himself a dolphin, but I say he's more like a bottom feeder."

MK giggled, her eyes never leaving Mack.

Oh boy, Ari mused, and she peered at Jesse's cart, noticing a lone, red stocking at the bottom.

"Christmas shopping?" she asked. "Shouldn't you be working on the case?"

"What, FBI agents can't have a little fun?" Jesse joked. "But in truth, we've only got two weeks before Christmas and I have a huge family. If I don't give out gifts, my own family will kill me before the actual criminals will."

"Have you bought anything yet?" she asked, amused by the desperate look on his face, so unlike the confident FBI agent she met in the park the other day.

"Not a thing."

"Me neither," Mack chimed in. 'I've only got a father and a sister to buy for. He's got both parents, three brothers, a sister, two nephews, and a niece. That's nine gifts!"

"I can count, Mack," Jesse grumbled.

"Well," MK looked between the two of them. "We can help you, can't we, Ari?" She didn't wait for an answer. "Let's get started!"

"Really?" The men looked enormously relieved, which Ari found to be slightly hilarious.

"Really. Ari, you take Jesse, and I'll take Mack, and we'll meet back here in a half hour."

Ever the jokester, Mack looked at MK and said, "If you can help me get this done in thirty minutes, I would consider marrying you."

"He'll ruin your life," Jesse warned.

Ari giggled, heading down the next aisle. "You poor things. Come on, let's do this." Jesse dutifully followed her.

"So, are there any new developments in the case?" she asked him.

"Only if we're off the record."

"Absolutely!"

He sighed. "None, but the leads are growing by the day."

"That's a good thing, right?"

"Sure, but too many leads can become a tangled web that's often a more difficult problem to deal with."

He sounded like he didn't want to talk much more about it, so Ari decided not to push her luck. "So, who are we buying for?"

she changed the subject.

"Well, let's start with my nephews."

"How old are they?"

"Uh, well. . ."

"You don't know?"

"Not really," he admitted, and she laughed at him. "They're about this tall." He hovered his hand around waist-height.

"Okay. . .grade school." She steered them into the toy aisle and picked up a few games. "How about Yeti in My Spaghetti? Chloe loves that game. Guess Who is fun too."

"That sounds good. Put them in the cart."

She snorted. "You didn't even look at them! Alright then, who else?"

"My sister, Bella."

"What does she like?"

He frowned, as if deep in thought. "She likes womanly things."

"Womanly things?"

"You know," he motioned toward the bubble bath and soaps. "That stuff."

"Well, this is pretty," Ari said and picked up a white wicker basket that contained a bottle of bath gel, body lotion, and bubble bath in a dreamy scent of roses and vanilla. "Wow! This smells amazing."

"You like it?"

"I do."

"Put two in the cart."

"Done!" she said brightly, smiling up at him with dazzling eyes sparkling like the day sky.

She'd braided her dark hair at the temple that day with the strands drawn behind her head, leaving the rest of her hair to fall down her back like a black satin sheet. She'd also picked out her favorite white puffer jacket, jeans, and black boots to match, giving her more confidence under Jesse's piercing gaze. A little rush went through her.

"Did you say you have a niece?" she asked, breaking their gaze.

"Eleana."

"How old is she?"

"Good question."

She sighed and shook her head. "What grade is she in?"

"I think fourth or fifth?"

"Oh! Well, that's easy. That's Chloe's age. Those girls are often into makeup at that age. Does her mother allow her to wear it?"

He shrugged. "I'll text her." He pulled out the phone, texted his sister, and a few minutes later said, "Yes, but only on special occasions."

"I'm the same way with Chloe. I'm getting some for her this Christmas, but I want her to start with the bare minimum. Girls can go overboard with it and. . .well. . .never mind. I think this would be a perfect little starter set for her."

"Sounds good. Put it in the cart."

"Who else?"

"My brothers. I have three of them."

"Three brothers? Wow! You do have a big family. Do any of them drink?" she asked as they pulled up to a shelf full of insulated wine coolers and tumblers.

"Two out of the three. They might like these," he said, turning a cooler around in his hands for a moment. He put two in the cart.

"What about the other brother?"

"Lorenzo? He's a priest."

"Oh."

"He won't want anything."

"Get him a spiritual bouquet. My Gram gets them for people all the time."

He was nodding slowly, as if this was a novel idea, and Ari could barely keep herself from laughing. How could someone as capable as him be rendered so utterly inept by an activity as common as Christmas shopping?

"What are you laughing at?" he asked, a smile tugging at the corner of his mouth. "You're having fun at my expense, *mi belleza*."

"I'm not laughing," she put on a mock straight face.

"Yes, you are. You're laughing at me under your breath." He winked at her, and she giggled again.

"Pay attention," she said.

"Oh, I'm paying attention alright."

Her face reddened, and a fluttering started in her stomach. *Why does this man make me feel like a teenager at a boy-band concert?*

"What about your dad?" she hurried on.

"I know what he wants. He wants a gun, and he wants me to show him how to use it. I'll get him a Glock after Christmas, after his background check."

"Okay, so all that's left is your mom. What does she like?"

He frowned. "This is very hard for me. She asks for nothing. She only knows how to give."

What a beautiful thing to say!

"Well, is there something she *needs*, maybe in the kitchen? Does she like to cook?"

"Oh, yes. Mexican women know how to cook," he nodded knowingly.

They inspected the houseware department, but nothing Ari picked up looked right to him. It was obvious Jesse's mother was very special to him by the way he seemed so particular about her gift.

MK texted Ari a few minutes later. "Where r u? 30 minutes is up."

"Uh-oh. Time's up!" Ari said and gave Jesse a playful wink. "We better get back. They're waiting for us."

Mack and MK were standing arm-in-arm when they all met up in the center of the store.

"All done!" MK said brightly. "How about you?"

"Almost," Jesse said. "Just need one more for my mother."

"Oh," MK frowned. "Let's think about it over lunch." She glanced between the two men and said with her characteristic boldness, "As long as there are no wives or girlfriends to upset two weeks before Christmas. I mean, we wouldn't want to ruin your holidays. Why not join us?"

MK, you have no shame.

Mack laughed. "You're on, little lady. We're footloose and fancy-free."

Jesse shook his head. "Who are you kidding? We're not footloose and we're definitely not fancy," he said, flashing a handsome, white-toothed grin, "but we're free. So, let's go ladies."

They decided to meet up at a café down the road, and MK chattered like a schoolgirl the whole way while Ari drove. "Be still my foolish heart! Am I dreaming? Are we awake?"

"Will you act your age?"

MK ignored her. "And they're both *available*. I mean, what are the chances of that? Two guys who could be models for *Gentleman's Quarterly* and we happen to stumble upon them?"

"Well, not exactly. I've been working with them on Marty's case. Cal did say they live around here. But they're really likeable guys, aren't they? We hit it off immediately." She told MK what happened in the park the other day. "Within five minutes, I felt like I had known them for years."

MK nodded. "Yeah, you'd never know they were FBI agents.

They're real normal guys. And I'd say your heartthrob has eyes only for you."

"What?"

"Oh, come on! When are you going to get over Jack?"

Ari winced. "What does Jack have to do with this?"

"You just walk around with blinders on all the time. Men practically fall over themselves trying to get your attention and you don't even notice! Jack warped you, which is a shame, because you never had anything in common with him anyway."

"Yes, I did."

"Like what?"

"We were both insecure," Ari stated.

"Seriously?"

The women looked at each other and burst out laughing.

Ari pulled into a parking spot a few spaces down from Mack and Jesse. "And I don't even think about Jack anymore. Ever," she corrected, slamming the car into park.

A few minutes later, they were sliding into a booth inside the café—she and Jesse on one side, MK and Mack on the other. They talked and laughed and then teased Jesse mercilessly when the waitress started flirting with him.

"*Mi amigo* gets all the ladies," Mack joked when the waitress walked away.

Jesse just rolled his eyes.

"Well, she must have a lot of confidence in herself," MK said, "especially when he's sitting next to Miss Universe."

Jesse choked on his water, and Mack laughed outright.

"I hate you, MK," Ari hissed. "She says stuff like that to embarrass me."

Jesse elbowed her and smiled good naturedly at her flustered expression. "But she speaks the truth, *mi belleza.*"

"What does that mean?" MK inquired innocently.

"It means 'my beauty' in Spanish."

Ari's cheeks blushed hotter than they had since she was a teenager. MK caught her eye from across the table and laughed mischievously.

I'm going to strangle you.

"Let's change the subject," Ari jumped in before MK had a chance to say something even more embarrassing. "Remember, Jesse's still looking for something for his mother."

"You know, I had an idea driving over here," Jesse said. "Your grandmother is Jacqui Dalton, right? The genealogist?"

"That's her."

"My mother has always wanted to know her lineage. She is a Castillo. Do you think your grandmother would consider working on this for her? I would pay her whatever she asks."

"Let's see what she says." Ari whipped out her cell phone and texted Jacqui.

Just then, the waitress came back with their order.

"Those hamburgers are the size of your heads," MK joked. "If only I could eat like that!"

She and MK went through their usual ritual of placing an order, then deciding they liked the other's choice better. They would switch plates, eat for a few minutes, then decide to go back to their original choice. The men munched away, amused by their antics.

Ari's phone beeped and she looked at it. "It's from Gram," she said, and Jesse's hamburger paused a few inches from his mouth. "She says, 'Absolutely. I would be honored.'"

"Seriously? Let me see." He reached for her phone. "May I?"

She gave it to him and watched the delight dance across his face as he read it, then texted back, "*Muchas gracias.* I will be in touch to arrange your payment. JJS."

Gram texted back a moment later. "No charge. Just find Marty's killer."

He slid the phone back to her. "I'll pay her; I insist. My mother will be ecstatic. She's talked about this for years."

"You can put something in a card, like a certificate of some kind," Ari suggested.

"The secretaries will do it for you, Jesse," Mack offered. "They fall all over themselves trying to do things for you."

"*Santa Maria. . .*"

Ari giggled. This was the most she'd laughed in one day in a long time. She was almost disappointed when their lunch came to an end.

"Well, we need to stop at the SPCA on the way home, MK. Just want to see what they have."

"Uh-oh. Is someone getting a puppy for Christmas?" Mack asked.

"My daughter is finally getting the kitten she's always wanted. It's a surprise."

"Kitten?" Jesse nudged her again and she looked at him. "Bella has kittens right now. I think there are two left."

"Really?"

"I'll text her."

A few minutes later, she was looking at a photo of two tiny orange tabbies sleeping in the corner of a box, their little legs wrapped around each other. "Oh, how precious!" She showed MK.

"I thought you only wanted one, Ari."

"I do, but look at them, will you? Only a serial killer would be heartless enough to separate them," she said, and everyone laughed, including her. "Well, how much does she want for them?"

"Nothing. They're free. She had four, and these are the only two left. If you want them, they're yours."

She looked over at MK, who shrugged. "It's up to you. You're the one who's going to be cleaning the litter boxes."

"No way. Chloe already knows this is her duty."

"What if she doesn't?"

"She will. She may be a silly little goose, but she's obedient and she keeps her word." She turned to Jesse. "Okay, I'll take them. Can Bella hold them until Christmas Eve? Gram and Chloe are going to a Christmas concert at the parish. It would be the perfect time to sneak them into the house and hide them in my bedroom until Christmas morning."

He texted Bella. "That's fine. I will bring them to you."

MK and Mack exchanged phone numbers as Jesse paid the bill and walked her out to the car.

"Okay then, *mi belleza*. I will see you at 7:00 p.m. on Christmas Eve with the two *gatitos*." She reached for the door when he touched her arm, drawing her attention back to him. "Thanks for the help," he said sincerely. When they looked at each other, their eyes lingered just long enough to send a little flutter through her insides.

What is wrong with me?

"You're welcome, Jesse," she said and couldn't help but wonder if he felt it too. "It was fun."

"Yeah, it was," he said, feigned tipping a hat as he walked away.

They weren't even out of the parking lot yet when MK began swooning. "I'm in love. Mack and I are going out, and you and Jesse are going to see each other on Christmas Eve. Isn't this great?"

Ari couldn't argue. She liked having the attention of a man again, a man like Jesse Sandoval. But she was also a realist. "You heard what Mack said. All the women like Jesse."

"I can see why. That's what I call a *man*," MK breathed and started fanning herself.

Ari felt her cheeks warming again.

Why am I acting like this?

MK whistled through her teeth. "Yeah. He's drop dead gorgeous alright, but," she looked at Ari and winked mischievously, "so are you, *mi belleza!*"

THIRTEEN

ROCK'N ANGELS WAS A UNIQUE GIFT SHOP on the outskirts
of Monmouth where Ari had been buying her crystals for years. It
was owned by a sixty-something former hippie who called herself
Crystallina Bright. The walls were littered with posters of her and
her rock-star former husband in their younger years. She still wore
her brown hair the same way, long and straight and parted in the
middle, and the same style of clothing—tight jeans and a Boho-style
peasant top that spoke of a bygone era of rebellion and "free love."

"I am so excited about this article, Ari!" She gushed as soon as
Ari walked through the door. "And what a perfect time! Right before
Christmas!"

"Nobody knows crystals the way you do, Crystallina." Ari put
her camera and cellphone down on the counter of a case full of gems.

"Wow!" Crystallina said as they hugged in greeting. "You are
tense, girlfriend!"

"Why do you say that?"

"I've known you for a decade, Ari. I know when your Zen is off."

Ari blew out a puff of air. "I guess you're right. It's been a rough
month."

"The hate crime?"

"You know about it?"

"Who doesn't?" Crystallina reached into the case for a piece of
calcite. "Creepy, if you ask me. Here." She dropped a pale blue, milky

stone into the palm of Ari's hand. "This is blue calcite. It's the absolute best for calming the nerves."

Ari held it between her hands, closed her eyes for a moment and took a few deep breaths. "You're magic, Crystallina."

The woman laughed throatily. "You're welcome. So, is it true about all these Satanists around here?"

Ari peeked open an eye. "That's what they tell me, although I have yet to find one to interview."

"No way would I go near one of them. No thanks. I ran into some in Sedona a couple decades ago at the height of the LSD craze. Let me tell you, those people were messed up. They hated everybody. There wasn't an ounce of love in them. We were chanting 'make love not war,' and they were hollering 'death to God'. I mean, who does that?"

"Lots of people, from what I hear."

"Feeling better now?"

"A lot. Thanks." She handed the stone back. "So, tell me how you got started in this business."

"For me, it began forty years ago with my first stone massage. It was when I was living out in Arizona. We had a commune where we raised all our own food, herbs, all kinds of root plants for healing. I got hurt trying to dig a stone out of the ground. My shoulder was killing me. Some of my sisters in the commune took me to this crystal healer. He made me lay on a blanket and laid about two dozen stones all around me. He put a bright red carnelian on my navel and a quartz crystal on my abdomen."

She went on to describe how he set a large, smoky quartz crystal next to her head. He called it the "energy source." Another crystal shaped like an obelisk, which he referred to as a "power crystal," was placed at her feet. He then concentrated on the energy emitting from the 'energy source' so that it would pass through the power crystal which he would then direct into the stones on her body.

"Within a few minutes, I was totally healed," Crystallina said, her green eyes sparkling with pleasure.

"Wow!" Ari was impressed. "So how does it work?"

"Well, crystals are known to interact with the body's vibrational energy. They can actually redirect the energy flow in the body with their energetic vibrations, and this is what can heal areas of the body where the energy field has become blocked or stuck. And they can also absorb other forces of nature like the touch of humans, which is why some people will cherish a particular stone because a loved one has touched or 'imprinted' it. Isn't that fascinating?"

"You know I love crystals!" Ari said as she began photographing the stones. "Where does this information about crystals come from? Is it scientific?"

"Mostly from practitioners and the writings of Edgar Cayce, who had a vision about a large crystal structure that supposedly supplied power to the lost city of Atlantis. His writings were pivotal in opening the eyes of the world to the many uses of crystals."

Ari was familiar with Cayce, an American clairvoyant, and had avidly read every one of his books.

"Which would you recommend as gifts for Christmas, Crystallina?"

The owner went on to recommend a list of stones she thought would make nice gifts and by the time Ari left the shop, she was excited about such a good start to the series.

From there, she headed downtown to the office of Edward Manning, Ph.D. Edward was a well-known geologist and fellow at an international scientific think tank. Ari was anxious to hear what he had to say about crystals and their use in alternative medicine.

"I'm afraid there is no scientific evidence to support the efficacy of crystals in any of these applications," the geologist said, and Ari's face must have fallen because an apologetic look suddenly flashed across his own pale, round face. A slightly built man in his late fifties, Edward had thinning, brown hair and thick horn-rimmed glasses that made him look the part of a scientist. "Who wouldn't want them to work as they're advertised? But they don't because the so-called energy they're supposedly infused with, sometimes referred to as chi or vibrational energy, has never been scientifically substantiated."

Where have I heard this before?

"But what about electrical, magnetic and nuclear energies?" Ari argued. "I realize these are different forms of energy, but they say crystals can conduct and even store these types of energy."

"That's partially correct. Quartz crystals can conduct some forms of energy, and even produce a slight electrical charge under certain conditions. But the stones don't 'store' anything, which is really the basis for their use in the alternative market."

He was making too much sense, and it was rattling her nerves, not just because his comments would have a dulling effect on the article, but because they were unexpectedly challenging her own beliefs.

"What kind of scientific studies have been done to prove what you're saying?"

"Plenty," he said and rattled off a list of impressive studies.

But she was not about to go down without a fight for her precious crystal collection. "What do you say about these stones being used for healing since ancient times? Surely there's a reason why people turned to them."

"I'm sure they had good reason to do so, Miss Dalton. But they must not have been very effective if people in ancient times rarely lived past the age of forty. This is hardly a reason to resort to one of their methods of healing. It obviously didn't work very well for them if they died so young."

Touché.

"Many people claim they've been healed by crystals. I used them when I was suffering from depression a few years ago and honestly felt better. Was it all in my mind?"

She could tell he was trying to control the expression on his face so as not to insult her.

"Look, if a person feels as if a certain crystal is helping them, they can certainly use them; they just need to understand that whatever relief they are feeling is due to the placebo effect."

"So, it is all in my mind?"

He shrugged. "I'm afraid so."

Her high spirits were deflated by what Dr. Manning had explained, and she couldn't help but chide herself for not investigating this before now. How could such a well-trained investigative reporter like herself have failed to do her homework on the validity of crystal healing? She had been using them for years and had genuinely believed they contained some kind of power. How many times had she held those crystals in her hands and felt the warmth, the energy? How could it all be in her mind?

Later, she finished the first article and was honestly disappointed to have to include Dr. Manning's counsel because it would leave readers with doubt about the use of crystals for healing. Summoning the best of her journalistic skill, she spun Dr. Manning's closing comment about using them if a person felt better, with the hopes that people would not give up on the use of crystals.

When the article was done, she deliberately filled the tub with hot water and a frothy essential oil bubble bath, then carefully laid her amethyst stones along the edge of the tub. She called this her "power bath." After a particularly grueling day, she would lay in the tub, absorb the calming energy from the stones, and let it soothe her nerves.

She gingerly climbed into the tub, let herself adjust to the hot water, then laid down with her head cradled on the rim. With her eyes closed, she whispered her mantra a few times to clear her mind.

A feeling of lightness and bliss slowly penetrated her body, making her feel snug and cozy and good all over. She lay very still and let images from the day parade across her mind: Crystallina and Dr. Manning, Annette at her desk, the yellow lane markers on the highway flashing past her car window.

Jesse. His image suddenly loomed from her memory, the way his eyes sparkled and his white teeth flashed when he laughed in that deep, throaty, unpretentious way of his. It was the kind of easy, natural laugh that could only come from someone who was well-accustomed to humor.

The mere thought of him made her sigh with pleasure.

But not for long. Almost immediately, another thought rushed across her mind like an inner voice speaking from some dark corner of her heart. "What would a man like him see in a broken, wounded person like you?" it taunted. "He's smart, handsome, successful, and you're nothing but a train wreck with good hair."

She tried to shake off the thought, but it seemed so plausible, so completely believable. Of course, a successful FBI agent like Jesse Sandoval would want a whole and emotionally healthy woman. He deserved as much! With her brokenness and sad history, she could never be anything but a burden to a man like him.

"Who cares how he makes you feel?" the voice in her head continued to torment. "He's out of your league. Your parents ruined you. You're broken in places that no shrink will ever be able to fix. What man wants a broken woman?"

An intense sensation of heaviness settled over her spirit, dragged it downward into a place where all was dismal and hopeless. The same feeling of darkness that had settled over her the other night, when those thoughts of suicide took hold of her mind, returned and was suddenly surrounding her with a foreboding sensation, as if she was in the presence of something very dangerous.

"Give it up. End it. Think of the peace. The pain will stop. You'll just float away from here the way you did when you died and were floating above the table."

No! I'm not going here!

She jumped out of the tub, slid across the wet floor, and steadied herself on the sink. With one sweep of her hand, she swept the crystals off the rim and shoved them back into their white mesh purse. All the while, she had the eerie feeling that something was chasing her, an energy, a spirit, of some kind.

Why is this happening to me?

After drying and putting on some clothes, she deliberately went out into the living room to watch television with Jacqui and Chloe, but mostly to pretend that all was well. It took almost an hour for her to calm down and drown at least some of her dark thoughts in a silly sitcom.

When it was time to go to bed, she was afraid to do so, to close her eyes, to do anything but lie there feeling utterly alone and vulnerable to the dark feelings she expected to return at any minute.

They never did. She fell asleep out of exhaustion and woke up the next morning with the sinking feeling that something was terribly wrong.

It's time to go back to counseling.

FOURTEEN

DAYS WENT BY without any dark thoughts of suicide. Ari began to rationalize what was happening to her, that it was just another manifestation of her usual self-deprecatory thoughts about herself brought on by the memories dredged up by Marty's death. Before long, she forgot about it and let herself be caught up in the final festive days before Christmas that were full of parties, cookie baking, gift wrapping, and tree decorating.

Strangely enough, for the first time in years, she actually looked forward to Christmas and wondered if it was because she was going to see Jesse again. Normally, she hated this holiday because it meant facing her parents and enduring the latest snub from her ex who usually ignored her altogether and just sent something to Chloe via Amazon. The last two years it had arrived late. This year, his gift was early and was embarrassingly inappropriate for his growing daughter.

"What do I want a Pillow Pet for? That's for babies," Chloe snarled with the same disdain with which she greeted his last four Christmas gifts which were toys meant for girls half her age. "Why did he send this to me, Mommy?"

"Who knows? Oh Chloe, don't let him bother you. He's a mess."

"Aren't dads supposed to love their kids? Why doesn't he love me? What's wrong with me?"

"Nothing!" Ari said at once. The last thing she wanted was for

Chloe to grow up thinking her father's neglect was her own fault.

"Then why doesn't he love me like he's supposed to?"

"He just doesn't know how to show his feelings. I'm sorry, honey."

"I'm not sorry. I hate him!"

"Don't say that!"

"Why not? He's a jerk. He never even comes to see me."

Jacqui decided to step in, sitting down next to Chloe on the couch and giving her a big hug. "Some people are just not capable of loving, for whatever reason. It's like they're missing that part, like someone who is missing an arm or a leg."

Chloe looked up at her with a quizzical look on her face. "What do you mean?"

"Some people suffer injuries when they're growing up. Maybe their mother or father was unkind to them, and they never really learned how to love. I think that's what's wrong with your dad."

Good one, Gram!

"What did they do to him?" Chloe wanted to know.

"We don't know. We just know that he never really learned how to love. But the point of all this is that it's not your fault, my little angel. It has nothing to do with you. It's all him." She gave Chloe a kiss on the nose. "Why don't we donate it to Toys for Tots?"

"Okay!" The girl said at once, and shoved her bad feelings back into that secret place inside where all neglected children bury their pain.

By the time Christmas Eve rolled around, Chloe had forgotten all about the Pillow Pet and her father's indifference. Ari treated her to a "make-over" by styling her hair and doing her makeup for the Christmas concert. She dressed her in a pair of black leggings, ankle boots, and a bright green, oversized sweater.

"You look so grown up!" Ari smiled at her. "Like a teenager."

"Am I pretty?"

"Of course you are."

"Am I as pretty as you?"

"No! You're as pretty as *you!*" Ari knelt on the floor in front of her, shifting Chloe's sweater so it sat straight on her shoulders, and looked into those big round eyes that were now sporting eyeliner and mascara. "You're one of a kind, Chloe. There's no one else like you in the whole universe. Be proud of who you are! Besides, why do you want to be like me? I'm always tripping over my feet because I wear a size ten shoe!"

"Big foot!" Chloe giggled. "You're funny, Mom!" Chloe hugged her tight, and Ari let herself enjoy it, the feel of her, the smell of her, the sound of her.

She's growing up so fast. Soon she'll be off to college. I'll miss you so much, Chloe.

"Let's go Chloe. We'll be late!" Jacqui stuck her head in the door. "We should be back by eight o'clock."

"Go on, Chloe! Text me when you get back, Gram."

Jacqui knew the kittens were being dropped off at seven o'clock. Just in case something went amiss with the arrangements, she knew to text Ari first to be sure the coast was clear before bringing Chloe upstairs.

Once they were gone, Ari concentrated on setting up the litter box, food, and water bowl in the corner of her bedroom. In the midst of this, Jesse texted, "Be there in 45."

She felt instantly flustered. Men didn't usually make her nervous, but this one did, that is, whenever he crossed the line from being an FBI agent to being just a man.

Maybe it was her sugar. She checked but the meter reported a near-perfect sugar level.

Get a grip.

She dressed in a pair of black leggings and a fluffy white sweater and gave her hair a long, thorough brushing. Although she meant to slip into a pair of black flats, she forgot all about it until the bell rang.

"Merry Christmas, Ari," Jesse said as she swung open the door and pretended to be nonchalant about the fact that she was still wearing the ridiculous rabbit ear slippers Chloe had gotten her for her birthday.

You forgot to change your shoes! You look like a ten-year-old!

"Merry Christmas to you too, Jesse. Come in, come in."

"Nice place," he said, looking around and setting a big Fava boot box on the kitchen island. Perched on top of it was the same white wicker basket full of bath gel and lotion that he bought for his sister. "This is for you," he said, picking it up and proudly holding it out to her. "You should like it. You picked it out yourself."

"You're pathetic," she laughed in spite of herself.

"I can't seem to get a compliment out of you."

"Just keep trying," she teased. "But thank you! You really shouldn't have."

"But I did, thanks to you." He leaned on the countertop and motioned to the box. "These little *gatitos* want out of the box. They were sleeping for most of the drive, but they woke up when I got out of the warm car."

"Poor little things," she cooed and stuck a finger into one of the holes Eleana had cut into the side of the box.

"Eleana cried for two hours. She kissed them a hundred times before I got them out of the house. I told her they were going to a good home, not to their death."

Ari laughed. "Girls that age are so emotional. Chloe is the same. Little drama queens. Let me get you something to drink. Wine?"

"No, I don't drink. Water is fine."

She got him a glass.

"I like your slippers."

She cringed.

Figures he'd notice.

"I mean it! They're nice slippers."

"Are you always such a tease?"

His eyes sparkled with humor as he gazed down at her from his towering height. Why did the kitchen ceiling suddenly seem so low with him standing in it? "I'm afraid so. But I really do like your slippers."

"Will you stop?"

"I'm serious!" he said through a playful grin.

"You're teasing! I can tell!"

"How can you tell?"

"Your eyes twinkle."

"I'm glad you noticed."

She blushed, then blushed for having blushed.

I'm a disaster.

He was still grinning. "Alright, I'll stop teasing. In my family, we're all teases. It's a sign of affection."

Flustered now, she flipped a large swath of her black hair behind her shoulder and sighed. "Well, at least you're not making fun of me."

"Of course not!" he scoffed as if she should know better. "And speaking of my family, I want Jacqui to meet with my mother soon. Why don't you and Chloe come too?"

Ari shrugged, trying to appear nonchalant, even though MK would chastise her for not wanting to show too much interest.

"Men fall all over themselves trying to get your attention and you don't

even notice!"

"Sounds good to me. When?"

"Monday?"

"Sure."

"Do you like Mexican food?"

"We love it!"

"Seriously?" He was pleased. "We will prepare a feast for you then. How hot do you like it?"

She grinned up at him and said honestly, "So hot it makes my eyes water and my nose run."

He laughed out loud. "I like you, Ari Dalton. . ."

She smiled, smug with herself. "What time on Monday?"

"Let's say three o'clock. They're expecting weather that night so let me pick you up in the Rover."

"Okay."

"Let's hope I don't get called out of town." A bit of the humor fell from his face just then. "If I do, we'll reschedule it."

"Of course. Does that happen often?"

He nodded. "It does. But it's been quiet lately. People are keeping their hate under wraps, at least for now."

"Thank God, but I'm still looking for clues. I started the Mystical Marvel series, you know."

"I know. I read it."

She was surprised and wondered if she should be flattered that he bothered to read it. "Crystallina didn't know much, but a psychic friend of mine, Priscilla Tomlinson, claims to know about Satanists in the area."

He was suddenly interested. "Tomlinson, you say?"

"Yes."

"Where does she live?"

"Uh. . .in Monmouth, why?"

He didn't answer. "What did she tell you?"

"That she wants to find out more about them before giving me their names. She thinks they could be dangerous."

"She's right, which tells me she probably does know some." He was back to being the impersonal FBI agent again. "We'll look into it."

"What are you going to do? Priscilla isn't involved in this."

"Don't worry about it."

"I just don't want her to be interrogated and—"

"Interrogated?" He chuckled down at her. "That stuff only happens on TV. We have ways of checking people out that they don't even know about, which is why everyone hates us and accuses us of corruption. That is, until we catch their murderers, human traffickers, and child porn pervs. Then we're the heroes. We just can't win."

She laughed cynically. "You got that right. I'm sorry. I overreacted."

He was quiet for a moment, all the while watching her very carefully. He had an expertise in behavioral analysis, she reminded herself, which meant he was probably analyzing her for possible motives at this very moment.

Just don't cut me off from the case!

"I take it she's a friend of yours as well as a source for your articles."

"She is. And she's a psychic. She knows things."

"Yeah, right," he said with just a trace of sarcasm in his voice. "Just promise me you'll give me those names as soon as you get them. . .without looking into them yourself first."

She hesitated.

"Ari?"

"Yes! Yes! Of course I will."

"I'm serious."

"So am I."

He frowned down at her. "Why do you worry me, Miss Dalton?"

"I don't know, Agent Sandoval. Why do I?"

"Because I don't want you to get hurt," he said and his voice was very firm, until he added much more softly, "for more than one reason." The FBI agent persona vanished ever so briefly as genuine concern for her suddenly wrote itself all over his face.

His boldness was breathtaking.

"I'll be careful. . .I promise," she said with as much conviction as she could muster.

"I want you to promise to tell me first."

She could hardly say no. Besides wanting an excuse to see him, if she didn't go along with the rules, he would cut her off from the case and Annette would be furious. "I promise. I want this to be a cooperative effort with your team, Jesse, the way it was with Tony's team."

He nodded but was still watching her carefully as if debating whether or not to believe her.

Before he could change his mind, she hurried on, "So, is this the only hate crime you're working on right now?"

"No, but it's the one that has most of my interest, probably because there are so few leads. I'm not used to that. Typical hate crimes are usually pretty easy to crack."

"Why is that?"

"Because it's mostly kids behind them, punks who are just trying to shock people. They usually leave a trail of evidence, and when we get them in custody, they sing like canaries and point at everybody but their own mother."

She laughed dryly and shook her head. "Maybe getting locked up is the best thing for them."

"Or the worst, depending on where they're sent. Many gang members are in prison. That's where a lot of them hook up."

"What makes kids get involved in that?" she wondered aloud.

"Poverty, parental neglect, poor education. The gangs are their source of power. It makes them feel important."

"That's so sad. We could almost say it's not their fault, but sooner or later a kid has to make the decision to be his own person and not let his parents define him," she said wisely, and wondered why she didn't take her own advice.

"Well said, *mi belleza*. Do you mind me calling you that?"

"Not really."

"It's not too presumptuous of me, is it?"

He was back to his playful self again, grinning in that easy-going way of his that instantly put her at ease. "What are you up to, Sandoval?"

He laughed shortly. "I'm just trying to read you."

She blushed again but turned her attention to the kittens. They were meowing, scratching, and mewling.

"I think they're crying," she cooed and went for the lid. "Why don't I get the carrier and we can put them in there with some food and water?"

"Good idea."

She padded down the hall looking like a beauty queen in bunny slippers and returned a few minutes later with the carrier.

"Be careful, they're feisty," he warned and positioned the box next to the open carrier door. He slowly opened the lid, an inch at a time, until one of them popped his tiny head out and meowed loudly.

"Poor thing!" Ari cried. "He's so cute!" No sooner did she tip up the lid when the creature jumped out, skid across the countertop, and fell to the floor. "Oh no! It got out!"

Jesse tried to catch it, and when he took his hand off the box, the other kitten popped out and followed his brother to the floor. "*Caramba!*"

"Oh no! They're both out!"

"I told you they were feisty!"

One of them flew toward the sectional, and Ari ran after it, tripping over the ottoman and landing on her stomach in the middle of the living room floor. Before she could reach it, it darted under the sofa. She crawled after it, but it only popped out the other side and went skidding toward Jacqui's office. "There it goes! Catch it!"

"I got it!" Jesse called, and she sat up just in time to see him hoist one of the kittens up in the air, at which time the frightened little animal let loose a tiny stream of liquid. "*Caramba.*" He dropped it like a hot potato.

She collapsed to the couch in a fit of giggles. "You let it go!"

"It peed on me!"

"You're pathetic. . ."

"*Pequena broma,*" he said, lapsing into Spanish as he dove to the floor and grabbed the little creature, holding it out in front of him just in case. "Get the carrier before it pees on me again."

Just then, the other kitten made the mistake of running toward the slipper Ari had lost in the chase. Curious, it stopped just long enough to sniff at the shoe. Ari scooped it off the floor.

"I got it!" she cried triumphantly, rushing over to the carrier and shoving him inside along with his brother.

They both took a deep breath, looked at each other and burst out laughing. "That was almost a disaster," she choked.

"How did I get myself into this?" He looked down at the wet spot on the front of his thigh and made a sour face that looked almost hilarious on such a masculine man. "I see what you mean about the pee, and now I smell like it."

"Yes, you do."

"Thanks."

She burst out laughing, went to the sink, and soaked a dish rag in warm water and put a few drops of lavender oil on it. "Here. . .this might help."

"What did you put on it?"

"Lavender oil."

"I don't want to smell like a flower."

"It's not a flower! It's an herb."

"It smells like something a woman would wear."

"God forbid!" She made a face at him, snatched the rag back and handed him another one with Dawn dish washing liquid on it.

He smelled it first.

"You're so pitiful!" she giggled.

This guy is fun!

"I'm going to take that as a compliment," he said, grinning while he scrubbed at his jeans.

"You must be desperate if you call that a compliment."

"I am desperate. You never say anything nice about me."

"Stop teasing!"

"I'm perfectly serious." He looked up and laughed at the way she was grinning at him.

Just then Ari's phone went off. It was Jacqui.

"Oh no!"

"What?"

"It's Gram. They're on their way upstairs!"

She grabbed the carrier and ran down the hall, unaware that she was still wearing only one slipper.

She returned to the kitchen just as the elevator bell rang and

Jacqui's key turned in the lock.

There they were, standing side-by-side in the kitchen, looking like they'd just been caught doing something very wrong. Slightly disheveled, with Ari missing a slipper and the very tall man at her side obviously struggling not to laugh, they both feigned nonchalance.

"Hey Gram!" Ari said, and Jesse grinned.

Jacqui glanced between them, briefly, then decided she really didn't want to know what they had just been doing.

"What a pleasure to meet you, Mrs. Dalton," Jesse was saying and offering his hand.

"Jesse Sandoval?" She took his hand and smiled appreciatively. "The pleasure is all mine. I can't tell you how many of us are praying for you right now. Every day we ask God to guide your work."

"I appreciate that very much," he said sincerely. "And I'm grateful for your offer to research my mother's lineage."

"I'm happy to. Every search is a new adventure," Jacqui said with her usual grace. "She's a Castillo, you said?"

"Yes. My father's family is from Sonora, but they moved to Puerto Vallarta. That's where I was born."

"Well that explains your height," Jacqui said. "Puerto Vallarta is beautiful. It's on the Pacific coast, right?"

"Exactly. It's beautiful there."

Just then, Chloe strolled up to Jesse and gave him a thorough look from the top of his head to the tip of his black leather boots. Not one to be shy, she tipped her head back to look up at him. " Are you the FBI man?"

"I am."

Her brows furrowed as a look of fear settled over her face. "Did you get the bad people who killed Mr. M&M's?"

"Mister. . ?"

"Marty Mason," Ari informed him. "The kids called him Mr. M&Ms because he always had candy in his pocket."

"Not yet," he said, and his whole expression softened when he looked into Chloe's fearful eyes.

"Are they still around here?"

"No, *mi hija*," he reassured very firmly. "They are not close. You have nothing to worry about."

Just then, a very distinct meowing noise sounded from down the hall.

Ari cringed, then started coughing in an attempt to cover the sound.

"Mommy?" Chloe asked quietly and turned her head toward the sound.

Ari ran the water in the sink on full speed, coughing all the while. Another meow sounded.

"Mommy?" Chloe asked again, a little louder this time, and looked at her in wide-eyed amazement. "Mommy! Is that a—"

Ari let out a sigh, "Oh sweetie, it was supposed to be—"

"You got it! You got it!"

Chloe was suddenly jumping up and down and issuing the most piercing squeals that made Jesse wince and Jacqui cover her ears.

Ari put a hand over her mouth. "Chloe! The neighbors! Yes, I did get them. I was hoping to wait until tomorrow."

"Where is it?" Chloe shrieked, still jumping up and down.

"They're in my bedroom," Ari let out an exasperated laugh. Chloe dashed down the hall and Ari hurried after her. "Be careful, Chloe, they're very little!"

Chloe exploded into the bedroom, fell upon the carrier, looked inside, then gasped, "There's *two!* Oh, Mommy! You got me two?"

"I didn't have the heart to separate them," Ari explained.

Chloe looked at the two little golden balls of fur who were meowing and sticking their little paws through the grate. It was too much for her. Overwhelmed with emotion, she put her hands over her face and burst into tears.

"You got me kittens! Two kittens," she sobbed.

"Me and Gram did, and Jesse brought them over tonight while you were at the concert. But they're very feisty, and you must keep the door closed or they'll get loose."

"I will, I will, Mommy. I promise. I'll take such good care of them," Chloe cried.

Ari wiped her daughter's face with a tissue. "Now stop crying. Do you want everyone to see your boogers?"

Chloe giggled through her tears. "I love you so much, Mommy."

"And I love you too, baby. Forever and ever. Now take them into your room where they have to stay for a few weeks. They're too little yet and could get hurt around all the furniture."

"Okay, Mommy," Chloe sniffled and dutifully picked up the carrier, "I'll take good care of them. I promise! I can't wait to tell Missy and Emma. They'll be so jealous!" she babbled and sniffled her way out of the room. "Oh, Mommy! This is the best Christmas ever."

Ari smiled, pleased with herself as she watched Chloe carry her precious cargo into her room.

"Shut the door, Chloe. Always keep the door closed until they get bigger!" Ari said as she followed her in with the food bowls and the litter box. "You need to find a nice place for them in here. I'll help you set it up later, okay?"

Jesse was just getting ready to leave when she rejoined him and Jacqui in the kitchen.

"Oh well, Gram. So much for our plan of waiting 'til the morning."

"Yes, but they probably wouldn't have been quiet all night,"

Jacqui said.

Ari and Jesse told her how the kittens had gotten loose minutes before she and Chloe returned from the concert, and Ari's grandmother laughed happily. Ari could tell by the way she looked at Jesse that she liked him, maybe even admired him.

A few minutes later, she was walking Jesse out to the elevator.

"I can't thank you enough, Jesse. This was really nice of you."

He decided not to hit the elevator button right away. Instead, he leaned against the elevator wall, crossed his arms over his chest, and let his full attention fall upon her in a way that made her feel nervous all over again.

"So," he said and there was mischief in his eyes. "Boogers and bunny slippers. . ."

She laughed in spite of herself. Thank God for his sense of humor. "Figures you'd hear me say that. Now I'll never hear the end of it."

"Probably not."

"Lovely."

"You made her laugh. She's a sweet kid."

"I want her to be happy," she said, suddenly serious. "Christmas is always hard for us, for her. Her father doesn't pay much attention to her, and the holidays is when that becomes a lot more obvious."

"I'm sorry to hear that."

"He sent her a stupid Pillow Pet this year." She spat the words out of her mouth as if they were snake venom. She was completely unaware of how ravishing she looked in a rage and how the man in front of her could hardly take his eyes off of her.

"I take it you don't get along with your ex."

"Hardly," she scoffed.

"Well, me neither. Cynthia and I haven't spoken in years."

She looked up at him, interested. "Were you married?"

"No. But let's not talk about her. That's the past. My mind is totally fixed on the present right now," he said, pressing the button, and the double entendre was not missed on her.

She liked his confidence. A lot. Probably because it was so different from the needy men who always managed to wiggle their way into her life.

"I look forward to Monday," he was saying as the elevator door opened. He stuck a foot in it to hold it open as the couple across the hall stepped out and smiled at her. "Now if you'll excuse me, I need to change before midnight Mass."

She giggled, her eyes dancing prettily. "Merry Christmas, Jesse."

"Merry Christmas, *mi belleza*," he said, stepping into the elevator and watching her until the door closed between them.

Swoonish should be a word.

FIFTEEN

"WHAT A GENUINELY NICE MAN," Jacqui said later when they finally found a moment to sit down. Chloe was in bed, the kittens were fed, and the house was finally quiet. "You two would make a nice couple."

"Gram!"

She smiled with a very uncharacteristic caginess, then shrugged her shoulders. "I'm just saying, you're both tall and dark and would make a striking couple."

"Well, thank you, but we're just friends."

"For now." Gram reached for her laptop sitting on the coffee table between them. "But tonight, I have something special for you," she announced, flipping open the laptop and bringing something up on the screen. "It's something I've wanted to talk with you about for almost ten years now."

Ten years?

"Really?"

"Yes. I've been waiting for the right time, and I have the feeling that it's now, so I decided to give this to you as my Christmas gift." With the laptop still facing her, she leaned forward from within the comfortable embrace of a white brocade wingback and looked Ari directly in the eye.

"Ari, you know the greatest sorrow of my life has been the way your mother and father treated you. And I know it's going to be painful for you to see them tomorrow, but there's a whole lot more to you than your parents. And I think it's time that you start to realize this."

Ari just looked at her, confused. "What is this about, Gram?"

"You have a very interesting lineage."

"I do?"

"Yes!" Gram said brightly. "Take a look at this."

She flipped the laptop around and there on the screen was an image that made the breath catch in Ari's throat.

It was a black and white photograph, yellowed with age, of a woman who looked exactly like Ari, only she was dressed in nineteenth-century garb. She had the same eyes, the same dark hair, only hers was piled on top of her head in dramatic curls with several winding down her neck and tumbling to her shoulder.

"Oh wow. . ." Ari breathed.

"Uncanny, isn't it?"

"Who is she?"

"Are you ready for another shock?"

"I guess so."

"Her name is Ariella Ward, and she lived 160 years ago very close to where we're living now in the Kensington section of the city."

"She has the same name too?"

"Yes," Jacqui said and slipped into her professor persona. "It's an unusual name, almost rare. It's Hebrew and it means 'Lioness of God.' The name is from your mother's side of the family, the Pritchard line. I came across it when I was researching the Dalton line in the family, and when I found the name 'Ariella' and the picture, I was instantly intrigued and had to look further."

"Mom always said it was a family name, but she never really knew why."

"Because she probably didn't know herself."

"Does Mom know about her?"

"Yes."

"And?"

"She thought it was amazing, for about five minutes," Jacqui recalled. "This is just one of several 'Ariellas' that I have found in the Pritchard family tree."

"You mean there's more?"

"There are, my love. There are six Ariellas that I found who are more than likely a part of your bloodline. Once we get beyond the Middle Ages, this kind of research is challenging, even for me. Thankfully, it's an unusual name, and the bearers of that name usually did something notable and were associated with notable people, which enabled me to find more information. I was even able to find portions of personal diaries in some cases, which helped me to piece together the story of their lives. And there were other characteristics that concern medical records, so I was able to find information from medical journals and notes as well."

"Medical?"

"You'll see. What it means is that you have a very definite legacy, a legacy of women who all look like you, have the same name, and other characteristics in common that you'll discover as we unveil these women."

They were silent for a long moment as Ari's eyes shifted between the woman on the screen and her grandmother's face.

"Let me tell you about Ariella Ward," Jacqui pointed her attention back to the woman in the photo. "She lived during the great Gilded Age of the late nineteenth century, a time of great political instability. First was the assassination of President James Garfield in 1881 after only four months in office. He was succeeded by his vice president, the lackluster Chester Arthur, who was defeated in 1884 by the rather uninspiring Grover Cleveland.

"As bleak as the political landscape looked at the time, this was also an era of very rapid and exciting advances in the sciences and technology. Thanks to American entrepreneurs, candles and gas lamps were replaced by the electric light bulb. The typewriter replaced the quill. The telegraph and telephone were taking communication to a whole new level. The railroad was replacing horse and buggy, and industries such as steel and textiles were producing mass amounts of products to satisfy the demands of the growing population of the country and the world at large.

"But this progress had a very dark side. Greedy men, known as robber barons, cashed in on the incredible growth of this era in steel, banking, and the railroads and built enormous fortunes for themselves at the expense of the working class. Mass immigration brought in cheap labor, which they exploited for their own gain, subjecting workers to sub-human working and living conditions.

"It was on this dark side that Ariella, who was known as 'Ella' to her family and friends, was born in 1864, a year before the Civil War ended. Her father, Jonathon Ward, died of cholera during the war, and her mother, Dolly Sadler-Ward, passed away fifteen years later of brown lung, which she contracted while working in a cotton factory just ten miles from here in what is now known as Olde Kensington. Ella was taken in by her mother's sister, Elisabeth Sadler.

"As you can see by her picture, Ella was a lovely woman, but she was raised in abject poverty. Even though she was of English ancestry and native born, she was a Catholic, which placed her at the same low level of regard as the immigrant population. In the news accounts that I read about her, she was very involved in the movement to organize the beleaguered masses of laborers into powerful unions that could affect change and improve the living conditions of the poor. She wholeheartedly embraced the blossoming feminist movement of her time, which surrounded the fight for women's equality and the right to vote, but she was also quite fascinated with the scientific advances of her time, especially astronomy. Largely self-taught, she was known to be of brilliant mind, and yet had the 'voice of an angel' who was said to be able to 'cut a man off at the knees, as he'd mistake it for a sweet embrace.'"

Ari grinned in spite of herself. "I like her already!"

"You'll love her! It's impossible not to! Even though she was a devout Catholic who considered becoming a sister in order to better help the poor, God had another plan for her, and it was to align her with a true prince of a man with whom she would lift herself, and many others, out of poverty while doing great things for the Church. They say hers was a true Cinderella story, but I disagree. The hand of God was surely at play in bringing together these two persons so perfectly suited to fulfilling the sacred mission of furthering the establishment of basic human rights for all. Do you want to know more?"

Ari nodded. "I do!"

"Okay, let's get ourselves some hot chocolate, and I'll tell you all about this courageous young woman whose story starts in a most unusual way—with a simple pair of boots. . ."

SIXTEEN

"ELLA! SLOW DOWN! I can't keep up!"

"Because you're too busy chattering. Hurry, Cora! It's freezing."

The two women huddled inside their cloaks, a blanket drawn over their heads to keep off the snow that was falling fast and heavy as they made their way up the slippery sidewalk. Despite the early hour of the morning, the streets were already busy with millworkers like them hurrying to their factories while delivery carts rambled down the road, their horses snorting in annoyance as they struggled through the deepening drifts.

"I wanted to stop at the second-hand store on the way home tonight," Cora said, her round cheeks already bright pink from the cold. She wore an old gray wool bonnet too small for her head. It barely covered her ears and left a long, loose strand of curly blonde hair to whip around in the frigid winds. "Will it be open, do you think?"

"Probably. They need to work just like us."

"I need a frock for church."

"Church, eh?" Ella looked at her and smiled slyly. "Or for Dickie?"

Cora blushed, rolled her big, green eyes, and sighed, "Do you think he notices me?"

"He smiles whenever we come into the bakery."

"He's probably smiling for you. All the men smile for you, Ella, you being so pretty and all."

"I'm no prettier than you."

"But you're not as plump as me."

"You're not at all plump! Besides, that's what corsets are for! Just tighten it!"

"It's as tight as I can stand it."

They reached the last house on the block and stopped to wait for Margaret "Megsie" Whitman to come out.

"Oh! Hurry Megsie!" Cora implored just as the door opened and Megsie rushed outside.

She looked unusually tiny this morning, barely five feet tall in her boots, a threadbare gray cloak clutched close around her petite frame. Her pale skin seemed all the whiter while buried inside the shadowy folds of her hood, the dark circles under eyes making her appear almost sickly. But she wasn't. For as frail and delicate as she looked, Megsie Whitman had the stamina of an ox. She almost never missed her quota at the factory, even when it meant working a sewing machine treadle for a twelve-hour shift.

"I almost overslept!" she said apologetically and wedged herself between them so they could huddle close under the blanket. "But I wouldn't miss this day for anything."

"It's Ella's big day!" Cora chirped. "You get to speak to the owner of Marsden Mills today and plead our case!"

Of course they'd chosen Ella. Much like her mother, she was highly intelligent, very well-spoken, and on fire for the cause of worker's rights. She could out-talk any man on the subject and do it in her trademark sweet voice that barely rose above a whisper, even in the midst of her most impassioned speeches. Tall and statuesque and exceedingly lovely to look upon, she managed to maintain her humility with a daintiness that made even the toughest men trip over themselves in her presence.

"Pray the good Lord will be with me," Ella said, blessing herself and secretly praying for strength as she'd done incessantly for the last three days. "I can't lose my job. Auntie Bess would go into a swoon she might never come out of."

"They won't fire you," Megsie said sweetly. "You're the only one who knows how to fix the sewing machines."

"And balance the books," Cora added.

"And keep the cutters happy," Megsie reminded.

"But you know how Mr. Marsden is," Ella fretted.

"Yes. Old, crabby, and ornery! If anyone can soften his heart, it's you, Ella!"

"My feet are soaked," Meg sighed.

"And mine are numb," Ella added. "The heel's falling off my boot and the snow is making it worse. I'm wobbling like an old horse with a bad shoe."

Their teeth were chattering by the time they burst through the factory door at Marsden Mills. Warm air hit them in the face, filling their nostrils with the scent of wet earth and their lungs with the soot of spent charcoal. They gathered their half-frozen hems and hurried up the rickety wooden stairs into the expansive second floor that was already bustling with activity. A spacious room with crude wooden floors and brick walls, it was equipped with long rows of sewing machines, each with a worktable and baskets to catch finished jackets before being sent off to the basters, finishers, and pressers.

"Ella!" Mr. Champs shouted as soon as they appeared on the landing. "Molly jammed her machine already!"

"The bobbin's not wound right!" the fourteen-year-old girl said, standing as far away as possible from the fuming overseer.

"I'll tend to it!" Ella tossed off her cloak and hurried across the room. She had worn her finest black wool skirt today, a clean pin-striped blouse, and a freshly starched white linen apron, all acquired from Jamesby's Second-Hand shop on Oxford Street.

"Everything has to be running smoothly today!" Mr. Champs barked at no one in particular. "Mr. Marsden's coming. He'll be wanting to inspect the machines, the workers, the quotas, the books. . ." The more he spoke the more flustered he became until he started pawing at his handle-bar mustache that was as black and greasy as his hair. He always pawed at his face when he was nervous.

"It'll be fine, Mr. Champs," Ella reassured in her sing-song voice that could lull a raging bull to sleep. "I looked over the books last night and everything is in order."

"I'll be hoping you tell him something good about me, Miss Ella," Mr. Champs growled. It was the closest he could come to groveling.

"And will you be saying something good about Ella, Mr. Champs?" Cora challenged. "After all, she practically runs the place while you take all the credit."

"Mind your tongue, Miss Hughes!" he grunted, prickled by the statement because it was true. Porter Champs, popularly known as "Portly Porter," was getting paid for running a mill that a twenty-year-old Catholic activist woman with a brain as sharp as a needle was managing because he hadn't the wits for the job.

"Never mind, you two," Ella said kindly. "I'll speak the truth, Mr. Champs," she reassured while peering deep into the bobbin compartment to check for any blockage.

"That's what I'm afraid of."

He had reason to fear. In spite of how much she helped him, Champs disliked Ella because of her involvement in the labor movement. Just like all the managers who groveled at the feet of the robber barons who were driving the country's working class no gentler than cattle, he tried to break her back by increasing her quotas, forcing her to skip lunch, or making her stay as late as ten o'clock at night. But he wasn't stupid enough to fire her because he hadn't the wits to keep the books and manage the workforce. It was Ella who mopped up after him even though he was paid three times what she made in a week.

"If you behave in a way to keep your conscience clear, you should have nothing to fear," Ella smiled prettily while snapping the compartment shut.

"You papists do nothing but preach," he scowled.

"Now, now," she looked at Molly. "Step on the treadle, Molly. Let's see how it works."

The machine hummed into life, the needle rising and falling and picking up the thread just as it was designed to do.

"There now!"

"Back to work, girls!" Mr. Champs shouted.

As the hour for Mr. Marsden's arrival drew near, Ella withdrew to the outdoor privy, now covered in snow and ice, and prayed for the strength and courage to say what had to be said.

I know you're with me and you hear the cry of my heart. Keep my intentions pure. Don't let me give way to anger or resentment or any other evil sentiments toward the greed and despotism of the Marsden family that makes life so miserable for us. I forgive them because you ask me to do so. Have mercy on them, Lord, that they might see the error in their ways. And have mercy on me that I might find the strength and courage to say what must be said without fear or anger.

"We must be active but not angry," her mother had coached five years ago from what was to become her deathbed. Ella could still see the animation on her mother's face as she lay in the darkened bedroom full of the musky scents of mustard plasters and a tincture of belladonna. "Love must guide our protests, otherwise, the labor movement will become a feeding ground for criminals and miscre-ants whose bad behavior will be attributed to the whole movement. We cannot allow this to happen. If we want justice, we must be just in the way we make those demands."

Memories of her mother made her heart feel heavy, but only until Mr. Marsden arrived and the atmosphere in the mill turned suddenly tense and excited. Beneath the din of their machines, they heard footsteps rushing up the stairs as one of the basters an-nounced importantly, "Mr. Marsden is here but it's not the older, it's the younger!"

"Randolph?" Cora gasped.

"No. No. It's Reese, the eldest. The heir!"

"I read about him in the papers!" Cora said, her eyes flashing with excitement. "They say he's dashing!"

"Cora! Control yourself!" Megsie giggled at the girl who was feigning a swoon.

"Pipe down, ladies!" the baster said as if being the bearer of the news gave him some kind of authority. "They'll be coming up before you know it."

Ella was thoroughly relieved at the news. Caleb Marsden was a pickle of a man if there ever was one. Surely his son would be more amiable.

Although they were careful to keep their machines whirring, their eyes remained riveted on the door, which finally opened to reveal a rattled Mr. Champs, who was furiously pawing at his mustache.

He was followed by a very tall and distinguished looking gentle-man in a black, knee-length frock coat cut in the fashionable dou-ble-breasted Prince Edward style. It was impeccable except for the sprinkling of snow on its wide shoulders. His dark hair was as care-fully trimmed as the beard that traced the broad outline of a strong, square jaw. Clear, dark gray eyes looked out from beneath a pair of heavy brows as he looked around the room, at the rows of sewers, the crude shelves full of neatly basketed sewing notions, the dusty floors, and slightly sagging ceiling.

His stance, his dress, his manner reeked of power, money, and prestige.

Ella swallowed hard. Maybe the elder Marsden would have been better after all.

Every eye followed him as he walked into the office where he took off his coat and laid his hat on the desk with Mr. Champs following after him like a nervous gosling. But then he abruptly turned around and came back out into the sewing room.

"I want to see the machines," he murmured.

"Yes, sir. Go right ahead sir."

He walked up to the first sewer—Cora, who smiled at him like a lovestruck schoolgirl—and carefully inspected her machine, running his hand over the surface, watching the needle move up and down.

"I could go faster but my treadle sticks, sir," Cora peeped.

"Does it?" Mr. Marsden asked in a friendly tone of voice, then turned to Mr. Champs and said, "Get some oil and fix her treadle."

"She's always complaining."

"I'm not!" Cora protested.

"Let me see," Mr. Marsden ignored them. "Can you please step aside?" he asked Cora in a surprisingly cordial tone of voice.

"Certainly!" Cora said and stepped aside so hastily she nearly fell into the scrap basket.

Mr. Marsden put his foot on the treadle and tested it, then squatted down and inspected the apparatus under the table. When he stood up, his hands were greasy. Molly nearly tripped over herself to get him a piece of discarded wool.

"Here you go, sir."

"Thank you, Miss. . ?"

"McGovern. Molly McGovern."

He feigned tipping a hat and she curtsied clumsily. "Sir."

"Get the oil and fix this treadle," he ordered Mr. Champs, then added. "I'll look at the books now."

"Yes, sir."

The moment he disappeared into the office, every treadle stopped as the women gazed at one another, utterly awestruck.

"Fetch me the salts," Cora gasped, and they all giggled as she ran her hand along the spine of her machine where he had touched it.

"He's so nice!" Megsie whispered.

"A gentleman!" Ella said with unmasked surprise. Maybe this wouldn't be such a hard day after all.

"Stop your fawning! You women act like you never saw a man before," Mr. Champs hissed as he stooped over Cora's treadle and gave it some oil.

"Perhaps because we haven't!" Cora sneered.

Mr. Champs looked ready to strangle her. "Get back to work!" He headed for the office, swiping and scratching at his mustache, then disappeared inside.

As soon as the door shut, their oldest sewer, Mary MacLeod, said in her thick Irish brogue, "This one's far more handsome than Randolph, if you ask me. Randolph takes after his mum, short and portly. This one, he's got his father's looks, but who can tell? What happened to Caleb, all bent and plagued of body, is what happens after a lifetime of greed and indulgence."

"Handsome or not, he's also the son of the man who's paying us next to nothing and working us to the bone," Jane O'Toole muttered from her station a few tables away. "I'd look as good as him too if I had the luxuries he enjoys every day."

Mary laughed scornfully. "Baths in clawfoot tubs, lightbulbs in every room, expensive colognes, servants to fix his tea and warm his towels and wipe his dandy behind every time he steps out of the loo." The whole room erupted in naughty giggles. "What's he got to do all day but play cricket? And at night he's hobnobbing with the gentry folk or kissing the hand of Lady This or That."

They were all laughing when the door opened and Mr. Champs came out and put a finger to his lips to silence them. "Get to work!" he whispered fiercely.

"My machine's jammed!" Cora teased.

"Saints alive!" He paled visibly.

"She's fooling you!" Ella said and watched him let out his breath in a long and very relieved sigh.

"I'll wring your neck, Cora!"

"In front of Mr. Marsden? What would he think?"

"Shh! Let him work. He's reading the books. And he's an accountant so there'll be hell to pay if anything is off in our ledgers." He looked at Ella just then to let her know she'd be held accountable if there were any problems.

An hour went by before the door opened again. This time, it was Mr. Marsden who stood in the doorway, clothed now in just his waistcoat and a shirt so white it made everything around him look even filthier than it was.

"Mr. Champs?"

"Right here, sir!" Mr. Champs popped out of the only chair in the room and nearly bowled the man over in his haste to rush into the office.

"I'll see the workers' representative now," he said in that deep voice that made Mr. Champs sound like a cackling hen in comparison.

"Miss Ella?" Champs called out loud. "Mr. Marsden will see you now."

Ella's heart sank an inch lower in her chest as real nervousness took hold of her.

"Never be afraid to fight for what's right, Ella!" her mother's voice rang in her ear as she took off her apron, blessed herself, then headed into the office.

SEVENTEEN

WHEN ELLA ENTERED THE ROOM, Mr. Marsden half-rose out of politeness, but didn't look up from the books that were spread across the desk. He quickly sat back down and seemed far more interested in them than in her.

"This is Miss Ariella Ward. . . .er, we call her Ella around these parts," Mr. Champs informed him. "She has been chosen to speak to you on behalf of the workers in the mill."

"Very well. What do you have to say, Miss Ward?" Mr. Marsden asked, still studying the books in front of him. Ella was hardly offended by his seeming lack of interest because it was so typical of his class. The wealthy had no time for the poor, except to shoo them away like nagging insects at a posh country picnic.

But she would not be so easily shooed. As gentle and kind as she was known to be, Ella Ward had a will of steel and bowed to no one but God.

"The workers in this mill have selected me to ask the Marsden family to consider rectifying some of the unseemly conditions in this mill," she began.

"First, we work twelve hours a day and sometimes longer to meet our quotas and yet are not paid enough to live. Women and children are paid only half of what men are paid for the same work. There are few safety precautions in this building and when one of us gets hurt, there is no recompense. We get no medical assistance and lose our wages. The air we breathe in this shop is full of lint and dust and soot from the furnace, which could be easily rectified with more windows to provide ventilation. This is particularly grievous to me because my mother died of brown lung after having worked in such conditions in Horstman's Mill."

For some reason, he looked up just then, caught sight of her, then blinked and looked more closely. There was a flash of surprise on his face that she didn't quite understand. It made her wonder if she had just said something terribly wrong.

"My condolences," he said after a long moment. "I lost my mother too."

"I'm sorry," she said and looked him in the eye for just a brief moment before properly dropping her gaze to some spot on the floor.

"Now what is it that you'd like me to do about these conditions?" he asked, and she could feel his eyes studying her so closely she became instantly self-conscious about the faded pinstripes on her over-laundered blouse.

She almost hoped Mr. Champs would say something but he was standing in the doorway, only half listening to their conversation.

"We would like eight hours to work, eight hours to rest, and eight hours to enjoy our families," she finally said.

"Yes, I've heard that slogan."

"It's not just a slogan, sir, it's a blueprint for a healthy life that is worthy of the human species."

"Is that so?"

She heard the chair scrape across the floor as he stood up and walked around the desk to stand before her. The closeness of him, the intensity of his attention, made her heart pound in her breast, but it wasn't just from fear. It was from something else that she couldn't quite name other than that he was very manly, very handsome, very powerful, and very close. Maybe too close.

"It is, sir," she said in the most even tone she could muster. "Surely there are ways to protect your profits that would not result in forcing so many otherwise hard working and decent Americans into abject poverty."

"Pray tell, what are those ways?" he asked.

"How difficult would it be to add a few extra windows for ventilation in the sewing areas? A railing on the stairs might have prevented numerous falls that resulted in broken bones. If you provided the lumber, we would build it ourselves. Reducing hours does not necessarily mean reducing output. A healthy and rested workforce will only produce more, not less, ready-made garments. And most of us sewers would be more than happy to take work home so that we can spend more time with our families."

For a brief moment, when she lifted her eyes from the floor, she could not have known how struck he was by the beauty of them, by how pale they were, like the color of arctic ice, and how he found them to be all the more striking when set against the jet black of her hair and brows.

And yet, as frosty a blue as they were, there was nothing cold about her because she was careful not to allow any hostility in her voice or mannerisms. Instead, she remained calm and poised and spoke in a voice that was so soft, so dulcet, so genteel and articulate, that the man before her was instantly intrigued by the contradictoriness of her. By the shabby clothes contrasting her highborn speech, by the filthy surroundings against her flawless porcelain skin, the harshness of her circumstances compared to the delicacy of her figure, and the dullness of her world compared to the seeming brilliance of her mind.

Ella was too innocent to realize how the dichotomy of her could seem so strangely riveting to a man like Reese Marsden, a man who had long since grown tired of being surrounded by empty-headed women of privilege who wanted for nothing yet desired everything.

Mr. Marsden leaned against the desk and crossed his arms over his chest. Ella wondered at his attention, at what it might mean, hardly aware of how she suddenly looked to him like a fragile white rose in a garden full of slugs.

"It's not cheap to cut through the walls of this building to put in more windows," he challenged her.

"It's cheaper than losing laborers who are too sick to come to work," she countered intelligently.

"And if we reduce hours and the workers get lazy, then what?"

"You fire the lazy ones and hire those who are willing to work hard in exchange for a better life. There's not a sewer in this mill who wouldn't give you twice as much effort in exchange for few less hours away from their families each day."

He thought for a moment, then changed the subject. "You don't sound very Irish."

"Because I'm not. I'm of English descent and native born."

"Native born? What are you doing in a mill? Native born workers are sought after in much higher trades than this."

"Not if they're Catholic."

"Oh. I see." He walked around the desk and retook his seat. "What is the opinion of the workers about the management in this mill?"

Mr. Champs suddenly stood upright and returned his attention to their conversation. He looked almost pleadingly at Ella, who just smiled demurely and said, "He is what one would expect of a man of his caliber."

Mr. Marsden let out a gusty laugh that made his whole face

brighten. The stiffness dropped away, his eyes twinkled, and his handsome lips split into a wide grin. "Well said, my lady!" he awarded and rapped the desk in delight. "Pray tell, Champs, did she just insult you or praise you?"

"Only heaven knows, sir."

"I'm actually starting to enjoy this visit."

"I'm glad to hear that, sir."

Ella curtsied and asked, "Will there be anything else, Mr. Marsden?"

"Not unless you have more grievances to air."

"I believe I've said enough. If you'll excuse me, I have work to do."

"Of course you do. It was my pleasure to meet you, Miss Ward."

"Likewise."

She turned to leave, but right as she did, the heel on her boot gave way and broke off, sending her stumbling into the door jam.

"Good heavens! Catch her!" Mr. Marsden leaped around the desk and was upon her in a moment. "Miss Ward! Are you alright?"

"I am!" she said, utterly embarrassed. "This old boot. . ."

He bent down and picked up the heel. It was as worn as an old door stop.

"I'll get it repaired," she said, took the heel of out his hand, and left the room, shutting the door softly behind her.

EIGHTEEN

AUNTIE BESS WAS STANDING AT THE WINDOW when Ella came home that evening and hastily dropped the curtain to open the door.

"Why are you hobbling like that?"

"My heel fell off."

"Poor thing. So, what did you tell Mr. Marsden? Did you tell that no-good pod-snapper where he ought to rest for all eternity?" she asked with her usual colorful language.

Ella laughed, stripped off her boots and wet stockings and padded barefoot into the kitchen where she stood before the stove to thaw the hem of her skirt, which was half frozen with snow.

"Out with it!" Auntie Bess demanded as she waddled behind Ella as fast as her short stocky legs could carry her. Dressed in a threadbare gray wool skirt and shirtwaist, her gray-streaked black hair crammed into an old white snood, she quickly filled a bowl with pepper pot and brought it to Ella.

"Hold onto this 'til your hands warm, girl," she ordered as Ella perched on a stool in front of the blazing fire. The young woman recounted the entire conversation to her aunt.

"So, you faced the young'n then?"

"I did. The heir. His name is B. Reese Marsden, Esquire."

"La-di-da!" her aunt scoffed. "Uppity like his father, eh?"

"Actually, he wasn't at all uppity. He was almost likeable, even when I said the worst."

"You have your mother's nerve, girl."

"I was never impolite."

"Just like she taught you. The best way to be impolite is to be polite about it," Auntie Bess flashed a sneaky smile that revealed her yellowed teeth.

Ella could only smile at this beloved woman who so generously opened the humble doors of her old wooden duplex on the corner of Duke and Marlborough to the orphaned Ella. Even though they were pitifully poor and eked out a living on the sewing and laundering that Auntie Bess took in and the five dollars weekly pay Ella earned at Marsden's Mill, it was a happy home.

As usual, when her chores were done, Ella went up to her bedroom, stoked the stove, and buried the aches and pains of poverty in the latest issue of *Science* that she had dug out of the trash behind the Kensington Hotel. It featured an article about a scientist named Andrew Ainslie Common who set up a reflecting telescope in his backyard and managed to photograph sixty-minute exposures of the Orion nebula. His photos showed stars too faint to be seen by the human eye.

Such advances fascinated her, especially in astronomy, but American entrepreneurs were inventing marvels at a rapid pace. In the past four decades alone, they had invented the rotary printing press, the electric light bulb, the typewriter, the suspension bridge, the phonograph, telegraph, and telephone. It was such an exciting time to be alive, and reading about these inventions made her yearn to learn more, see more, experience more.

After reading a page from the good book, which all Catholic ladies were expected to do every day, she prayed to the God who was ever close to her and had been all her life. From the time she was a child, it had never been difficult to pray because she could always sense the nearness of God, as if He was just waiting for her to glance His way. She did it as often as possible throughout the course of the day. Fr. Kieran called it the Practice of the Presence of God and encouraged her to continue the practice although she couldn't imagine life without it.

And so, she lay abed, reliving every memory of the day and sharing it with Him while pleading that this young heir might actually help them. For some reason, she felt hopeful, and wondered if this was God confirming her deepest desires to bring justice and relief to the long-suffering lower class in what was supposed to be the land of opportunity.

Oh Lord! Hear the cry of the poor, of those of us who have no one but You to help them!

The following morning, she was startled awake by a loud rap on her door. "There's a package for you on the stoop, Ella!" Auntie Bess called.

"A package? But I'm not expecting anything."

"You better come downstairs."

There was something peculiar in her aunt's tone of voice that made Ella hurry through her usual morning ritual. She rinsed her face in the basin, put on a fresh chemise and pantaloons, laced herself into a corset, and pulled a pair of wool stockings over her knees. She tied them in place with tattered strips of ribbon and donned a thick cotton blouse and a muslin underskirt, along with the heaviest woolen skirt she owned to keep the cold off her legs while outdoors.

As for boots, she planned to make do with the broken pair but would wrap her foot in rags to keep out the snow and ice. If she could make it to Jamesby's today, she'd try to find another boot that didn't cost more than the thirty cents she had left from last week's pay.

She rushed downstairs and found a box wrapped in brown paper sitting next to her breakfast of boiled eggs and hot cakes. An envelope was tucked under the tightly tied twine.

She opened it and pulled out an impressively embossed card that read, "B. Reese Marsden, Esquire." Her heart skipped a beat. She flipped the card over and saw that there was no message on the back.

"Lord, have mercy!" Auntie Bess blessed herself. "It's from him?"

"I suppose." Ella tore through the paper and opened the box to reveal a pair of brand-new black leather button boots that reached past her ankle. Stunned, she sat down on the kitchen bench and slid her feet into the boots, which fit almost perfectly.

"Are my eyes deceiving me?" Auntie Bess was fanning herself with a table napkin. "Or are those boots the new kind with a right *and* a left foot?"

"They are! And what a difference it makes!" Ella turned this way and that, admiring the boots, the leather, the fashionable buttons, then carefully took them off and put them back in the box.

"What are you doing?"

"I'm sending them back."

"Whatever for?"

"I can't possibly keep such expensive boots when the rest of our neighbors are wearing rags on their feet, as I'll be doing today with my old boots."

Auntie Bess put her hands on her hips and huffed in a way that made her cheeks puff and redden. "Ariella Maria. You'll do nothing of the kind. You're keeping those boots!"

"I'm not," Ella said sweetly, but firmly.

"That's not what your mother would do!"

"Pray tell, what would Mama do with these boots?"

"She'd keep them, is what! The man owes you as much in cheated pay! That's what she'd say. It's the least he could do."

Ella struggled to find an argument. "Well, I suppose. . ."

"I suppose you'll keep them and start wearing them today."

"But it's not proper for a lady to accept a gift from a gentleman," Ella reminded her, which made Auntie Bess look even more peeved.

"Of course it isn't, but this isn't a gift. It's pay in exchange for work."

"That's not what the card says."

"The card says nothing!"

It was true. Mr. Marsden did not indicate any motive for the boots, which meant she was free to assign her own.

"Alright then. I will keep the boots but under one condition."

"What is that?"

"I'll pay for them in installments."

"Don't be foolish! You can't afford these boots!"

"Enough said, Auntie," Ella said as she picked up her fork and started eating. "I'll write him a note under your signature."

"I won't mail it."

"Then I will."

No sooner did she arrive at the factory when everyone started noticing her new boots. Somehow, she managed to deflect their questions so as to avoid lying and committing a sin and was glad when the day wore on and everyone gradually forgot about them.

Except for Mr. Champs. Just before she left for the day, he stuck his head out of the office and motioned to her. "I want to see you in here, Miss Ella! Straight away!"

"I hope he's going to give you a raise for what a good job you did yesterday!" Cora whispered.

"The only way I'll get a raise out of him is if the Lord God Himself appears and orders him to do it," Ella grumbled.

"And even then, he'll probably claim it was the devil in disguise and pocket the money himself," Jane giggled.

As soon as she entered the office, Mr. Champs shut the door behind her and instantly fixed her with a mean scowl.

"What are you up to, young lady?"

"Pardon me, Mr. Champs?"

"Where did you get those boots?"

"My boots? What do you mean?"

"You and I both know where they came from."

"I don't understand," she said carefully.

"Let me help you. Mr. Marsden had his driver trace the outline of your footprint from the dust on the floor of the office yesterday, then ordered his driver to take it somewhere and 'buy a pair that meets these exact specifications and have them delivered first thing in the morning to this address,'" he said, imitating Mr. Marsden's deep baritone. "At the time, I thought it was the strangest thing, and now here you come strutting into work with a brand-new pair of boots. Coincidence? Hardly. Now tell me why he did that."

"I have no idea."

"Don't lie to me, Miss Ella. I don't want to have to fire you."

"Fire me? For what?"

"What did you offer Mr. Marsden in exchange for those boots?"

"Mr. Champs!" She gasped, genuinely shocked at what he had just implied. "No such thing transpired between us! You were listening to the whole conversation."

"With half an ear!"

"Perhaps you should use both ears next time as well as keep your mind out of the gutter!"

"Never mind acting so high and mighty. We all know about you mill girls. . ."

"Do you now?" she asked and could feel the anger flushing up her cheeks. "We might be poor in material possessions, but we are rich in the things of heaven." She squared her shoulders and fixed him with her most indignant look. "Shame on you, Mr. Champs!"

He struggled not to look sheepish.

"And for your information, I am paying for these boots in installments!"

"Never mind! I don't believe a word of it, and I'm adding two jackets to your daily quota tomorrow, girl. You can stay until they're finished every night."

"Two more jackets? That's not fair!"

"I don't need to be fair to a papist mill girl."

"Is this the thanks I get for helping you?"

"I don't want your thanks. You'll help me because I say so and you need a job. No one else will hire you. Who wants Catholic scum in their shop? Especially not Catholic scum who involve themselves in labor unions. Now get out."

Lord, give me the strength to seal my lips!

Later that night, Auntie Bess was furious when Ella told her about the conversation with Mr. Champs.

"Why, that witless fopdoodle!" she spat, crossing her arms over her chest and fuming. "Who does he think he is making such a filthy accusation against a woman of such untarnished character as yourself?"

Ella sighed. "Oh, Auntie! He's just being Mr. Champs."

"He should be fired!"

"Of course he should, but he won't. If anyone gets fired, it will be me. Besides, his wife is expecting their fourth."

"I don't know how she could climb into bed with that crusty slob."

Ella choked. "Auntie! Let's try to be civil about it or we can't receive Communion on Sunday."

"I'm going to tell the Lord God Himself what I think of Mr. Champs and his dirty mind!"

That made Ella giggle.

After Ella finished eating, she spent a few hours laundering and hanging their clean garments to dry overtop the stove in the kitchen, then sat down to write a letter to Mr. Marsden.

"To the honorable Mr. B. Reese Marsden, Esquire. Please accept this payment as my first installment toward the very fine boots that you provided to me this morning. I promise to make a monthly payment of twenty-five cents until I have paid the list price of the boots, which appears to be $2.50. If the cost is higher than the aforementioned, please advise me, and I will be happy to continue the installments until said matter has been resolved. With gratitude and the utmost respect, Miss Ariella Maria Ward."

She folded the note and handed it to Auntie Bess. "Here's the note to Mr. Marsden with my first installment. After what Mr. Champs accused me of, I suggest we be perfectly proper about this, which means you will have to write a cover note."

"Alright, alright," her aunt sighed, "I'll write something up tomorrow and mail it on Monday."

Ella smiled knowingly. "You'll leave it on the desk for me, and I'll post it on Monday."

"But I—"

"Auntie? I've had a rough day and want nothing more than to take a hot bath and read the latest issue of *Revolution*, which I managed to dig out of the trash behind Mrs. Cooper's house a few days ago. We women must stay informed so that when we win the right to vote, we can vote these do-nothing men out of office."

"Hmph! That'll be the day. And you, a feminist trash picker. What would your mother say?"

Ella giggled. "She'd say, 'That's my girl!' and we both know it!"

Auntie Bess finally forgot her irritation and laughed at the memory of her sister. "That she would. But she might have something to say about what happened with these boots."

"Oh? What would she say?"

"That some might call it romantic for a man to go to the trouble of measuring a lady's footprint in the dust in order to buy her a new pair of boots."

"What?" For a moment, Ella was so surprised she didn't know what to say.

"You heard me. Like he didn't have anything better to do than measure your footprint?"

"Auntie Bess! You've been reading too many romance novels!"

"And you've not been reading enough of them."

NINETEEN

"AUNTIE BESS IS RIGHT!" Ari said overtop a steaming mug of hot chocolate as her grandmother paused telling the story. "I think that's incredibly romantic, don't you? I mean, men just don't do things like that anymore."

"But they do still hand-deliver kittens on Christmas Eve," Jacqui replied with a sneaky smile.

"Gram! I told you. We're just friends," Ari insisted but she blushed in spite of herself.

"Many a fine romance starts out with friendship. Your grandfather and I were on the same debate team in college and used to love to debate one another because we thought so much alike. And then all of a sudden, one day, we just. . .noticed each other."

"I never knew that!"

This was turning out to be a very interesting evening. Not only was Ari discovering unknown facts about her family, but she was also getting a first-hand look at Jacqui's unique talent of making history come alive in story form.

"You should write a novel about this, Gram!"

"I've thought about it, but it would have to include the rest of the Ariellas that I've found. Now *that* would be an interesting book!" she said with a sparkle in her eye that was most unusual for the normally astute Professor Dalton. "Now, getting back to our story. Ella was very angry with Mr. Champs and her new quota, which made it difficult to keep up with her charities and the labor movement. But she refused to be bested by Champs and went into the mill at five o'clock in the morning to begin her sewing so she could make her new quota and still keep up with her charity work.

"In those days, the Church funded numerous charities to aid the poor immigrant population, the orphaned, the insane, delinquents, and unwed mothers. The St. Vincent de Paul Society, which exists to this day, was one of the most important charitable societies in the country at the time. And how desperately they were needed! Of the nearly twelve million families in the United States at the time, eleven million earned less than $380 a year."

"But that's less than eight dollars a week!"

"Shocking, isn't it? At the time, a quart of milk was thirty-two cents, beef was six to eight cents a pound, potatoes were fifty-six cents a bushel. A pair of shoes, which at the time were just beginning to be made with a right and a left foot, cost $2.50, so if Ella had to replace her own boots, it would have taken half a week's pay."

"I can't imagine what a terribly hard life they must have had. We're so spoiled with our cellphones and cars and supermarkets full of food," Ari pondered.

"It was a much different world then. We were just becoming the country we are today, and if it wasn't for the churches and their charities, God only knows how many people would have perished from hunger or the diseases than ran rampant through these communities that could not afford the health care available at the time, which wasn't very good for either rich or poor.

"But for all the Church did to help the poor, she did absolutely nothing to combat the injustices that caused these sub-standard living conditions. One of Ella's deepest concerns was how her Church could be so engaged in helping the poor and yet so uninvolved in fighting to correct the inequities that plagued this population. Instead of berating these robber barons for their blatant greed, the bishops and the Vatican did essentially nothing. In fact, the Archbishop of New York at the time, John Hughes, stood in front of his congregation one day and said, 'To the rich, moderation in enjoyment and liberality toward the poor. To the poor, patience under their trials and affection toward their wealthier brethren.'"

"Talk about tone-deaf!" Ari scoffed.

"Exactly! If Ella were here right now, she'd applaud you! Nothing upset her more than the church's indifference to social justice. It was during this time that many Catholics were coming to the conclusion that the times demanded more than charity and mercy; justice was also necessary if this blatant inequity was to be addressed. A day after Ella received this shiny new pair of boots from one of the wealthiest and most eligible bachelors in the world, the Church made a decision against labor unions that would compel her into the forefront of the fight for Catholic social justice.

"She was on her way home from the mill that night when she attended a local meeting of the Knights of Labor. Otherwise known as the KOL, it was the most formidable labor union of its time, boasting of some 700,000 members. On this night, the meeting that was usually devoted to organizing strikes took a sudden turn when its largely Catholic membership heard the news of the Vatican's decision. . ."

* * * * *

Fr. Kieran McDonough had an ominous look on his face when he motioned for the attention of everyone gathered in the narrow basement of St. Michael's parish church. Mostly Irish and German, their gaunt faces were bathed in the pale, yellow light of two overhead gas lamps hanging from the ceiling beams and casting long shadows up the stone walls. The smell of burnt gas mixed with the earthy scent of the damp mud floors and the musky odor of sweat-laden clothing made the cold air seem even more raw than usual.

Ella huddled deeper in her cloak and watched Fr. Kieran shift in his boots as if they were suddenly uncomfortable. A tall, elderly Irishman, he had thick, white hair that crept down the sides of his face in wide sideburns. Always slightly disheveled, his washed-out black robes hung on his thin frame and made him look as hungry as the rest of them.

"I hate to be the bearer of bad news, but it must be said," he began in his thick Irish accent, then sighed and spit the news out of his mouth as if it was sour milk. "It seems that Archbishop Taschereau of Quebec convinced the Vatican to issue a ruling forbidding Catholics to belong to the Knights of Labor."

"What?"

"Say you jest!"

"How could they betray us like this?" the crowd cried.

"Just hold on a minute!" Fr. Kieran put up his hands. "The bishops in America decided the ruling only applies to Canada, so we're safe for now, but it's a word of warning that the same edict could come our way soon enough."

Ella could almost feel the collective sinking of their hearts. It was one thing to be betrayed by their government, but when men of God turned their back on the people, it felt as scandalous as a blaspheme against the Sacred Heart of Jesus.

"Why would they do this to us?" Mr. Albert McGuiness, a master workman and the head of this assembly demanded. "Abandon us to the wolves?"

"They don't like all the secrecy, the rituals," Father explained.

It was true that the KOL had its share of rituals. Even meeting notices were shrouded in secrecy and issued in cryptic codes chalked onto the sides of buildings and pavements, such as the one announcing tonight's meeting. The code read "8=211/5," which meant a meeting of the 5th Assembly of Kensington would take place at eight o'clock on the evening of February 11. The usual meeting place was the basement of St. Michael's church. To enter the meeting, one had to pass through two "veils," or checkpoints, where they had to utter the password, "Discourage discord," before and after passing through.

"The rituals are harmless!" another man shouted. "It's just an excuse! They're out of touch with the people who fill their own pews."

"The Church only cares for those who put the most coins in her baskets!" a woman cried, and they could all hear the frustration in her voice.

"Which is a fool's folly," Ella spoke up, and everyone strained to hear her soft voice. "The Church's rosters have been exploding in recent years, and not because of the *nouveau riche*. It's the immigrants who are swelling her ranks. The working man and woman. If she wants to keep her pews full, she should pay more attention to their plight because their coins are what's building her churches."

"Here! Here!" the crowd cried.

"And how do you propose we move our bishops who are like stone pillars set in cement blocks when it comes to change?" Fr. Kieran demanded.

"We've a new bishop! Patrick Ryan! An Irishman!" a man called from the other side of the room. "Maybe he'll listen to us."

"It's possible," Fr. Kieran shrugged. "He's a good man."

"He'd listen if enough of us spoke up," Ella said, and they all looked at her. "The bishops listen first to whoever puts the most coins in their baskets, and they know it's the working man who supports them. They'll listen if enough of us demand action or else we'll not contribute a dime to the collection plate."

"Now, now, Ella!" Fr. Kieran warned, clearly thinking about his own collection plate. "That money is used to help the poor by funding our hospitals and food banks and clothing drives. Would you see them suffer?"

"Father, the time has come to stop buying bandages for our wounds," Ella said with a passion as fierce as it was dainty. "We need to stop the blade that cuts us, or we'll never be done bleeding!"

"Here! Here!" the crowd shouted.

They might be a frustrated and motley bunch, but they had a common fire in their hearts. Everyone in the room, male or female, young or old, Black or white, Protestant or Catholic, shared an unflinching desire to put an end to the injustices inflicted upon the poor by the prevailing *laissez-faire* economics.

"If we all joined together and wrote letters to the bishops telling them of our desire to see them act on our behalf, they may be more inclined to lend us an ear!" Ella said.

"Don't give them a bloody dime!" one man called, and several cheered him, but Ella put up her hand.

"Father's right. We can't cut off funds from the very ministries that are keeping so many of us alive. Let's start by just threatening to cut our donations. This gives us some bargaining power for the future," Ella said smartly. "If we could rally the congregations in our parishes here at St. Michaels, St. Boniface, and Our Lady of the Visitation—"

"We could ask our relatives in city parishes to do the same," one woman offered.

"And the Protestant churches can petition their own bishops!" another joined.

"Yes!" Ella said with rising excitement. "We could gather hundreds of these letters and perhaps organize a march to hand-deliver the letters to the bishops. An impressive show of our numbers might just spur them to act on our behalf."

"Here! Here!" several shouted.

"Think of what the Church, with all its power and influence, could do for us if she took our side?" Ella continued. "She could influence our lawmakers to pass legislation that protects workers from this abuse. Perhaps we could have a law similar to the Factory and Workshop Act passed just a few years ago in England that stipulated adequate ventilation must be provided workers to protect them from harmful gasses and vapors and dust, the same poisons that killed my mother and so many others from brown lung! My dearest brothers and sisters, we may be poor, but we're not powerless! Especially not when we join our hands together for a common cause."

"I'll write my letter tonight!" one man offered and set off a chorus of similar promises.

"What say you, Father? Have we your blessing?" Mr. McGuiness asked.

"And if I say no?"

"You won't!" he said with a boisterous laugh. "Or your plate will be the first to suffer!"

"A-ha! Blackmail, is it?" Fr. Kieran asked, but he was grinning all the while.

By the end of the meeting, they had decided upon a deadline of one month to collect the letters at the various parishes. By then, the weather would be starting to break for spring, and they would plan a march to the bishop's residence for anyone who wanted to attend.

* * * * *

Jacqui set her mug on the coffee table and sat back in her chair. "No one, not even Ella, had any idea what an impact this letter-writing campaign and the accompanying march would have on the Church. She would soon find out, but not before Mr. Champs would face his day of reckoning over Ella's boots."

"Oh, no! What happened?"

"It seems that our dear Auntie Bess took it upon herself to add a little something to the cover note that was required in those days when a single lady wanted to write to a single man. Everything was chaperoned in those days, even letters. We can only assume that Ella didn't read the note before it was posted, and Mr. Marsden was none too happy about what he read when he received that piece of correspondence and Ella's twenty-five cent installment on the boots."

TWENTY

"YOU MUST LEAVE ME to finish the jackets on my own. I can't have all of you working late every night just for my sake," Ella told her concerned co-workers who were beginning to worry about how many hours she was working these days.

"But Ella, you'll be here all night—again! You're exhausted! What's gotten into him? Why is he picking on you like this?" Cora demanded.

Ella didn't dare explain what had Mr. Champs so upset. It would only spark gossip. Night after night, Ella worked until nearly nine o'clock, got home just long enough to eat, wash up, and go to bed. Within a week, she was so tired she could barely keep her eyes open during the day. For the first time in two years, she failed to make her quota and began to seriously worry about losing a job that had once seemed so secure.

Oh, Lord! You were treated unfairly too, and it led to Your death. Be with me now as I bow under this heavy cross. Help me to carry it. I have no one but You! Lend me Your strength!

It was Friday afternoon, and she was only three jackets short of her quota.

"I may get home by eight o'clock tonight!" she whispered to Cora.

"I'm staying to help you! We all are! You're exhausted, Ella! You can't keep up this pace."

"I can't lose my job. We'll not make it without my pay."

Cora bent her head and whispered, "You know what this is all about. What did you do to make Mr. Champs so angry?"

"Nothing! It was just a misunderstanding."

"About what?"

"I can't talk about it!"

"Meg knows, doesn't she? You confide in her but not in me."

"Oh Cora, let's not talk about this right now. I need to go home and get some sleep."

"Alright," Cora huffed.

A loud bang sounded downstairs, and they all looked up.

"What was that?"

"The boiler again?"

Heavy boots sounded against the stairs. All the machines stopped whirring as the women's eyes pinned on the door. It burst open with a bang that made them all jump a foot.

Reese Marsden strode into the room, clad in his black frock coat, gray pin-striped trousers, and highly polished black boots. They could tell by the stiffness in his jaw and the way he was clenching his bowler hat in a tight fist that he was angry. Perhaps even furious.

His dark eyes were piercing as they scanned the room, pausing for just an instant when they landed upon Ella, then continued to look around.

"CHAMPS!" he boomed, and they all jumped again.

"Right here, sir!" Mr. Champs called from the cutting room next door. He scrambled into view, one arm in his jacket while the other hastily buttoned his badly stained gray waistcoat. "To what do we owe this—"

"Get in the office, please," Mr. Marsden abruptly cut him off.

"Yes, sir," Mr. Champs blustered, looking suddenly terrified.

Mr. Marsden followed him into the room and slammed the door

shut behind him.

"Good Lord!" Cora gasped. "What in heaven's name is going on?"

"I have no idea!" Ella said, but she was now the most awake she'd felt all day.

"He looks mighty mad," Jane said.

"And handsome as the devil," Mary remarked, and they all giggled.

The muffled sounds of men's voices went on for about five minutes before the door opened and Mr. Marsden motioned for Ella.

"Miss Ward?"

All the blood rushed to her feet. "Sir?"

"Will you come in here please?" His voice was suddenly very gentle.

"Me?" she peeped.

"You're not in any trouble. Just come in here, please."

It's about the boots. What else could it be?

She came into the room to find Mr. Champs standing alongside the desk, his face drained of all color.

Mr. Marsden gently shut the door behind her, walked to the desk, and perched himself on the edge. "You'll forgive me for what I'm about to say because it's distasteful and a lady should not be subjected to it. But my hand has been forced, thanks to the good work of your aunt."

"My aunt?"

"Yes, she told me about the accusations that were made about the two of us, that you offered me. . .favors for the boots I provided. Is this true?"

She blushed crimson. "Oh. . .well, I. . ."

Only the hardest of hearts could not be wrenched by the sight of how hard she was struggling, standing there with her hands clenched in front of her, dark circles under her eyes and lines of exhaustion stiffening the otherwise delicate contours of her heart-shaped face.

"Miss Ward? I'm so sorry for your discomfort, but this must be settled."

She swallowed hard. "Well, he, uh, said something of that nature."

Mr. Champs scoffed from the corner, but it sounded more like the anguished moan of a wounded animal.

"And since then, he has been," Mr. Marsden stopped, fished something out of his pocket that looked very much like the yellowed stationary found in the desk at the Sadler-Ward residence, "'. . .Upping her quota with the intent of working my niece to the bone every day as punishment.'"

Auntie Bess! What have you done?

He folded up the paper and shoved it back in his breast pocket. "Is this true?"

"Yes, my quota was raised, sir."

"To what?"

"Two more jackets a day."

"And how many do you have left for today?"

"Three, sir."

"And it's nearly one thirty in the afternoon. When do you expect to finish them?"

"About eight o'clock, if my machine doesn't jam."

"And what time did you come into work this morning?"

"Five o'clock, sir."

"I see." He stood up, towering above her as he came to stand directly in front of Mr. Champs. Leaning down from his great height and speaking directly into the face of the terrified overseer, he said very slowly and carefully, "What I choose to do with my money is my business, Mr. Champs. The fact that you not only besmirched this woman's reputation, but mine as well, is reprehensible to me, and I will not stand for it. Nor will I abide by this *bullying* of a defenseless woman who has done absolutely *nothing* wrong. I did not give her the boots to make her life any more miserable than it already is, Mr. Champs."

"No sir. Of course not, sir. Allow me to apologize, sir."

"It's too late for that."

Mr. Champs' eyes suddenly filled with dread.

"You're fired."

Ella gasped into her hand.

The overseer looked momentarily stunned.

"Get out."

"Sir!"

"NOW!"

Champs flew out of the room, Mr. Marsden catching the door before it slammed shut behind him.

Ella didn't know what to say, just stood there staring at the floor in shocked silence until she finally found her tongue. "Mr. Marsden. . .please, this isn't necessary."

"Of course, it's necessary, Miss Ward," he said, picking the bowler hat off the desk and preparing to leave. "I am not my father, and I do business in a different way."

"But he's about to have his fourth child and—"

"My dear woman, are you defending this man after what he did to you?"

"If we could just discuss it. . ."

"Fine. But I'm expected on the other side of town in less than an hour so it will have to be another time."

"Yes, sir."

"Tomorrow, my coach will pick you up at one o'clock."

"What? But I. . .I have to work."

"You have the day off. . .with pay," he added, popping the bowler hat on his head and opening the door to let her precede him into the shop. "Until then."

A moment later, he was gone.

TWENTY-ONE

"GOOD GOD ALMIGHTY! His coach is here and it's a Quinby coach with the Marsden crest on it!" Auntie Bess cried the following afternoon as a luxurious carriage pulled up out front. She fumbled in the pocket of her black cloak for a bottle of smelling salts and took a deep whiff. "The whole neighborhood is watching. ELLA! Quit dawdling! The coach is here!"

"I'm right here!" Ella said.

Auntie Bess jumped with a start and put a hand to her heart. "Don't be creeping up on me like that! My poor heart."

"You mean, your poor *meddling* heart," Ella said and preceded her aunt out the door.

A smartly uniformed driver hopped to the ground, dutifully held the door open, and assisted them inside. He offered a plush blanket for warmth and waited until they were settled in their seats.

"Is everything to your liking, misses?"

"It is," Ella said. Auntie Bess nodded fitfully and looked afraid to move for fear of sullying the expensive red velvet seats.

They were both dressed in their finest. Auntie Bess wore a black wool bodice and matching skirt along with the best boots she owned, which they had hastily polished last night. She wore two petticoats, which only made her frame appear stockier, and a black bonnet covered her normally unkempt hair, which was neatly braided today and pinned to the back of her head.

Ella wore the only winter dress she owned, which was a woolen bodice and skirt in a pale blue color with black piping around the collar and decorating the hem. It was a straight skirt with a slight bustle on the back and a short train that needed some last-minute repairs last night. A blue bonnet, fashionably tilted to the right, was perched on top of the thickly woven braids that were wrapped around her head.

The minute the coach lurched into motion, Auntie Bess put the salts to her nostrils and inhaled again. "Who would have thought he'd react like this? Most of the robber barons could care less about us."

"Then why did you write him?"

"Because it was the right thing to do! It was the boots that started it all!"

"And had you left well enough alone and just sent a short cover note with my first installment as we agreed, we wouldn't be carted off to the Marsden home today, would we?"

Auntie Bess looked at her, flustered and suddenly contrite. "I meant no ill by it! I was defending my niece, my only family, the girl I promised my dear sister I would guard with my life."

Ella sighed, rolled her eyes, and looked out the window. She had heard this lament thousands of times already.

"Champs was killing you, Ella!"

"He would have let up eventually."

"And what harm might he have done to your health in the meantime?"

"I'm fine."

"You slept ten hours last night, and I don't think you moved a muscle all night. Hardly needed to make the bed this morn."

"Yes, I was very tired."

They fell quiet as Auntie Bess looked out the window and watched the familiar buildings of Kensington give way to the larger establishments that lined the main road into the city.

"I still think it's romantic."

"Auntie Bess! You must put this out of your head! Mr. Marsden has no romantic interest in me! He's a Marsden, and I'm a mill girl."

"Stranger things have happened. . ."

"Yes! In the circus! Now stop with this nonsense. I need to pray!" Ella took out her Rosary, blessed herself, and began to pray fiercely enough to ward off the questions whirling through her own mind about Mr. Marsden's intentions.

The Marsden-Lowell House was a tall and imposing brick colonial structure on the waterfront. Tucked into a wooded lot at the end of a long winding drive, it was a serene and quiet location despite being only blocks from the city. Several carriages were parked along the winding drive, and their driver maneuvered the Quinby into a spot adjacent to the front door. He alighted and helped them to the ground just as the front door opened and a pleasant, elderly man in a handsome black cutaway jacket stood on the threshold. With a polite smile, he bowed and waved for them to come inside.

"Misses Ward and Sadler, I assume?" The women nodded briskly. "Very good. Master Marsden is expecting you. Right this way."

He led them down a hallway flanked in paneling that matched the highly polished oak floors, a red oriental runner padding their footsteps as they followed along. The faint scent of well-oiled leather hung in the air, but Ella hardly noticed. Her attention was drawn to the light fixtures on the walls, all of which sported one of the new lightbulbs from Mr. Edison. The mere sight of them filled her with wonder.

"Have a seat in here and he'll be with you shortly," the butler said, showing them into an anteroom decorated with a divan and two wingbacks upholstered in brightly striped blue and white silk. Side tables sat atop a spotless white rug, while a dazzling glass lamp sent shards of brilliantly colored lights throughout the room.

The sound of men's voices could be heard through a set of double doors. If Ella listened carefully enough, she could discern the telltale baritone of Mr. Marsden.

Auntie Bess took out her salts just then and snorted loudly.

"Put that away!" Ella whispered. "Let's not be acting doltish."

Her aunt huffed indignantly but she could hardly care about her feelings at a time like this. Ella had never felt so tense in her life and thought her very skin would crack it felt so stiff. There was no other option but to turn to her only source of comfort and strength.

Lord, help me. This is such a strange world and I do not know my way. Help me to remember why I'm here so that I can fight for Your beloved sons and daughters, and help me to remember that I am a daughter of God and therefore have no reason to feel ashamed of who I am.

The doors parted so suddenly they both jumped. Two smartly dressed men walked out, bowed politely to the two of them, and continued on their way.

Reese Marsden was sitting behind a massive mahogany desk in an office lined with shelves full of leather-bound books and trinkets of glass and shining metal. Overlooking the desk was a huge picture window that provided a panoramic view of the river where chunks of ice floated lazily in and out of view. He finished what he was doing, slid the papers aside, and stood up. Obviously unaware that the door was open, he leaned heavily on the desk for a moment, a lock of dark hair falling across his brow as he closed his eyes and seemed to collect himself.

For some reason, Ella's heart was touched by the sight of him, by how worn and burdened he looked, not at all like the commanding young heir of the Marsden fortune.

He sighed then and pulled a watch out of his vest pocket. He glanced at it, then stood upright and looked out into the anteroom.

"You're here!" he said brightly while hastily throwing on his jacket. "I did not hear my man announce you."

He strode out of the room, his eyes pinned upon Ella as he approached "What a pleasure to see you again, Miss Ward. I trust you're no worse the wear for the trials of this past week?"

"I'm fine," she said and smiled demurely at the tops of his expensive leather shoes.

"She slept ten hours last night!" Auntie Bess blurted, and Ella wanted to sink through the floor.

"Pray tell, this must be your good Aunt Elisabeth?"

"It is," she said. "I call her Auntie Bess."

"And may I do the same?" he asked, smiling at her aunt who nodded so briskly Ella feared her braids would pop loose. "Why don't we go into my office where we can talk? Come. Follow me."

They seated themselves on the other side of his enormous desk, both nervously perched on the edge of their chairs, and watched him fold his hands on the desk.

"Now then, let us pick up where we left off yesterday, Miss Ward. You were beginning to plead for Mr. Champs, whom I understand is expecting his fourth child."

She took a deep breath and had a feeling he noticed because he never seemed to take his eyes off her for long. "Yes, he is. And for this reason, I'd like to ask you to please not fire him. Perhaps discipline him in some way, but don't fire him."

"But I already have. His behavior was despicable. I won't have it."

"Even worse goes on elsewhere. Far worse."

"In our mills?"

"No, sir."

"Are you sure?"

"I am," she said and looked up just long enough to meet his eye and let him see that she was not hiding anything. "When you are as poor as we are, Mr. Marsden, to lose a job too often means death to the little ones. They cannot thrive on such meager rations and suffer all kinds of maladies—scurvy and rickets, cholera, and the fevers. Please, sir! It's his babes that I plead for."

"I see," he said. "Does he bully his wife and children the way he bullies his workers, I wonder?"

"I cannot judge him."

He was quiet for a moment, and she could feel his attention on her, not knowing how much he was wanting to look into those spectacular eyes of hers that were like looking through the gates of heaven. "No, of course not. You're obviously a very pious young lady. Catholic, you say?"

"Yes, sir."

She heard him open his desk drawer, then stand up just long enough to slide something across his enormous desk.

It was twenty-five cents.

"I'm returning your installment."

"But—"

He put up his hand for silence, then asked pleasantly. "Do they fit?"

"Yes. . .yes, they do, but you should know that it's not proper for a lady to accept a gift from a gentleman. My honor is one of the few things I own."

"I wouldn't think to offend your honor, Miss Ward," he said so genuinely it was almost flattering. "Consider these boots to be back pay. Is that suitable to you?"

"It is!" Auntie Bess exclaimed, and Ella gave her a sidelong glance that made Mr. Marsden grin.

"Your guardian has spoken."

". . .A bit too much lately, I would say."

"Now, now, that's her duty! Had she not written to me, that useless, puff-gutted, shag bag of a. . .er, pardon me."

Auntie Bess burst out laughing.

Ella put a hand to her lips and grinned at her lap.

He cleared his throat, adjusted his collar, and finished more politely, "Mr. Champs would have driven you to the point of exhaustion and perhaps an early grave, which would have been a true loss to the world."

She smiled at her lap. "I think the world would not miss another mill girl."

"But you're not just a mill girl, are you?"

She looked up, confused by the question. "Sir?"

"You've been running the mill for Mr. Champs for two years now. Is that right?"

"Well, I. . ."

"And he allows it as long as it benefits him but scorns you for your involvement with the labor unions. Is that right?"

It was, and Ella wondered how he knew this. Who did he speak with at the mill? For a moment, she sincerely feared for her job, especially if his informant knew about her union membership. But she was not about to cower. Not while sitting before the son of Caleb Marsden, one of the worst offenders of worker's rights.

"It is sir. I believe wholeheartedly in the equitable treatment of workers. As exciting as the progress this country is making in the arts and sciences, she lags far behind in the area of basic human rights. There is no reason why we must starve while the robber barons build more houses than they'll ever need."

"Is that what you think I am? A robber baron?" Mr. Marsden raised a brow.

Auntie Bess kicked her in warning, but Ella ignored her.

"You'll forgive me, but I do, sir."

A tense silence fell over the room and Ella was almost certain that he was about to fire her. She could only hope it would not be as brutally as he fired Champs.

"You're forgiven," he finally said, and her insides sank in relief. "But only because you don't know any better."

"Sir?" She looked up in surprise and caught a twinkle of humor in his eyes just then.

"I'm the *son* of a robber baron," he pointed out. "There's a difference. In my case, a big difference. For example, one could say that I'm as different from my father as you are from Mr. Champs."

She laughed in spite of herself.

"In fact, my father and I don't see eye to eye on anything. And we never have, I might add. I'm the heir by birth, not choice. He's the epitome of a robber baron, and I strive to be the opposite. I sympathize with the plight of the worker and one of my dreams has been to enact sweeping changes in the way our mills are run. Of course, until my father passes into eternity, I can't do much except experiment here and there, which I have done in other places with great success, if you will permit me to brag."

He stopped just long enough to acknowledge her surprise. "But before I can make a decision about Mr. Champs' replacement, I need to know if you are as hostile to the owners of the American industrial complex as some of the members of the labor unions."

"There's not a hostile bone in this child's body," Auntie Bess said before Ella could answer.

"I didn't think so," Mr. Marsden said smoothly, "but I had to ask because the one thing I cannot condone are the violent strikes of these unions. They don't just hurt individual owners, they hurt entire industries, which in turn deprives millions of innocent, hard-working Americans of the goods and services they've come to expect from us. I believe there's a better way."

"As do I, sir," Ella said forthrightly.

"Oh? Then why did everything you said to me last week sound like it could have come out of the mouth of Terence V. Powderly himself?"

She should have guessed he would be entirely aware of Powderly, the grand master of the Knights of Labor. A staunch Catholic, the ranks of the KOL had swelled to more than half a million under his leadership. Although people of all creeds and races were welcomed in the union, the Catholics were particularly proud to serve under Terence Powderly.

"Whether you agree with him or not, you can't deny that he's a brilliant man," Ella offered.

"Yes, he is, but we all know the Knights of Labor can get violent sometimes."

"Violence is never espoused or tolerated," Ella said quickly. "Those who perpetrate it do so on their own, not under the auspices of the KOL."

"How do you know that?" he asked.

"Because she's very well read," Auntie Bess said quickly to spare Ella the misfortune of having to reveal her membership in the union. In some places, this was grounds for automatic termination.

"That much I figured out on my own," Mr. Marsden smiled

knowingly.

"She reads everything she can get her hands on and even digs discarded journals out of the trash behind the Kensington Hotel!"

"Auntie Bess!" Ella looked at her, mortified. It was even more humiliating when she glanced at Mr. Marsden and found him grinning in amusement at the two of them.

"Pray tell, what journals do you favor so much that you must dig in the trash for them?"

She paused, then decided she might as well be honest at this point. "*Journal of Science, The Lancet, Revolution, The Intellectual Observer, American Geologist, The Journal of Psychology, The Ladies Home Journal,* and. . ." She stopped for a moment, then added, "Twice I found a copy of the *Journal of the Royal Astronomical Society,* which I found particularly fascinating!"

For a moment, Mr. Marsden was so surprised he looked at her as if she was a creature from another world. She was supposed to be a mill girl, a woman of no consequence, of rugged bearing, dull mind, and poor breeding. But instead, she was well-spoken with an intellect capable of appreciating the most advanced science of the day.

"Fascinating indeed," he said with no hint of wonder in his voice. "I suppose you've heard of Andrew Ainslie Common?" he asked, deliberately testing her.

"Oh, yes!" she said brightly, and her eyes danced with wonder as she recalled, "I just read about him a few weeks ago. He recorded exposures of the Orion nebula that showed stars too faint to be seen by the human eye!"

He was utterly enthralled. "Yes, and he used a photographic dry plate process and a thirty-six-inch reflecting telescope in his backyard to do it."

"Can you imagine?" she asked, forgetting all about her discomfort while focusing on such a captivating subject.

"I don't need to imagine it, my lady," he said. "I have a scope of the same power. Do you want to see it?"

"Here? On the premises?" she asked, unable to contain her excitement.

"Yes! In my observatory. Come along."

Auntie Bess had no idea what they were talking about but waddled after them as he led the way out of the office through various lovely sitting rooms and parlors and dining areas until he reached a spacious sunporch in the back of the house. Next to the window at the far end of the room was a large telescope on a tripod, its lens tilted up toward the heavens. Beside it was a table strewn with astronomical maps, books, and journals.

Ella's eyes widened in wonder. "Oh, my!"

"Would you like to look through the scope?"

"Yes! I would!"

He showed her how to use the eye piece, how to focus the lens, adjust the tilt of the scope. "You can't see anything now, but I can see far into outer space from here at nightfall."

"And the planets?"

"Whichever ones are visible this time of year."

"But that would be nearly all of them! Isn't that right?"

"It is," he said and looked at her with unmasked admiration. "Mercury, Jupiter, Mars. . ."

"Venus, Saturn, Neptune, and Uranus!" she finished and was suddenly very proud of herself.

For a moment, she didn't feel like a mill girl anymore, especially when he was looking at her the way he was, like a friend would look who was sincerely enjoying the companionship of another.

"I have a book for you to read," he said suddenly and picked a volume off the top of a stack of books on the table. It was entitled, *The Textbook of Astrology* by Alfred J. Pearce. "You can borrow it for as long as you'd like," he said and handed it to her.

Of all the wonders Reese was privileged to witness in his life, never did the man see such delight on a human face as he saw on El-la's in that moment. Her pale blue eyes sparkled, her cheeks flushed, and her soft pink lips curled up into the most winsome smile. What man could resist such a beguiling woman?

"I have no words, sir. . ." she breathed. "I will cherish every page of it."

"I'm sure you will," he said, and a quietness came over them as they looked at each other in what seemed like a new light.

As friends.

Just then, she remembered a warning from Megsie when she re-vealed the truth about the boots, about how wealthy men like Mr. Marsden often groom low-born women with gifts, "*For, er,* softer play, *if you will.*"

Her guard went up. She looked away quickly. "I won't keep it overlong."

"Keep it as long as you'd like," he said and led them back into his office.

She decided it was best to change the subject. "About Mr. Champs. . ."

"Yes, well, my plan is to have you replace him on a temporary basis," he said, taking a seat behind his desk.

"Me?" She was shocked.

"Why are you so surprised? You've been running the place for the last two years, at least that's what the workers tell me. They all hold you in the highest esteem, you know."

She could only stare at him, speechless.

"Come now, Miss Ward. You're too humble."

"But I. . .I. . ."

"It would only be temporary. I may move an overseer from one of our New York mills to Kensington, but this could take a while. In the meantime, I need someone to keep the place running. Who better than the person who's been running it and letting Mr. Champs take all the credit?"

"Mr. Marsden, I so appreciate your confidence in me, but won't you please reconsider Mr. Champs?" she pleaded with him, wringing her hands.

"I'm afraid not, Miss Ward. He will not be the overseer in any of my mills. First, because of his unscrupulous character. If anything, I'll allow you to persuade me to give that cussed, bootlicking, purse-leech of a man a job working the furnace."

Auntie Bess giggled into her hand.

Ella tried not to grin.

"Second, because he and I don't see eye to eye. To be quite honest with you, I was rather impressed with your suggestions and believe they are quite similar to my own thoughts about how to manage the labor force in a more equitable way. There is great wisdom in incentivizing employees. It's a far more progressive tactic than brutalizing them day in and day out. Hasn't mankind progressed beyond slave-driving to get their work done? I should hope so. And now that control of the Marsden Mills has fallen almost completely on me due to Father's failing health, I intend to begin implementation of some of these incentives at select mills. Call it an experiment if you will."

"An experiment?"

"Yes, I have expansion plans for Kensington, and the workforce there is quite stable. It may be the perfect place to enact some of these incentive plans. And you, being so well-liked, and with a mind similar to my own on these matters, may be able to partner with me to convince them to try it."

Ella frowned, uncomfortable with aligning herself with a robber baron's son, even if his ideas were attractive to her. "That depends on what the incentives are and if they will benefit more than just the owners of the mill," she challenged as boldly as she dared and was surprised at how forthcoming he was.

"Pay bonuses for increased output, weekly instead of daily quotas with the allowance of reducing work hours when quotas are met. Once done for the week, the workers could either take the hours off or work for bonus pay. If this works, I would consider adding ten more machines and four more cutters with the hope of doubling the output in ready-made clothing in one year. These are just some of my ideas. How do they sound to you? Would this offer the workers some relief?"

"They would indeed," she said. Impressed with the proposition, she sat back and thought about it for a moment before asking, "What about the safety issues?"

"If you take the job, I'll remedy the ventilation just for you."

She only half-smiled at his gallantry. "And compensation for injuries?"

"You drive a hard bargain, Miss Ward," he said and looked at her with obvious admiration. "Let's take it a few steps at a time, shall we?"

Auntie Bess cleared her throat. "Excuse me, but what kind of pay is she going to get for this work?"

"Her pay will double to ten dollars per week."

"Men make considerably more," Ella blurted, and Auntie Bess looked ready to reach for her smelling salts. "Mr. Champs made

$14.50 a week. I know because I helped him with the books."

"Yes, but he was experienced in overseeing."

"And he was a man."

"That too," Mr. Marsden conceded. "But we have a woman overseer in our Boston mill and your salary is commensurate with hers."

"Yes, but that doesn't mean it's equitable. Perhaps she's not being paid enough either," she said in that sing-song voice of hers.

"Touché!" he applauded and could only shake his head in wonder at her. "Twelve dollars a week," he said. "That's my final offer."

She sat back for a moment of quiet consideration. "When do you need an answer?"

"Well, we don't have an overseer at the moment. . ."

She sighed. "Alright, I'll try it, but on one condition."

"What is the condition?"

"That Mr. Champs be given a job at the mill. We can't leave him destitute, Mr. Marsden."

For a moment, he could only look at her in amazement. "I wonder if anyone fights for you the way you fight for them."

"I do," Auntie Bess said without a moment's hesitation. "I fight for her because she means the world to me."

Ella was so touched by her aunt's rare admission that it brought tears to her eyes.

"I can see why," Mr. Marsden was saying. "Your niece is an extraordinary woman."

"That she is, sir."

"About Mr. Champs," Ella reminded them both.

"Yes, well, you can hire him back as a furnace keeper," Mr. Marsden said and Auntie Bess choked on a laugh, then tried to make it look like she was coughing. Mr. Marsden wasn't fooled and grinned broadly, proud of himself for amusing her. "But on one condition.

He must apologize to you for his offensive behavior, and then thank you for interceding for him."

"Oh, dear!" Ella hid a grin behind her hand. "He'll not take kindly to that."

Mr. Marsden laughed devilishly. "I should like to be there to see that useless scalawag groveling for your forgiveness. Do be gentle with him, my lady."

Ella giggled at her lap.

"Now then, have we a deal?"

She sighed. "We do, sir."

He stood up, walked around the desk in two strides and offered his hand. She shook it and did her best to appear businesslike, even though she felt almost dazed by all that had just transpired.

"I'll be in touch about how and when I'd like to implement these incentives. Until then, please be discreet about our private discussions."

"Of course," she agreed, standing up.

Mr. Marsden called out the door. "Roger! Escort my guests to the carriage. I'll be in touch, Miss Ward. I pray you'll be well."

A half hour later, the two women were bouncing along the road back to Kensington. Auntie Bess put away her smelling salts and spent the whole ride home gushing about Ella's new pay, the luxurious Marsden house, and how much she appreciated Mr. Marsden's colorful vocabulary.

"He might be the son of a robber baron, but I like him, Ella."

"So, you think I can trust him then?"

"About your business affairs? Time will tell. But there's one thing for sure about Mr. Reese."

"What is that, Auntie?"

"He's smitten with you."

"What?" Ella looked at her aunt, shocked.

"Anyone can see it."

"You're wrong. I'm just another charity of his. Nothing more."

"You're just naïve about men," Auntie Bess tsked.

"I'm not!"

"You are! You turn down everyone who comes to call on you."

"Because I don't like any of them and there's no point in leading them on."

"What if Mr. Marsden asked to come 'round?"

"He won't."

"But if he did, what would you say?"

"Well, I—I. . ." Ella stammered and was genuinely shocked at how difficult it was to answer this question. The mere idea of a man like him being interested in her in that way made her feel strangely rattled somewhere deep inside. "I don't know, but why discuss it? It will never happen," she quickly dismissed.

"We'll see, won't we?"

TWENTY-TWO

"ELLA COULD NOT HAVE BEEN more wrong," Jacqui said, and Ari cheered out loud.

They had long since finished their hot chocolate and were snuggled into the sofa, each wrapped in her own fleecy throw. Perhaps seeing Jesse tonight, the way he teased her, flirted with her, looked at her with those big eyes so full of feeling and spoke in that deep, gusty voice of his, saying, *"That's the past. . .my mind is totally fixed on the present right now. . ."* put Ari in a mood for romance that she hadn't felt in a long, long time.

"You see, Reese Marsden was a very lonely soul," Jacqui explained. "He was born an heir to more than just an estate. It was to a lifestyle and one that he despised. His mother, Mary Leigh Lowell-Marsden, was a lovely woman, very pious. A Lutheran, I believe. She and Reese and his sister, Esther, were kindred spirits. They were more intellectual, thoughtful, and philosophical about life. In those days, they were known as 'progressive,' not because their politics were liberal, but because they were considered to be reformist in their thinking.

"On the other hand, his brother, Randolph, took after his father in his ambition and ruthlessness. He wanted the inheritance, and Reese would have given it to him if not for the pleas of his mother who believed the only hope to make the Marsden legacy into something more than just a family of money-grubbers would lie in the hands of her first-born.

"As opposed as Reese was to the robber barons' way of life, however, he was a brilliant financier. Some of the world's wealthiest people sought him out for advice on investments. They said he almost had a sixth sense about what to buy and what to avoid. This made him very popular in his father's circles, much to Reese's dismay, because other than his financial prowess, he had little else in common with the upper class. He was far more interested in the sciences, particularly astronomy. Of course, his father would hear none of it and was determined to see him marry a wealthy socialite and thus add more millions to the family coffers. Reese was surrounded by people whom he considered to be empty, driven by greed for wealth and status rather than for the advancement of mankind.

"And then he met Ella. There was something about her, how unique she was, her inquisitive mind, how closely her ideas were aligned with his own, how devoted she was to creating a better world rather than a larger bank account, and, yes, how beautiful she was, that instantly captivated him."

"He doesn't sound too bad either," Ari said with a sigh. "These days we'd call a guy like him 'hot'. And he's got all that money besides! She'd be a fool to turn him away. But what about Mr. Champs? Did she make him apologize?"

"Yes, she did. But by now, you should know Ella enough to understand that she had the heart of an angel. Mr. Champs was lucky to get off as easy as he did the day he was summoned to the mill to meet with Ella in the office that now belonged to her."

* * * * *

Mr. Champs looked particularly slovenly that morning, as if he'd been drinking all weekend to soothe his wounded ego and dull the fear of being without a job. When he came into the office, he had to be reminded to remove his hat, which he did begrudgingly.

"Now then, I've been instructed to read you this letter from Mr. Marsden," Ella told him as soon as he arrived. She gently shut the door so as not to humiliate him any more than necessary and carefully read the note written in Mr. Marsden's firm, clean script.

"*Mr. Porter Champs is to beg forgiveness of Miss Ward for having besmirched her reputation and then subjecting her to a hostile work environment as punishment for accepting back pay deemed warranted by the owners of the mill. In addition, he is to thank her for going to the trouble of traveling to the Marsden-Lloyd House to personally intervene in the matter of his re-employment. It is only upon these conditions that he is to resume work at Marsden Mills, Kensington, as a furnace assistant, with the pay of seventeen dollars per month. B. Reese Marsden, Esq.*"

Ella noticed that his pay was exactly $4.30 a week, seventy cents less than her former pay, and wondered if Mr. Marsden did this on purpose.

Mr. Champs stood scowling at the floor while the letter was read and did little more than shift in his boots when his pitiful salary was read aloud.

"Now then, Mr. Champs. Do you accept these conditions?" Ella asked kindly.

"But this whole matter—"

Ella motioned for silence. "Please do as Mr. Marsden has asked, Mr. Champs. Your livelihood is on the line."

"And now I must answer to a woman? All the men are grumbling. . ."

"They grumbled when you were in charge too, Mr. Champs."

He looked surprised, which made her want to laugh, but she pitied him too much to let him see her amusement. "Now then, will you accept these conditions?"

"I suppose so. What choice have I?"'

"You can get another job."

"No one's hiring right now."

"Then take this job and if you keep yourself out of trouble, perhaps you can work your way into a better paying job."

"It took me ten years to get where I got."

"And less than five minutes to tumble back to where you started."

"Over a pair of lousy boots!"

"Which were none of your business."

"He only gave you the job so he can get information out of you about the labor unions," Mr. Champs snarled.

"I'm sure he has his reasons for what he's done, Mr. Champs. Far be it for us to discern them. Now then, what say you about the position he's offering you?"

"Alright, alright. What do I have to do?"

"Make the required statement."

He cast an ugly look at floor, shifted slightly in his boots, then grumbled, "I'm sorry for having besmirched your reputation, Miss Ella, and for punishing you for your involvement with the boots. . .and I am grateful for your pleading on my behalf for a job at this mill."

"That's good enough. Now go downstairs and tell Bart you've been hired back to assist him at the furnace."

Ella's promotion was the talk of the mill the first few days, especially amongst the men who were not used to working for a woman and claimed it was unnatural for men to have to answer to women. It brought to mind one of the tenets of the suffragette movement that detailed why women should have the right to vote. "Because the objections raised against their having the franchise are based on sentiment, not on reason." There was absolutely no reason why the woman who had been running the mill while hidden behind the britches of a man should be prevented from running it now that she no longer had cause to hide.

Thankfully, their respect for Ella and the fact that the position was only temporary eventually won the day and convinced them to swallow their manly pride and go along with things.

As busy as she was with the books, the securing of fabric, and the allocation of materials amongst the workers, her desire to ease the plight of the workers found her discovering a myriad of ways to make their lives easier. She added a few benches to the lunchroom so they would not have to sit on the dirty floors anymore. The doors to the building were opened every few hours to allow for better ventilation. She convinced a few men to fashion a crude banister out of rope to make ascent on the steep and rickety stairs a bit safer. Between these innovations, every spare moment was spent behind her old sewing machine where she would sit and sew jackets that could be added to the output of the mill.

A week after she started in her new position, Mr. Marsden returned to the mill to announce the new incentives.

"I am proposing that the quota system be changed from daily to weekly," he told the workers who gathered in the cutting room. "You will each have a set quota for the week, and you can work as many hours as needed in order to complete your quota. If you finish your quota before the weeks' end, you can either take that time off or make additional garments for bonus pay."

The workers were clearly delighted by this announcement. She could tell by how their eyes widened in unexpected delight and grinned at one another.

"I am also planning to add ten more machines to this mill and four more cutters with the hope of doubling the output of ready-made garments in one year. In addition to men's jackets, we will also be making waistcoats. If we're successful in that, everyone's salary will be raised."

A low murmur of approval raced through the room.

Mr. Marsden waited for them to quiet before he continued. "Once implemented, Kensington will be the second of the Marsden Mills to operate under these new conditions. The other mill is located in the Boston city center. In less than a year, it became one of the top producing mills in the country. I have found that workers work best when incentivized rather than driven like cattle and, thus far, my theories have proven true. I would like Kensington to be the mill that finally proves my point and perhaps convinces other manufacturers to do business differently for the good of us all."

It was only after the employees were reassured that their quotas would not be raised, and they would be paid for a full day even if their quota was met and they went home early, that the new incentives were wholeheartedly embraced.

"That seemed to go very well," Ella applauded him when they retired to her office after the meeting.

"Do you think?"

"I do!"

"Very good. And things are going well for you?"

His personal attention always made her nervous. She smiled at the floor and tried to appear nonchalant when she shrugged, "I suppose it's going well. There was not too much of a fuss, just from some of the men."

"Let me guess. They don't want to work for a woman?"

"Precisely. But they're working just the same."

"Because they have no choice," he finished for her.

He sat down at the desk, and she presented the week's books, which he glanced over quickly. "Output is up, I see," he murmured and followed the lines of the ledger with a carefully manicured finger.

"I'm still sewing."

"You shouldn't. You're the manager." He looked up at her.

"I may be the manager, but I'm one of them, and I want them to know that."

"Why is that important to you?"

"So, they'll know that relations between management and labor need not be a strained one. It can be mutually enriching. They learn from me, and I learn from them. They help me and I help them. Isn't that the way it ought to be?"

He looked at her for a long, quiet moment, before returning his attention to the books. "As usual, I find it difficult to disagree with you."

Although Reese planned to eventually turn over the work at the Kensington mill to a team of managers, he took a personal interest in the project and met with Ella almost weekly. They discussed the business of the mill, the workers, the latest trends in the textile industry, and never finished a meeting without some reference to their favorite subject of astronomy. Ella had devoured the book he'd lent her and was reading the second volume. Whatever she did not understand, he would patiently explain, sometimes sketching illustrations on the desk blotter to make it clearer.

After a few weeks, she found herself looking forward to his visits, to how often he complimented her for the job she was doing and how willing he was to listen to her ideas and share his own. Now that they were becoming more relaxed in one another's company, she found him to be a very friendly and down-to-earth man, a brilliant and witty conversationalist who seemed able to converse on a wide variety of topics but in a way that was never arrogant or condescending.

Even the millworkers liked him. Some even adored him, such as the perpetual flirt, Cora Hughes.

It wasn't long before word began to circulate around the streets of Kensington that the working conditions at Marsden Mills were the best in the city due to exciting new innovations in the way they produced the ready-made clothing that was becoming all the rage in the country. It was far cheaper to buy a suit or a frock off the rack than it was to have one made by a tailor or seamstress. Thanks to the sewing machine and other modern manufacturing techniques, the ready-made market was exploding with clothing that was well-made, fashionable, and affordable.

As well as her professional life was going, Ella's personal life was even better. Her heart was light and her hopes high as she ventured into what felt like a whole new life with enough money to buy more food and some much needed clothing. Auntie Bess didn't need to take in as much laundry or sewing anymore and was busily planting the family vegetable garden in preparation for the summer growing season. Ella threw herself into local charity work, helping out at the unwed mother's home and working with the parish on a plan to set up a settlement house for homeless families.

By far, the most gratifying experience was the letter-writing campaign to the bishop. The response was unprecedented. Within two months, they had collected hundreds of letters with more pouring in every week. They settled on the day of Sunday, April 18 to march to the bishop's residence and deliver satchels full of letters.

Ella had never felt so exhilarated as the day they marched to the bishop's residence in a crowd several hundred strong. They were a rousing sight, marching and praying, singing and waving their placards. All along the route, people came out of their houses to wave them on, carriages pulled over to let them pass, and pressmen ran alongside the marchers with their notebooks at hand.

With the exception of when she received the Sacrament, she had never felt the presence of the Lord as powerfully as she did on that day. It was as if she was walking in lockstep with Him, her spirit buoyed by a powerful influx of grace that empowered her stride and made her heart fill with hope.

"How good You have been to me, Lord! Who am I that You should care about me, that You would send me such a welcome relief in the goods of the world, that You would send into my life such a good and gracious benefactor, that You would allow our humble plans to amount to this great march for the good of Your Church and the world? No matter what comes of this, I will never stop thanking You for the joys of this moment in my life!"

When they finally reached the steps of the bishop's residence, they were met by a short, stocky man sporting the robes of a monsignor. It was Monsignor Bellafonte, the bishop's secretary.

"We've come in peace!" Mr. McGuiness announced when he saw the trepidation on the monsignor's face. "By the mercy of God, we walked several miles to deliver you these letters from parishioners all over the city to his imminence, the Archbishop of Philadelphia."

The monsignor shielded his eyes to look upon the massive crowd that stretched almost as far as the eye could see. He read their placards demanding "Fight for Catholic Workers!" "Vatican! End Your Silence!" "Blessed are the Poor!" He watched in astonishment as union members carried five large duffel bags full of letters to the porch where they were ceremoniously laid at his feet. He could only look at them in confusion.

"What is this about?" he demanded.

"The Catholic workers of this city have organized themselves in order to more effectively petition the Church to do more to help alleviate the injustices being perpetrated against the faithful by the employers of this city," Mr. McGuiness read from a set of carefully prepared notes. "We're grateful for the charity, but this does nothing to stop the injustice! And the Church allows it to go on!"

"What would you have us do?" the monsignor asked none too kindly.

"Petition our governors to enact fair laws, encourage the Vatican to issue instructions to the faithful on how to operate their businesses in ways that respect all human life, rich or poor! The Church has a mighty voice in this world!" Mr. McGuiness shouted. "Let her use it to help the poor! And unless she does, we are considering reducing our weekly donations. The time has come for action! We're asking for some response to these issues by May 1, the feast of St. Joseph the Worker. May the good St. Joseph watch over and guide us all."

The monsignor looked flustered, glanced between the letters and the crowd, then announced. "I will take this up with the bishop upon his return!"

He did as he promised, and a letter dated May 1 was read aloud in every pulpit acknowledging receipt of the letters and promising to bring the matter to the attention of the bishops at their next conclave.

"Which means they'll do nothing," Auntie Bess huffed at the coals hissing and spitting as they died out in the metal belly of the kitchen stove several nights later.

"Then we may have to do as we threatened, and do it *en masse*," Ella said gravely.

"Our churches are poor enough."

"Well, they may be getting a lot poorer," Ella said, reaching over and stopping the hand that was finishing the last of the day's basting work. When she looked into those half-buried blue eyes, she saw a quiet desperation that tugged at her heart. "It's the only way, Auntie. We must stand firm!"

"God help us all," her aunt said and blessed herself.

TWENTY-THREE

"IT WAS A HEADY TIME FOR ELLA," Jacqui said while paging through the documents on her laptop. "Even though we might think the march on the Church was a failure, she would soon find out that similar copycat movements had begun to spring up in other diocese throughout the country. This was particularly true in New York where a priest named Edward McGlynn was getting very involved in the local labor union movement. Ella's idea was catching on and she was encouraged by it."

"Yes, but, as usual, the Church did nothing but have a letter read on Sunday," Ari said scornfully. "Things haven't changed much in the last 170 years, have they? She's still as out-of-touch as ever."

"The Church has definitely made her share of mistakes over the years. This will become obvious when you hear the stories of the other Ariellas who all lived through troubled times in the Church's history that are remarkably similar to the problems she's facing today. But this doesn't mean the Church's teachings are wrong; it means the people leading the Church are wrong. Those are two different things."

"Why doesn't she ever pick the right people?"

"Because we're sinners and there was only one Jesus Christ. We're a fallen people, which is why the history of the Church's mistakes is really a history of man's mishandling of the beautiful truths that were entrusted to her. Maybe one day we'll get it right, perhaps when

Jesus comes back at the Second Coming and does it Himself."

Ari burst out laughing and so did Jacqui. "This is historic, Gram! We finally agree on something about the Church!"

"Alleluia. Maybe the Second Coming is closer than I thought!"

"Very funny. But seriously, Gram, with how poorly Catholics were regarded in Ella's day, you'd think Reese would have been more uncomfortable with her involvement in these Church protests. You said yourself that newspapers were some of your prime sources, which means the population knew that Ella Ward was a Catholic and involved in the labor movement. The only way Reese could have tolerated this is if he was already in love with her."

"Well, we know nothing about his private deliberations, but we do know that there were strong feelings between the two of them almost right away," Jacqui said. "God obviously intended for them to be together because those feelings only grew stronger as the months wore on. It finally came to a head one day in early summer. . ."

* * * * *

For the second time that afternoon, as they worked alongside each other at the desk, Ella felt Mr. Marsden's attention on her. She looked up, met his gaze, and smiled into it the way she always did when this happened, which was quite often lately. A sudden quiet would fall over them as they stopped talking, stopped working, stopped thinking about anything but each other. This strange and heady pause would envelope them and make Ella wonder if there was something he wanted to say to her. But she was unfamiliar with the ways of men and would just let it pass, as it always did in the same way. She would smile, and he would smile, and they'd go back to their work as if nothing had happened.

"Surely we've made enough profit to afford to put in those new windows," she said after the second pause of the day.

"Yes, yes, we can afford it, but not because of the profits from this mill. Our overseas investments are paying off twice what we projected," he said and went on to tell her about his financial dealings, even though she hadn't the slightest idea what he was talking about. But she listened anyway because of how animated he became when he spoke about it.

When he was finished, she asked, "Does that mean we can have the windows now?"

He blinked and returned to the original subject. "Yes, yes, we can have the windows now."

"The summer is upon us. It's a good time for construction."

"Hire the workers."

"I'll choose men who are out of work."

"Of course you will," he said. "As would I."

They paused and looked at each other once again, but this time, she asked, "What is it, Mr. Marsden?"

"I wish you would call me Reese," he murmured.

"What?" She blinked, surprised by what he just said. "But it's not proper."

"When we're alone and working it is. . .or it should be."

She was momentarily flustered.

"I mean no disrespect," he added.

"Of course you don't," she said quickly. "You have never been disrespectful toward me or any of us and we appreciate it, Mister. . .er, Reese."

"Very good. Now then, what were you asking me?" he inquired gently, his eyes never leaving her face.

"I. . .just wondered, when you look at me like that. . ."

"Like what?"

She suddenly lost her nerve. "Oh, never mind."

"No, say it."

"Like the way you did just then. I wonder sometimes if you want to say something to me."

He was quiet for a moment, studying her with an expression that seemed to soften right before her eyes. "I do want to say something."

"What is it?"

"I want to say something that does not concern this mill or our business relationship."

"Like what?" she asked so innocently a man would instantly know that she had little or no experience with men.

"Like how I'd like you to come to dinner and meet my sister."

"What?" She was stunned.

The reaction seemed to amuse him, made a little smile play at the corner of his lips.

"Are you jesting with me?" she gasped.

"I'm not!"

"Yes, you are! You're grinning. I can see it!"

He struggled to keep a straight face. "Well, will you come?"

"When?"

"Saturday night. There's a meteor shower at nine o'clock."

"There is?" She forgot herself and gripped his arm in excitement even though unmarried men and women were not permitted to touch. "Could we look at it through the scope?" She remembered herself and quickly let go.

"Of course! It might even be visible with the naked eye. We could watch it from the dock."

"I'll have to bring Auntie Bess. I can't come unchaperoned."

"Of course not. Bring her along."

"What time?"

"My coach will pick you up at four o'clock."

All the way home, Ella's heart felt like it was dancing in her breast, although she wasn't exactly sure why, just that maybe Auntie Bess was right. Maybe Mr. Marsden did feel some affection toward her after all.

"Mr. Marsden invited me to dinner to meet his sister and to watch a meteor shower on Saturday night," Ella announced the minute she walked into the kitchen that night.

Auntie Bess nearly dropped the cutlery she was carrying to the table. "You don't say!"

"I don't know what I'll wear!"

"I told you to get some new frocks. We can afford it now. But just in case, I made you something!"

"You did? What?"

She watched her aunt hike up her skirts and rush upstairs, returning a moment later with an armful of creamy white taffeta adorned with tiny pale blue flowers.

"Isn't it fetching?" Auntie Bess said and held up a lovely frock with a square neck, elbow length sleeves, and a fashionable bustle on the back. "I made the bustle myself and added the trim, the ruffles and the pleats and—"

"Auntie! Wherever did you get this dress?"

"I made it myself! I found the fabric at the fabric store and just took out a bit of our savings. You don't mind, do you?"

"About the savings? No, of course not. But why did you make this for me without telling me?"

"Because I knew you'd scoff at me, but I wanted to be ready just in case Mr. Marsden came 'round," her aunt said with a wink.

Ella sighed. "Oh Auntie, I'm not sure what this is about. . .

perhaps it's just friendship?"

"Don't be ridiculous. He's always been smitten with you, but you're just a child where men are concerned."

She couldn't argue with her aunt. "I suppose you're right. I really don't know what to think about it."

Auntie Bess paused, the fabric still draped over her arms. "Do you have feelings for him, Ella? The kind that makes you feel all fluttery inside like you swallowed a butterfly and it's fluttering around in your stomach?"

Ella nodded. "Something like that. When he looks at me a certain way, but I don't want to sin, so I push them away."

"Those feelings aren't a sin, girl! They're part of our human nature! They're only sins when you do wrong thing with them."

"But I'm a mill girl and he's one of the wealthiest men in the world."

"You know what they say. Love is blind."

"But I—"

"No more arguments," Auntie Bess said firmly, then ordered, "Hurry up and eat so I can get you fitted properly."

As incorrigible as Auntie Bess could be, she was also an excellent seamstress who had an eye for fashion and managed to transform Ella from a humble mill girl into quite the lovely lady for their Saturday evening excursion. Using a magazine bought from the local bookstore, Auntie Bess fashioned Ella's long black hair up into a lovely arrangement of braids and curls, then adorned it with two pale blue feathers that were almost a perfect match for her eyes. Ella had never felt so lovely as she did while wearing a dress fashioned for her by the person who was most dear to her in all the world.

But nothing made her feel as beautiful as the way Reese looked at her when he greeted them in the lobby of his home. He strode into the room, took one look at her, and paused in his tracks.

"My lady," he said. "You look positively ravishing."

She blushed at the floor.

He crossed the room, picked up her hand and kissed it very gently. The touch sent a shiver down her spine.

A tall, mousey-looking woman stepped up to his side and allowed him to introduce her.

"My sister, Lady Esther Marsden," Reese said with his usual elegant manners.

"Miss Ward. I've heard so much about you," the woman said. "And Auntie Bess, how good of you to come."

Esther Marsden was very slender with thin, brown hair and a fashionably pale complexion. Ella found it difficult to find any resemblance to her brother with her small, close-set eyes perched atop of very long nose and thin lips. Her features were sharp and angular compared to Reese's and, although she was not an attractive woman, her smile was as friendly and genuine as her brother's.

They were led into a lovely dining room with a long table and sidebars that had been set with fine china, glassware, and a bottle of chilled champagne. A servant popped the cork and filled them each a glass.

Ella noticed that Reese stood alongside her the entire time as they spoke about the mill and his "experiment" with employee incentives, about how the workers were responding, the early signs of increased output, and how hopeful he was of yet another success with more humane business practices.

"Reese has always been ahead of his time," Esther said. "So much like our mother. She was committed to various charities and was a staunch feminist who believed denying women the right to vote was criminal. She could recite all twelve reasons why women should be permitted to vote!"

"With each one being as important as the next," Ella said brightly. "It is the foundation of all political liberty that those who obey the law should have a voice in who makes the law."

"Here! Here!" Reese said and lifted his champagne in toast. "To all the women at this table who are ahead of their time! May the world stand up and listen!"

Dinner began with savory soup followed by roast turkey and stuffing and fresh garden vegetables. There were rolls with creamy, fresh-churned butter, jams and jellies, and sweet pickles.

The conversation flowed freely throughout the meal and into the dessert service held in a spacious parlor. Ella marveled at how relaxed and at home she felt in the house that had, at first, seemed so luxurious and other-worldly to her. Perhaps it was because of Esther, who was so warm and gracious and witty in her anecdotes about her and Reese when they were children.

"One day, when Reese was ten and I was eight, we decided to set sail around the world," she began while Reese shook his head in his brandy. "We were in the little rowboat with yellow ducks painted on the side that our father had bought us for Christmas one year."

"We christened it the 'Quackadoodle,'" Reese informed, then pointed at Esther. "It was her idea."

She scoffed indignantly. "Yes, and then you proceeded to crack an expensive bottle of vintage champagne over the bow! Father was furious when he heard what you did."

They all laughed.

"Well, it didn't keep us from paddling off downriver until the tide caught our little boat and set us ashore at Penn's Landing in the middle of a naval warship exhibition," Esther continued. "There we were, in our little boat with the yellow ducks on the side, amidst dozens of armed warships with sailors standing at attention along the rails."

"Esther started crying for our mother, and I couldn't think of what to do, so I just stood up and saluted the sailors," Reese recalled, and they all laughed again as he reenacted his younger self. "A few of them saluted me back and, in a short while, our little vessel was fished out of the water and brought ashore."

"That was the end of our trip around the world," Esther giggled.

The lighthearted story warmed Ella's heart, as did the way Reese and Esther treated their servants. There was a friendly familiarity between master and servant that was clearly not for show but was quite genuine and very much aligned with the way Reese treated the workers at the mill.

Ella's entire life had been spent believing the wealthy were a cold-hearted, greedy, and conniving people, and yet, in the course of just a few months, this tall and elegantly handsome man with his sensitive heart and visionary mind was introducing her to a whole new breed of wealthy men. Reese Marsden gave her hope that those with money and power might actually be a force for good rather than for oppression.

These thoughts occupied her mind as she watched him interacting with his sister, whom he was obviously very fond of, and with Auntie Bess, and with whatever servants came to refresh his brandy or offer another tray of sweets. He was gentle with all, yet in a strong and confident way that made her wonder if she had ever met anyone quite like him before.

She was even more intrigued when he checked his watch, then caught her eye and announced that it was nine o'clock.

"It's time," he said and offered his arm. "Let us retire to the observatory."

"Yes, let's," Esther said and linked arms with Auntie Bess. "I don't know a thing about the stars!"

"Me neither, but Ella has been watching them since she was a babe."

The lights in the observatory were dim but Reese's movements were sure as he set up the scope in the exact position he wanted, then drew up a pair of chairs. He straddled one, put his eye to the scope, and began to scan the heavens.

"Ah! There we are!" he said and gazed intently into the lens. "The heavens are exploding!" he said excitedly. "Come here, Ella—quickly!" She rushed to his side and took his seat the minute he abandoned it. "Look straight up!"

"I see it! Oh! I see it!" She gasped and watched the bright white flashes of light streaking across the sky. "Oh, my! There are so many of them! They're coming from all directions! Auntie! Quick! Come see!"

"No, no. I'm afraid I'll break it. You look, Ella."

"Esther?" Reese asked.

"Just a peek!"

Ella abandoned the chair long enough for Esther to look into the lens. "Oh, my heavens! It's spectacular!"

"Isn't it?" Ella asked excitedly. "I've never seen anything like it!"

Esther smiled warmly at her. "I can see Reese has found a fellow enthusiast in the stars. Would we be rude if we returned to those sweet cakes in the parlor while you two indulge yourselves in the heavens?"

"Not at all," Reese said.

Although Ella should never have been left alone without a chaperone, Auntie Bess was not about to pass up on more delicacies and quickly followed Esther out of the room.

A moment later, Ella was once again peering into the lens, watching the tails of what appeared to be dozens of meteors streak across the sky.

"Where are they all coming from?" she wondered, never taking her eye off the lens.

"Very deep in space, we cannot fathom the depths of it. At least not yet."

"I read that they're building more powerful telescopes. Is that true?"

"It is. But I believe we'll be able to see this tonight with the naked eye. Let's go out on the dock, shall we?"

He took her hand and led her across a gravel path and onto the plush green lawn that sloped down to a wooden dock. It rocked peacefully on the placid waters as they walked out to the end where benches sat alongside the rails.

"This is what I do sometimes at night," Reese said, letting go of her hand and stretching himself out on his back on the bench. "Try it."

Ella went to the opposite bench, laid down, and did the same.

When she looked up into the sky, the meteor shower was at the height of its brilliance and made a spectacular show.

"Oh! Look at it! It's like. . .like something out of a dream," Ella sighed and was so captivated by the sight she could do nothing but gape at the sky in enchanted wonder.

"Don't you wish to know about all that's out there?" Reese asked.

"I do. I love to read about it."

"I do too. And you're not bored with it?"

"No, why would I be?" she asked and looked over at him. All she could see of him was the glint of his eyes.

"I don't know any woman with a mind like yours, Ella. The

women I see have no regard for the sciences, or anything that interests me, for that matter."

"Then why do you see them?"

He sighed. "Father."

"Oh."

"He fancies us to be American royalty. How quickly he forgets that he started out with a fifty-dollar investment, a single-room shop, a wife, and a newborn son to take care of."

"Really? So, you had poor beginnings?"

"Yes, but I don't remember them. By the time I was old enough to understand, he had made a mogul out of himself. I grew up with servants, luxury, money, everything but what I really wanted."

"What is that?"

"My own life."

They looked at each other in the dark. "What would you do with it, Reese?"

"First, I would attend Oxford and get my degree in astronomy. Then I would come back to the continent and set up a staff who would take over the mills and run them the right way, where everyone profits, not just my family. And I would consider becoming a lobbyist and use my money to influence lawmakers to create laws that will favor both business and the working public. We can never be a great nation if we continue to do so at the expense of so many of our own citizens."

Ella was so excited by what he just said that she sat up and said with great passion, "That's a brilliant idea! This is exactly what is needed! You must do it!"

"You think so?"

She rushed across the space between them, knelt beside his bench and said with all the passion in her soul, "You know how the workers suffer. You've seen it! And yet, it would only take a few well-written laws that could make such a difference in the lives of thousands—even millions. With your money, your connections, think of what you could do!"

She suddenly realized how close she was leaning over him, how her hands were clutching at his lapels, at how they were suddenly looking at each other in the dark in that telltale way that always made her wonder what he was thinking.

"I daresay, you're fetching in a passion, Miss Ella Ward," he whispered just as his hand swept up the back of her head and ever so gently pulled her toward him.

Ella knew what he was about to do and yet the moment their lips met it was impossible to stop him, to stop herself. And so, she allowed him to kiss her, so softly, so warmly, so wondrously that it made some deeply private and unknown part of herself bloom into life. Never had a man touched her like this and, as uncertain as she was about how to respond, her instincts guided her until she was slowly, haltingly, kissing him back. The moment she did so, his arms came around her in a way that made her sigh at the taste of him, feel of him, scent of him.

"Ella. . ." he whispered against her lips, "my beautiful, brilliant Ella. . ."

She drew away, too breathless to speak and could only look at him in a kind of wide-eyed wonder that instantly revealed she had never been kissed before.

The sight of her compelled him to apologize. "Can you forgive me?"

"For what?"

He grinned, his white teeth flashing in the moonlight. "That was most inappropriate of me."

"It was wonderful. . ." she sighed, then remembered herself and sat up. "Oh, I mean, yes, yes it was. . .most inappropriate."

He laughed softly. "Come here." He helped her off the dock and onto the bench beside him. "I knew this was going to happen."

"What?"

"Us."

"But we—we can't!"

"Why not?"

"I'm a mill girl!"

"Not to me," he said. "You were only a mill girl until you opened your mouth to speak on behalf of the needs of the workers. From that moment on, you became the only woman whose company I ever really enjoyed. . .aside from my mother and sister, that is."

She was so astonished by what he said she could only stare at him in abject wonder.

"I fought with myself for months over this. But everything about you, the way we work together, the way I feel when I'm with you, like I'm alive. . .the way I'm not in this life where I've been trapped since the day I was born. . ."

In that moment, as he sat on the bench, bathed in starlight, his hair tousled and his gaze so unguarded, Ella suddenly realized how alone and vulnerable he truly was. Her heart went out to him, and she forgot all about the reasons why she should run away from the idea that he was "smitten" with her, as Auntie Bess liked to say. It just seemed so unlikely. But what he just said made her want to rethink those possibilities for his sake as much as her own. Maybe this really was happening. Maybe B. Reese Marsden, the sender of the boots, the man who sent a nasty overseer running for cover and lifted her out of a life of abject poverty had a romantic interest in her.

"What are you thinking?" he asked her. "Say something, Ella."

"Are we in love?"

Her inexperience, her innocence, was so obvious it was touching. "Perhaps," he agreed softly. "Is that how you feel for me?"

"I push away what I feel for you, Reese."

"Why?"

"Because it's so implausible."

He reached, touched her cheek ever so tenderly. "Don't push it away anymore. Let us see it."

She nodded, then whispered, "But I can't do anything immoral, Reese. My faith. . ."

"No! I'm not asking you for that."

"But I'm a Catholic! How far can this really go?"

"Does the Church not have room for another Catholic?"

She could only look at him in amazement. "You would do that?"

"If it comes to that, I certainly wouldn't let it stop me. I'm an admirer of Orestes Brownson, you know."

"The Yankee convert?"

"The same. He was a brilliant intellectual. He put much thought into his spiritual life, you know. He rejected several forms of Protestantism and even embraced Transcendentalism before he came to the conclusion that Catholicism was the only way to curb man's unruly nature and ensure the success of democracy. I am inclined to agree with him. My mother did too, but she died before she could do anything about it."

"Do you think she might have converted?"

"It was looking increasingly likely toward the end."

"But what about your father?"

"Definitely not Father. He hates the 'popers,' as he calls them."

"Oh dear. . ."

"But he's dying, Ella."

"Oh." She said and let out her breath in one long, windy sigh. "What about the people at the mill, your business associates? How do we explain—"

He put a finger to her lips and planted an affectionate kiss on her brow. "All of this will work itself out in time. For now, let us just be about our own private business and, if the time should come for us to make an announcement, we will do so."

"I suppose you're right," she said, her eyes dropping shyly to her lap.

He was quiet for a moment, then asked softly, "Are you sure, Ella? If you don't have the same feelings for me—"

"But I do," she said and touched his hand as if to emphasize her words, her feelings, in that heady moment. "I just never wanted those feelings. I thought I was just another one of your charities, or that perhaps you were grooming me for, er, things that are not mentionable."

"Good God, woman. Where are you getting such thoughts? Am I that cold?"

He looked genuinely concerned and it actually made her giggle. "No, you're not. You've always been the perfect gentleman. That's why I've been so. . .so hesitant. I suppose I shall have to rethink all this now."

"I should hope so."

She smiled and so did he and, for a brief moment, they sat side-by-side on the bench while the meteor shower sprayed the sky above them with dazzling white streaks of light they no longer cared to notice.

TWENTY-FOUR

ARI WAS MESMERIZED by the way the romance between Ella and Reese bloomed so naturally from their mutual interests. It reminded her of Jesse, of the hate crime case that enveloped their lives at the moment, and of how much more seemed to be blossoming between them. Even now, she could almost feel his eyes on her as the elevator door closed earlier that night, how directly, how boldly he captured her gaze and plainly revealed an interest that went far beyond just the case. *This is the way a man should act when he's interested in a woman,* she thought to herself, *with boldness and confidence.*

"Courtship in the Victorian Age was beyond the pale, even by my standards," Jacqui was saying. "Unwed men and women were never permitted to touch, to be alone, to address each other by their first names, or even to look too long into each other's eyes. Of course, that doesn't mean the rules were always followed. Chaperones, especially those like Auntie Bess who wanted nothing more than to see Ella married off to one of the richest men in the world, had a way of wandering off and letting the couple have some quality time to themselves."

"But how did couples get to know each other back then?" Ari wondered. "Nowadays, people don't get married until they've lived together for a while just to be sure the relationship works in all of the rooms of the house, including the bedroom."

"Not so in Ella's day, but that's not to say women were in shackles.

The feminist movement was born during her lifetime, only it was a whole different view of how to improve the lot of women. Headed up by Susan B. Anthony and Elizabeth Cady Stanton, they fought for acceptance and equality for women for who they were—women. They wanted to be women, to be child-bearers, to be wives and mothers, as well as to be professionals, if God so called them, but they wanted those roles to be on equal footing with the roles of men.

"They also believed in holding men accountable for their behavior both in and out of the bedroom and were vehemently against allowing men to control what women did with their bodies. Forcing women to use contraception or to resort to abortion were practices they believed exploited women and allowed men to get away with abusing them. Shutting down their reproductive organs was not at all palatable to them. In fact, they viewed it as playing into men's hands who used these means to turn women into objects of pleasure rather than as people worthy of love and respect."

"They have a point. . .in a way," Ari agreed. "But we've come a long way since the Victorian era when dating couples couldn't even hold hands in public."

"By the way, there was really no such thing as dating either."

"What do you mean?"

"It was courtship. When a man called on a woman in those days, it was because he was serious about her and was looking for a life-long companion. These were hardworking folks who didn't have a lot of time on their hands. They courted with the intent of discovering if they were compatible enough for marriage. If not, they withdrew their interest in one another and moved on."

"Now that's something I could live with, mature men who aren't afraid of commitment," Ari said and found it difficult to hide the scorn in her voice.

Jack had always been commitment-phobic. She used to tease him about it only because she didn't want him to think she was pressuring him for a commitment, even though this was exactly what she'd wanted. Thank God she didn't get her way! Although Jack was a good-looking man by any woman's standard, he was indecisive, somewhat clingy, and totally unreliable.

Even after just a few brief encounters, Jesse seemed like the exact opposite. He was very comfortable in his own skin and much too confident to cling. As for how reliable he was, only time would tell.

"It's no wonder the feminist movement grew out of the Victorian era," Jacqui was saying. "Susan B. Anthony and Elizabeth Cady-Stanton published a journal during these years called *Revolution* which struck a chord with women of all ages and classes and was read by women in that era almost as faithfully as the Bible."

"But it still must have been strange for Ella to find herself accepted into the family of a robber baron, the same people she was marching against in the union," Ari speculated.

"She did struggle with it, but there were other wealthy tycoons of the era who were visionaries like Reese. Andrew Carnegie was a giant among the robber barons in his time, making as much money in steel as J. P. Morgan made in banking. But he chose to donate the majority of his fortune upon his death. One of his most famous sayings was, 'The man who dies rich dies disgraced.'

"Francis Drexel, the Roman Catholic mogul of Wall Street, sat on the board of just about every charity in Philadelphia, and his wife opened the doors of their home to anyone in need three afternoons a week. Thanks to this example, their daughter, Katharine, who would later become St. Katharine Drexel, learned early on that along with wealth came responsibility for the poor. So, Reese was not alone in his thinking, and Ella needed to come to grips with the fact that she could do far greater work with wealth than she could without it.

"But it was a very hard lesson to learn. . ."

* * * * *

It took nearly a full day to reach Maryleigh, the Marsden summer estate in Morrisville, which was named after Reese's late mother. He was more pensive than usual during the ride, and Ella knew why. He had been summoned to the estate because Caleb, his father, was close to death.

The news had come suddenly, unexpectedly, in the middle of a Sunday afternoon when they had been indulging in their new favorite activity—sitting on a blanket beside the river at Marsden House and reading.

"Is that the Chicago paper, Reese?"

"It is," he had said, knowing what she was going to ask about. "And yes, there's news about the Haymarket riot." He flipped open the paper, scanned the contents for a moment, then read aloud. "Eleven people are dead. Four labor activists and seven police. Apparently, the police panicked when someone threw a stick of dynamite into the gathering and started firing on the crowd." He read a few more paragraphs, then folded the paper and announced, "Eight men are in custody for the crime."

"Oh, dear. Nothing is going well for the unions these days. Even my own Church is against us." Ella glanced over at Auntie Bess who was sitting in a lounge chair under a giant maple tree, contentedly embroidering the hem of a new dress for Ella. "Archbishop Corrigan of New York suspended one of his own priests, Fr. Edward McGlynn, because of his involvement in labor reforms. The only good that came out of that affair was the public outcry it caused. I daresay, Catholics are tired of waiting for the Vicars of Christ to start acting like the Savior they represent."

"As they should," Reese agreed and was just picking up a local paper when the sound of hooves thumping down the drive made him pause. A few minutes later, the butler was handing him a slip of paper sealed with the Marsden crest in red wax.

"Father," was all he said after reading the note. "It's time."

He insisted that Ella go with him, that her assistant at the mill could fill in for a few weeks. Meg was the only person at the mill who knew about their courtship, and she agreed to tell the workers that Ella had to tend to family business.

Secretly, Ella dreaded meeting Caleb, especially after Esther described the bitter shouting matches between him and Reese. The mere thought made her genuinely worried, especially while Reese sat on the seat across from her through most of the trip, brooding out the window. It was so unlike him! Seeing him like this revealed much more than she realized about the inner pain and conflict that existed between him and his father. When she could stand the sight of his suffering no more, she reached across the seat and caressed his hand.

"I wish I could comfort you, Reese."

"You comfort me just by being here."

He looked at her, at the concern wrinkling across the lovely brow that was shaded beneath the brim of her straw bonnet. Her hat was adorned with pale yellow ribbons that perfectly matched the simple cotton frock she wore on this humid afternoon in early July. Even though Reese showered her with gifts, money, anything she wanted, Ella would always have the heart of a mill girl and consistently dressed with great simplicity and modesty. At first, he'd just accepted it, but as the months wore on, he began to openly admire this quality in her, how faithful she was to her beliefs.

A gentle tug on her hand brought her to the seat beside him where he could hold her close for a moment and kiss her soft brow under the watchful and always lenient eye of Auntie Bess.

"I love you, El."

"And I you, Reese."

By the time they turned onto Maryleigh Lane, the sun was setting over the Delaware River. As they approached the estate, Ella was momentarily struck by the beauty of the place, by the pristine green lawns that surrounded the majestic stone building perched just beyond the tree line on the water's edge. The building stretched for what seemed like a full city block, its three-story wings crafted with dozens of tall windows overlooking the scenery. It was spectacularly beautiful, like something that belonged in a museum painting.

Several liverymen surrounded the coach when it stopped on the paved drive, along with servants who greeted Reese with obvious affection.

"Master Reese! Welcome home, sir!" the butler said. He was a tall, red-haired man of middle age with a round face full of freckles, dressed in an impeccable black suit.

"Hugh! You're looking fit, my friend."

"The summer's been a mild one, sir."

"And Father?"

"The usual," he said and the two looked at each other in a way that suggested Hugh was very familiar with the relationship between Reese and his father.

Reese offered his arm to Ella, whom he introduced as "my lady" and Auntie Bess as "her chaperone."

"Your bags will be brought to your rooms and your maidservants will tend you from there," Reese informed them as he led them up the drive.

"Maid? What do I need a maid for?" Auntie Bess wondered.

Reese grinned and winked at Ella. "To give you a bath at night, lay out your clothes, help you to fix your hair, things like that."

"But I do all that myself!" Auntie Bess insisted.

Ella giggled to herself. "Yes, but the maids will probably do a better job of it."

"Hmph! We'll see."

The moment the door opened, Ella was taken aback by the opulence of the place. It was almost garish to look upon. The floors were a pale blue-gray marble. The same stone formed a wainscot that traveled halfway up the walls, topped by a gilded gold railing. Exquisite wallpapers decorated the walls up to the ceilings, where enormous chandeliers dripping in crystal flooded the expansive rooms in a dazzling light.

Several doors opened off the broad foyer into a variety of rooms, including a study, a library, a large parlor, and a dining room with a table long enough to seat at least thirty people. Off to the side of the dining area was a sunken solarium fitted with floor-to-ceiling windows that looked out over the Delaware river. The white wicker furnishings were covered in silken cushions of bright turquoise and exotic prints.

Ella and Auntie Bess' bedrooms were even more luxurious, with four poster beds, cherry armoires, nightstands decorated with fresh flowers, and satin lounges positioned before the windows where they could recline and watch the water. As breathtaking as it was, nothing could prepare Ella for the bathroom adjoining her room. It had indoor plumbing, a large clawfoot tub, a marble sink, and shelves full of expensive oils and salts. She had only read about these rooms in magazines and never thought she would ever see one.

The maid assigned to her was named Gretchen. A petite young woman with curly, brown hair carefully tucked under a lace cap, she reminded Ella so much of Megsie she felt suddenly homesick.

"Is everything to your liking, Miss?" Gretchen asked when she noticed Ella's stunned reaction to the bathroom.

"Of course!" Ella said breathlessly. "I'm just not used to such. . .such luxury."

"Oh?" the girl looked confused.

"I'm not of the wealthy class," Ella murmured, reaching out and giving the girl's hand a kindly squeeze. "I come from a modest background."

The girl's smile seemed to deepen. "As do I."

"We'll get along well then, won't we?"

"Yes, m'lady," Gretchen said and curtsied in gratitude.

"And we'll have none of that, Gretchen."

"M'lady?"

"Curtsying. And please, just call me Ella."

TWENTY-FIVE

DINNER WAS A MOST UNCOMFORTABLE AFFAIR. Even in a lovely dress and with her hair expertly braided and curled into the most fashionable coiffure, Ella still felt like a stray cat that had managed to sneak into the house through an open window.

The three Marsden siblings were standing around the server, sipping cocktails and murmuring amongst themselves when Ella and Auntie Bess entered the room. When Reese saw her, his eyes lit with pleasure the way they always did, but even his appreciation couldn't dispel her feelings of being terribly out of place. If he noticed her discomfiture, he didn't let on. Instead, he kissed her hand, allowed Esther to hug her, and then introduced her to his brother.

"The honor is all mine, my lady," Randolph Marsden said as he bent to deliver a respectful kiss to the back of Ella's hand.

A short, portly man with the same mousy brown hair and close-set eyes as his sister, Randolph bore no resemblance to Reese. One would never know they were brothers.

Dinner was a formal affair and it barely got underway before the tension between Reese and Randolph became painfully obvious. The two barely spoke to one another and if not for Esther's presence and upbeat conversation, the dinner would have been completely silent.

"Ward, you say?" Randolph inquired as they dined on roasted pork and vegetables. "I'm not familiar with that family."

"She's of English heritage," Reese answered before she could.

"English? I should have guessed. Someone with your beauty must certainly be descended from royalty," Randolph continued to press, and Ella could tell by the way the muscle was twitching in Reese's jaw that he was annoyed by the questioning.

"I believe we're all descended from royalty," Esther said quickly. "Aren't we all sons and daughters of a King?"

Randolph smiled faintly. "Indeed. And Miss Sadler?"

"The same," Auntie Bess said, her mind keen enough to discern that Randolph was not to be trusted with her background.

It only made Ella feel more awkward.

"I have been praying for your father's return to health," Ella said in an effort to change the subject. "Is there any chance?"

"None, I'm afraid," Esther said. "It's not only his heart. The doctors say he has a cancer of some kind that settled in his lungs. We know so little about this disease."

"Which is why there is no effective treatment for it," Reese added. "In fact, what we do have is so poor, Oliver Wendel Holmes summed up our current drugs most dismally. He said, 'If the whole *Materia medica*, as now used, could be sunk to the bottom of the sea, it would be all the better for mankind—and all the worse for the fish.'"

"Oh, dear," Ella said and quietly prayed for the man who was suffering on his deathbed in a room upstairs.

"And the pain treatments are no better," Randolph complained. "I daresay, he's in so much pain it makes him angry and almost delirious."

"The doctors are doing the best they can," Esther said with a sad sigh.

"They're using heroin. It's the most powerful opioid they've got," Reese said.

"And when it wears off?" Randolph asked no one in particular.

"The doctors have left us with all we need, so we needn't worry about it wearing off," Esther said. "Let's talk about something more pleasant at dinner. We have guests."

"I believe Miss Ward brought it up," Randolph defended himself.

Reese gave his brother a warning look that Ella did not miss. She shifted uncomfortably in her chair.

"She merely mentioned that she was praying for our father and inquired about his status. A simple thank you might be appropriate," Reese said tersely.

"I wasn't blaming her!"

"Martin!" Reese barked for the waiter, effectively cutting him off. "We're finished here. Serve us dessert in the solarium, can you?"

"Yes, sir."

What followed was another tense hour that Ella was only too happy to end by feigning exhaustion from their long trip. As exhausted as she was, sleep did not come easily upon an unfamiliar bed clothed in luxurious sheets that smelled like rose water and a hint of lemon. Not even the dark could cover the opulence in the room, the glistening lamps and plush curtains that fluttered ever so subtly in the cool night wind.

I don't belong here, Lord. Forgive me, but I don't even want to be here, not when my people are sleeping on straw and eating soup and potatoes and drinking filthy water. Why did You align my life with that of the very robber barons who are causing this grave inequity in our world? This luxury, these comforts, are as obscene to me as the vermin-infested huts of the workers I love. How can I possibly be a good wife to Reese if I can't stand even a day in this luxury? All I want is to go home to my simple, modest, happy little home on the corner of Marlborough and Duke. I feel so conflicted and confused. Help me, Lord, for my heart is breaking!

A parade of doctors in and out of Maryleigh the following day told Ella that the end was near for Caleb Marsden. Reese was particularly occupied with the doctors, lawyers, and various business leaders who were all preparing for the transfer of the estate from Caleb to Reese.

Despite how busy he was during the day, Reese was particularly attentive to her at dinner, engaging in a lively discussion about their favorite subject of astronomy. Even the caustic Randolph was impressed by her grasp on science and, for at least a short while, the tension in the dining room eased.

"What is it, Ella?" Reese asked later, when Auntie Bess decided to retire early and deliberately left them alone in the solarium. "Come here," he beckoned from where he sat on a bench in front of an enormous mahogany piano. He took both her hands and drew her between his legs. "Your eyes are sad. What is in your heart?"

She looked down into his upturned face and felt the tears begin to well in her eyes. "I'm just so uncomfortable here, Reese. It's so. . .so. . ." she looked around the room.

"Overdone?"

"Yes! All this money, wasted! It makes my heart ache just to think of it."

"Put it out of your mind."

"I can't! How can I forget them? The homeless children who live on stale scraps of bread under that old wagon on Fifth Street, the starving mothers trying to keep their babes alive on a diet of corn pudding and discarded soup bones?" She pulled her hands away, wiping at the tears in her eyes. "I just don't know if I can do this."

"Do what?"

Her heart ached at the sound of the concern in his voice. "Be with you," she whispered.

His eyes lit with alarm. "Don't say that, El." He reached for her hands, but she backed away.

"I feel so torn between my love for you and my love for them."

"Why does it have to be one or the other?"

But Ella still kept her distance, shaking her head. She felt so shaken inside, so physically and mentally and emotionally drained. "Because I'm one of them, Reese! I'm a mill girl! And a Catholic besides. Your world is full of people who loathe me and my church. How am I supposed to feel comfortable enough around them to live in this world?"

The concern on his face only made her feel worse. She watched him come to his feet, ever so gently pulling her closer as he cupped a tear-streaked cheek in his hand. In a soft, pained whisper, he said, "Don't make any decisions right now. Give it a few more days. And if you decide to go, I will understand, Ella. I've always understood you, the way you have always understood me. But I cannot tolerate the idea of your unhappiness." He swallowed hard. "As much as I love you, Ella Ward, I will let you go if that's what you truly want."

"I don't know what I want, Reese, except that I don't want to leave you!" she cried, feeling so confused and flustered and hurting inside, for him and for her. "But I don't want to live here either! Oh! I just don't know what I want! Please. . ." she backed away. "I have to go." Without looking back, she burst into tears and rushed out of the room.

Reese tried to follow her, striding out of the room just as Randolph stepped out of the shadows and into his path. He had obviously been eavesdropping on them.

"So, a mill girl," Randolph sneered, swaggering up to Reese. "A Catholic mill girl. Did I hear that right?"

Reese didn't say anything, just fixed him with a look that might have left another man frozen, but not Randolph. His brother was already stone-cold.

"Does Father know this? You bring home a cheap mill—"

He never finished the sentence. Reese's fist crashed into the side of his head with a force so stunning it sent Randolph staggering backward. He hit the floor just as Reese grabbed his lapels and hoisted him back to his feet, bringing their faces so close Randolph could feel his hot breath on his skin.

"I could cut you off from the old man's money and send you packing with nothing, little brother," Reese growled. "And I might just do it to teach you a lesson, not about what it feels like to be poor, but what it feels like to be saved by the only person in this house who would defend you. Ella Ward. Wouldn't that be something to see?"

Reese let him go with a backward shove so powerful Randolph hit the floor with a bang loud enough to bring the servants running. They caught only a glimpse of Reese as he stalked out of the room and slammed the door behind him.

* * * * *

"Are you out of your mind? A *mill girl?*"

Reese should have guessed the ever-ambitious Randolph would use this newfound information about Ella to try to wheedle the inheritance away from his older brother. Their father's sick-whitened skin, bloated from illness, was flushed with the heat of his outrage as he struggled to sit up in his bed full of crisp, white sheets and strategically placed pillows meant to bring him some level of comfort. The lamp from his nightstand made his bald head gleam and his sunken eyes look haunted with pain and frustration.

"Don't tell me you intend to marry her—a Catholic! No son of mine will marry a poper! You will choose a fitting mate for yourself!"

"I'm a grown man. I can choose my own wife," Reese seethed from across the room. He'd been summoned to his father's chambers as soon as Caleb had heard his sons fighting below.

"You're mad! You're out of your mind!" Caleb boomed with such force it made him sink into a fit of deep, wracking coughs. Reese approached the bed to help, but his father picked up a marble ashtray and flung it at him, barely missing his head as it crashed into the mirror over the bureau, breaking it into a thousand pieces.

Startled, Reese could hear the servants collecting outside the door, whispering and fretting over what to do. But Reese didn't care about what they thought. Ella was probably going to leave him anyway, and he would be stuck with this monstrosity of an estate and a life that he couldn't even imagine having to endure without her.

He turned toward his father. "Why don't you put us both out of our misery and give the damn fortune to Randolph?"

"Because he can't handle it!" Caleb roared back.

"And I don't want it!" Reese roared back. "I never did!"

"Why not? What more could you want?"

Reese ran his hands through his hair. "My own life, is what! I hate this place, the sickening waste of money going to your gilded toilets and elitist friends and the empty-headed heiresses you line up at my door!" He was raging like he'd never let himself rage before, aware that he was shouting, that the servants could probably hear, and maybe even Ella, who was sleeping next door. But he didn't care. Something had snapped within him. He felt too worn down, too desperate by the dreaded fate that now seemed ready to consume the very life from him.

He took a deep, steadying breath in an attempt to calm himself and the desperate rage that was roaring inside him. "I want to make this world a better place than it is, not fritter away my life padding my own pocket and sniffing imported snuff in a parlor with walls full of the latest taxidermy from Africa. That's *your* life. I don't want it to be mine."

"You sound just like your mother!"

"What the hell is wrong with that?"

His father shook his head in dismay. "You're such a disappointment to me. You and your stars and your galaxies. That's all you've ever been, Reese! A useless star-gazer full of dreams."

His word cut into Reese like knives. "It's the only joy I've ever known."

"Will you make me die like this? Ashamed of my own son, worried about my estate, about all that I've worked for?"

Disdain dripped from every word as Reese said, "You chose the life you lived, Father, not me."

"Then GET OUT! I've had enough of your defiance! Damn you, Reese! Damn you!"

* * * * *

Ella jumped as an object hit the adjoining wall and shattered loudly. She heard the door slam shut and Reese's angry footsteps pounding down the hall to the stairs and across the foyer below.

She sat up, having only drifted off to sleep a short while ago after lying awake weeping and clutching her rosaries and pleading to God to make His will clear to her. Not even Auntie Bess could console her. After a long while, she fell into a fitful sleep and had no idea what time it was when the sound of angry voices shouting in the room next door roused her. It was Reese and Caleb. They sounded furious, and she thought she had never heard such a bitter exchange between a father and his son as she heard tonight.

With tears streaming down her face, Ella rushed to the veranda and watched Reese cross the yard, his figure barely illuminated in the faint moonlight as he came to the water's edge. He stopped, bent over, his hands on his knees as he shook his head as if trying to shake off the upset he had just endured.

Judging by what she overheard, Caleb Marsden seemed to have no love for his son, no concern about how it made his child feel to be called a "disappointment" and a "useless star gazer" by his own father. Even though she knew Reese was unwavering in his commitment to correct his father's mistakes, he was still his father's son. She could not imagine how painful it must be to be treated this way.

As she watched him standing alone beside the water, this man of such power and prestige, who was thoughtful enough to trace the outline of a mill girl's footprint to buy her a new pair of boots, she felt so overwhelmed with love for him that it suddenly felt terribly wrong to even think about leaving him. No. She would never do it. She couldn't do it.

Lord, I asked You to make it clear to me what I should do, and You have answered my prayers. I can never leave him. I won't leave him!

Without thinking, she grabbed her robe and flung it on as she opened the door and raced past the servants collected at the door to Caleb's room. They all watched her run down the hall, her hair unbound and her feet bare, as she flew down the stairs and straight out the front door.

"Reese!" she cried as she ran down the drive and across the grass, not caring about the rocks and rivets that dug into her feet. "Reese!"

He spun around, shocked at the sight of her running toward him, her long black hair and flowing white robes billowing in the brisk summer winds. The moonlight illuminated her tear-streaked face until it gleamed like pure alabaster, lending her such an unearthly beauty she might have been something out of a man's dreams.

"Ella? What are you doing?"

When she came within a few feet of him, she stopped, reached out to steady herself on a tree, breathless and panting from the exertion of her run.

"I can't leave you, Reese. . .I won't," she gasped. "How could I have ever thought to leave you alone in this life?" She asked him, and then herself. How could she have even contemplated it? Never before had she felt such an intense, passionate love for him as she did in this moment. "You will not bear this alone, Reese. Wherever you have to walk, I will walk with you."

For a moment, he was so caught off guard by her that he did not know what to say. Instead, he took a step toward her, his eyes searching her face long enough to watch the tension slowly fade into a look of pure and utter love.

"Do you mean that, Ella?"

"I do, Reese. I mean it with all my heart."

He nodded, and then slowly, almost solemnly, dropped to one knee, took her hand, and kissed it before whispering up at her, "Ariella Maria Ward, will you marry me?"

"What? Reese!" she gasped, tried to hide her surprise behind a trembling hand. "Are you. . .are you really asking this of me? Right now? Tonight?"

"I am, at this very moment."

As she absorbed those words, and the implication of them, a lone tear coursed down her cheek. But then the momentousness of the moment overcame her, made her shoulders straighten and her chin raise, and her eyes beheld him with the same fiery conviction of the stalwart soldier she was in the depths of her pure, angelic heart.

"Yes," she said firmly, her hand no longer shaking. "Yes, I will marry you, Reese Marsden."

He smiled, his sad eyes suddenly sparkling with joy. "I have a ring, just not with me at the moment."

She laughed softly and smoothed his cheek. "I don't care about the ring."

"Of course you don't."

She giggled, and he laughed, and they fell into each other's arms and sealed their promise with a kiss that lasted for what seemed like a very long time.

TWENTY-SIX

"CALEB MARSDEN DIED THAT NIGHT," Jacqui said. "They found him dead in his bed the following morning of an apparent heart attack. He had cancer, congestive heart failure, and the gout. He was a very sick man who suffered much for his sins before the Lord called him home. He was buried in the family plot at Maryleigh, and Reese Marsden became the head of the estate."

"Randolph must have been furious," Ari speculated. "I bet he tried to the bitter end to steal his inheritance."

"He did and went so far as to blame Reese for killing their father with that violent argument the night before. But Reese was not a man to be bullied, and as soon as the funeral was over, he banished Randolph to Canada."

Ari giggled. "Good for him! I would have done the same. And even though Reese didn't want the estate, at least he had Ella at his side and, between the two of them, I can just imagine what good they were able to do with all that wealth."

Jacqui grinned at her granddaughter, her eyes shining with pride. "You're thinking like an Ariella!" she praised. "That's exactly what happened. Ella and Reese were married three months later."

"Tell me about their wedding. Was it lavish?"

"No, no. It was very quiet. They were married by Father Kieran Mc-Donough at St. Michael's Church in Kensington on October 23, 1886. It was the same day that Reese was accepted into the Catholic Church.

"Their honeymoon was very romantic by the day's standards. The new Mr. and Mrs. Reese Marsden traveled by train to Chicago in a luxurious Pullman sleeping coach to attend a week-long symposium on astronomy. Their days were filled with insightful presentations by some of the world's foremost astronomical authorities, and their nights were filled with romance and hours spent dreaming about how they were going to use their money and power to bring about reform in the labor market. . ."

* * * * *

They were only married a week, but Ella was already enjoying the marvels of the intimate play between a man and woman. Not only did it deepen her love for Reese, but the closeness between them, their genuine friendship, their mutual interests, were all the more enhanced by the miracle of married love.

"Reese, darling, do you remember us speaking about opening a settlement house in Philadelphia? For homeless families?"

"Of course I do," he said while admiring her across the table in the dining room of the Grand Pacific Hotel in Chicago. Dressed in a snow-white taffeta gown that bared her shoulders and brought out her dark hair, he could barely take his eyes off her.

"Have you changed your mind about it?" she asked sweetly.

"I can't remember what I said."

"That real estate wasn't a good investment.""

"Oh yes. It still isn't."

"But do you think we should wait much longer?"

"What's the hurry?"

"Families are living in the elements! Winter's coming!" she protested with her usual passion, her eyes sparkling like sapphires.

Just then, the waiter came up to the table with a tray full of her favorite *hors d'oeuvres*.

"You remembered!" she gushed as he placed a treat on her plate.

"How could I forget when the loveliest lady in the house prefers them?" the waiter flattered, clearly enchanted with her.

"You are too sweet, and can I have one more before you go?"

He nearly tripped over himself to place another treat on her plate, then bowed deeply and departed.

Reese looked at her and sighed. "I daresay, until I married you, I never would have guessed you had such a way with men."

A memory of last night's passion flashed between them, and she blushed, fanned herself, and whispered, "I'm rather enjoying it."

He laughed heartily. "I know you are!"

She giggled naughtily. "But don't let us change the subject. What about the settlement house?"

"Yes, yes, you can have whatever you want."

"Oh, Reese! Do you mean it?"

"I do," he winked, and added, "You can thank me later."

"Oh, I will, Mr. Marsden," she cooed in that innocent, suggestive way of hers. For being so new to the ways of women, she was already excelling at it.

Within their first two years of their marriage, Ella was managing several settlement houses in Philadelphia for homeless families, orphans, and the disabled—a situation that greatly pleased local prelates. Now that she was married to one of the wealthiest men in the world, diocesan officials were only too happy to grant her audiences with whomever she pleased.

Of course, she went straight for the top and had several lengthy discussions with the Archbishop, who reassured her that the Vatican's position on labor unions was indeed beginning to soften.

She and Reese convinced him to correspond with state lawmakers with the hopes of getting laws passed that would protect the rights of workers and, most importantly, to let the people know that the Church cared enough to do so.

Meanwhile, the Marsdens were also busy implementing new, innovative safety standards in every Marsden Mill in the country. Although these improvements required an enormous investment at first, the better working conditions attracted better workers. Before long, their garments had acquired a reputation for their fine craftsmanship, and consumers proved to be more than willing to pay a little more for a ready-made Marsden suit.

In no time, Reese had recouped all his initial investment in the reforms. In addition, his innovations were beginning to spread to other establishments. This was all in place by 1888 when the state of Pennsylvania passed factory inspection legislation and established a department to oversee enforcement. At long last, headway was finally being made to eliminate a major source of suffering for the working class.

"We can only hope that they'll actually enforce these measures," Reese said one evening at dinner. "This is why I believe we would be prudent to check our enthusiasm until we see what comes of it."

"Why must you always be so practical?" Ella feigned a complaint and wrinkled her nose in a way that made Esther giggle and Auntie Bess shake her head.

"Cautious is a better word," Reese grinned.

"You ought to do the same, Ella," Auntie Bess chided while heroically turning away a second helping of roasted lamb. She had gained weight in the two years they had been living at Marsden House in Philadelphia and the family physician, Dr. Paul Caulfield, had put her on a strict diet that made her even more ornery than usual.

"I'm very cautious, Auntie."

"Except when you're handing out gloves to the newsboys on Market Street after hours," Esther cut in with a wink.

"Douglass watches over me," Ella applauded their faithful driver, then added, "Speaking of, I've bought a few dozen wool caps to hand out next week. It's getting colder. Those poor newsboys need them."

Reese rolled his eyes at the heavens. "There's no stopping this woman, Esther. She's already distributed socks to every homeless man, woman, and child in the city."

"There's no one else to take care of them, Reese! If you would just consider allowing me to have another settlement house or two—"

"Which will quickly become three or four, as you well know. This is why I don't do it for you, my love. Real estate is not a good investment right now."

"It's never a good investment!" she protested in that fetching way of hers that made Reese ponder the merits of retiring early again. . .with her. It would be the third time this week.

Reese sighed, put down his napkin, and motioned to the server who was waiting to clear their plates. "Come quickly! Save me from my wife!" he joked, and the server chuckled under his breath.

Later that evening, they were sitting in the parlor reading before the fire, when Ella began to sort through the day's mail. Their copy of the *Sacred Heart Review*, the most widely read Catholic periodical of the day, was at the bottom of the pile. She flipped it open and read a headline that took her breath away.

"VATICAN REVOKES PROHIBITION OF LABOR MEMBERSHIP."

"Reese! Look!" She flew across the room, fell to the floor at his feet, and laid the paper on his lap where they could both read the historic event that had just taken place in Rome.

Little did the public know, when Cardinal Gibbons traveled to Rome two years prior to receive the red hat, he brought along with him a statement defending the rights of workers to organize. He claimed that this right must be granted in the face of the public injustices that were plaguing the nation's working class. He asserted that to deter these workers from their only hope of success against the monumental wealth and power they were up against was an even greater injustice.

While presenting this statement at the Vatican, the Cardinal brought up Fr. Edward McGlynn, whose suspension had caused a public outcry that mirrored the same uprising Ella had led in Philadelphia in 1884. He urged the Church to recognize how the people reacted to the way the Church treated McGlynn, as if she was the enemy of the people. Imagine how much worse their reaction would be if this prohibition remained in place, he'd said, ". . .[F]rom the condemnation of only one priest, because he was considered to be the friend of the people. . .what will not be the consequences to be feared from a condemnation which would fall directly upon the people themselves in the exercise of what they consider their legitimate right?"

After two years of consideration, the Vatican finally rendered a decision to lift the ban on membership in the Knights of Labor.

Ella read the last sentence, leaped to her feet, and twirled around in a moment of sheer joy. "Victory!" she cried. "The Church has sided with her people!" She ran around the room kissing everyone, including Esther, who was Lutheran, as well as the servants. "I must see Fr. Kieran right away. Surely, he knows, but if he doesn't, I'll tell him!"

"Ella! You can't go there now," Reese chuckled, standing up to follow her out of the room. "It's nearly eight o'clock!"

"He's always awake until midnight. Come with me, Reese!"

An hour later, they were pulling up in front of the rectory at St. Michael's church. Fr. Kieran answered the door, took one look at Ella's beaming face, and knew exactly why she was there.

"You read the news, Ella?"

"I did! Just now! We came right away!"

"Come in! Come in!" He swung open the door and led them into the parlor where he had been sitting before the fire. He pulled up a pair of old wooden chairs on either side of his own. "The Lord has worked a miracle!" he smiled.

"It's more like parting the Red Sea!" Reese quipped and they all laughed.

"Oh, Father! I do hope this means a change in the position of the Church. Perhaps this means the leadership of the Church will officially take the side of the workers."

"Of course it does, Ella. She thought about this decision long and hard before making it because of the implications. From this moment on, the Church will be on our side. And we owe so much of this to you, Ella."

"To all of us, Father. We all wrote letters, we all marched, hundreds of us!"

"Yes, but it was your idea. And the word spread to New York and Massachusetts and Rhode Island. The only reason why the people reacted as they did when McGlynn was suspended is because the marches encouraged them and gave them new courage."

"At the time, all I knew was that we had to do something, not just for us, but for the whole church."

"The Lord blessed your efforts, Ella, and all that the two of you have done in the last few years to petition the bishops. None of your work was in vain! Victory is ours!"

Just as Fr. Kiernan predicted, in the two years that followed, the

Church proved to be very serious about her support for the working class, and rumors were circulating that Pope Leo XIII was preparing a major encyclical on the rights of workers.

There was nothing Ella wanted more, but in the meantime, she continued to devote herself to the relief of the suffering immigrant community, as well as the various Marsden charities and the push for new child labor laws, which Reese was actively involved in.

After nearly five years of marriage, there was only one thing missing from her life.

A baby.

There were times when she encountered a mother with a child and would feel such a stab of longing in her heart that it brought tears to her eyes. They had made friends with many young couples in the city, all of whom had children, and she would sometimes struggle to prevent herself from falling into outright envy. This was especially hard when they were friends with a couple who had two children with a third on the way after only five years of marriage.

And yet the Marsden's cradle remained empty. Over and over, Ella prayed for the blessing of motherhood.

"Lord, You have given me so much. A husband whom I adore and who adores me, a happy home, the means to help others in need. And yet my arms have never known the pleasure of carrying my own child. If it is Your will that I remain barren, please give me the grace to accept it. But if it is not Your will, I beg You to let me conceive and give my husband a child!"

The spring of 1891 was just beginning to turn into summer when the Marsdens hosted a picnic on the scenic banks of the river outside their home. Their friends were mostly young Catholic couples and a few family friends who chose not to abandon the Marsdens after Reese's entrance into the Church. Although their social standing had suffered at first, it had since revived into a robust and strong circle of like-minded friends of various income levels. The eclectic crowd kept their gatherings colorful and full of various opinions that made their get-togethers interesting as well as fun.

On that particular day, the children were occupied with games and many of the adults were bicycling along the path at the river's edge. They were racing each other for prizes of fresh cider and treats. Because Ella had been feeling unwell the past few weeks, she remained seated on a blanket in the shade with several other ladies, nibbling on blueberry cobbler and watching the men guffawing around the cider barrels. Everyone was so happy and carefree that in spite of her fatigue, her heart lightened just to be a part of it.

"Let's stroll by the river," Susannah Caulfield urged. Being the wife of their family doctor, she urged. "You look a bit peaked, Ella. The breezes will refresh you."

"Oh, the aches of womankind," Ella sighed as she got to her feet. "They never seem to go away." The moment she stood upright, her head began to spin, and she felt herself stumble to the right. "Oh, dear—"

"Ella?" Susannah's arm snaked around her. "What is it, dear?"

"I don't—I don't feel very well," she murmured just as her legs crumbled beneath her.

As if from very far away, she heard Susannah cry out, "Paul! Paul! Come quickly!"

Reese was suddenly there, bending over her, lifting her off the ground and up into his arms.

"Good God! Ella!" Auntie Bess cried from somewhere in the distance.

Ella was vaguely aware of her head thumping against Reese's chest as he ran, of the panicked sound of their guests, and of a child crying from somewhere close by.

"Reese. . .what happened?" she whispered weakly.

"You fainted, El. I'm taking you inside."

They reached the house and Reese took the stairs two at a time, Dr. Caulfield right behind him.

By the time Ella felt the soft down mattress of their bed beneath her, the dizziness had finally started to abet. "I don't know what came over me. . ."

"You've not been yourself lately, El."

"It's just women's trouble. . ."

Auntie Bess was suddenly hovering over her, thrusting a bottle of salts under her nose. "Sniff, girl!"

She inhaled deeply, then shook herself and tried to sit up. "I'm feeling better now. It must have been the heat."

Young, capable, and a brilliant scientist, Paul Caulfield strode into the room, one hand holding his bag and the other shoving the tips of a stethoscope into his ears. He cleared the room and sat on the edge of the bed. "It's just for a few minutes," he told Reese, who reluctantly left with the others.

While their guests mingled in the lobby below, nervously chattering among themselves, Reese paced the upper hall, stalking the floorboards for what seemed like the longest half hour of his life before Dr. Caulfield finally opened the bedroom door.

"How is she?" Reese rushed to his side.

"You can go in," the doctor said and deliberately avoided looking Reese in the eye. "She's waiting for you."

Ella was sitting up in bed, dressed in a comfortable shift, with her hair slightly disheveled and her face beaming with what appeared to be unsuppressed joy. "Come," she said with a beatific smile. "Sit by me, Reese."

He did so, perched on the edge of the bed and wondered what she could be so happy about. "What is it? What's happened."

Ever so gently, she took his hand and laid it on her stomach. "I'm with child," she whispered softly.

For a moment, he was so stunned by what she said that he could barely move. He just sat there staring at her in dumbstruck amazement. "Are you. . .is this. . ?"

She giggled at his stammering, caressed his cheek with her hand, and repeated, "We're going to have a baby, Reese."

"After all this time?"

"Yes! I suspected, but I didn't want to say anything because we've been so disappointed so many times. But this time felt different, and it was! Oh, Reese! Can you imagine? We're going to have our own child!"

"It's a miracle!" he said as a triumphant smile split across his handsome face. "I can hardly believe it!" He snatched her into his arms, kissing her hair, her face, her beautiful white shoulders until she was giggling with joy.

Just then, the familiar thump of Auntie Bess' heavy feet sounded against the stairs. A moment later, she knocked loudly. "Ella? Reese? What's happening? We're all wondering, and Dr. Paul won't say, but he's grinning like a sly dog!"

They both laughed out loud.

"We'll be right there!" Reese said as he helped Ella into a robe. A moment later, he was standing at the top of the stairs, his wife in his arms, grinning like a champion at the upturned faces in the lobby below.

"God has finally blessed us!" he announced. "We're expecting our first child!"

The ladies burst into squeals of joy, the men hooted, and the children shrieked a bit too loudly. Even the servants were suddenly hugging each other in celebration.

Reese descended into the lobby, still carrying Ella as if she was some kind of rare jewel while their guests surrounded them and followed them into the parlor.

"Look at him, will you?" Auntie Bess chided Reese with good humor. "Acting like the biggest toad in the puddle, aren't you?"

Ella giggled gayly. "Reese, darling, you can put me down now!"

"I don't want you to strain anything," he cautioned.

"Ella's tough enough," Auntie Bess reminded him and watched Reese finally put Ella down on a settee by the window.

Unable to contain herself, Ella immediately popped to her feet and rushed into a group of excitedly twittering ladies, unaware of her husband's concerned gaze following her across the room.

"Be still, my brother," Esther said, giving Reese's shoulder a pat. "You can't carry her around for nine months."

"But I must tell all the servants she can't lift a thing and they must help her up and down the stairs and. . ." He stopped when Esther's words registered in his besotted brain, cleared his throat, adjusted his jacket, then scoffed at himself. "You're quite right, aren't you? Here I am, acting like I've never had a baby before."

They both looked at each other and laughed out loud.

"Thank heavens for that!" she said, her face lighting with heartfelt affection as she teased, "Congratulations, my dear brother. You will make a wonderful father!"

Later that night, Reese and Ella lay in bed, wrapped in each other's arms, their baby tucked safely between them. For the longest time, they were content to simply enjoy the indescribable bliss that enveloped them. The moment was so divine, Ella was certain it was the closest she had ever come to heaven on earth.

TWENTY-SEVEN

"OH, GRAM! This is the best story I've ever heard!" Ari said, her dreamy gaze sparkling with happy tears. "I just can't imagine their joy."

"It was truly the happiest time in either of their lives. For a time, planning for a new family member and designing a nursery became more important than the latest stock market curves and the sometimes-deadly antics of the labor movement.

"And just when Ella thought life couldn't get any better, news came from the Vatican that Pope Leo XIII issued an encyclical on capitalism and labor, entitled *Rerum Novarum*. This was what Ella worked her whole adult life for. It demanded that workers be paid a living wage enough to support a family and that liberal capitalism must have checks on its power. It gave workers the right to organize, but stipulated that they could not use violence. Families must be protected as the fundamental unit of society with socialism and communism vigorously condemned. This document was considered a turning point in the Church's history and the beginning of the formation of her social justice program."

"What a triumph for her!" Ari said. "She had incredible odds working against her, and yet look what she managed to do! I'm so proud of her! I'm so proud to call her my relative!"

Jacqui's heart lifted until Ari could almost see it shining in her eyes. "This is exactly why I wanted to tell you this story, to let you know who you truly are. You're not the unwanted child of Donna and Robbie Dalton. You're an Ariella!"

Real tears formed in Ari's eyes, but they lacked the haunted, wounded look she'd worn as a child and, lately, since the death of Marty Mason. Tonight's tears seemed to be inspired more by deep feelings of joy and pride.

Jacqui almost hated to go on. "But the story is not quite over," she said. "You see, Ella had an uneventful pregnancy up until about the twenty-eighth week. That's when things started to go wrong."

Ari fell still. "Oh no, what happened?"

Jacqui braced herself and said very quietly, very gently. "Increased thirst, frequent urination. . ."

"No. . ." The romantic bliss on Ari's face fell away like a delicate veil blown off in a harsh burst of wind. "Gram, please don't tell me—"

Jacqui nodded. "I'm afraid so. Diabetes Mellitus, brought on by the pregnancy."

Ari was shocked. "She had diabetes?"

"It's in your bloodline, Ari. In her case, it was gestational."

"But that goes away, doesn't it?"

"In many cases. And even if it doesn't, it's only Type 2 diabetes which is easily controlled by diet."

A flicker of hope flashed across Ari's face.

Jacqui was forced to quash it. "But they didn't know that back then. Thankfully, Dr. Caulfield was well-read on this condition and did manage to help Ella carry the baby nearly to term. It was born three weeks early. A little boy, whom they named Jonathon Ward. He was healthy and strong, but his mother was not. She never recovered and only lived for three months after his birth."

"Oh no, Gram. . ."

Now they both had tears in their eyes.

"He was the spitting image of his mother," Jacqui said and slowly turned her laptop around to display a black-and-white portrait of a tall, dark-haired man with pale eyes and a heart-shaped face photographed underneath a painting of his mother, Ariella Maria Ward-Marsden. The resemblance between the two was uncanny.

"Jonathon Ward Marsden, Esquire," Jacqui announced.

"The resemblance is just unbelievable," Ari breathed as the hair on her arms stood up.

Is this what my son might look like one day?

"The funeral was at St. Michael's and there were more than a thousand people there, everyone from the Archbishop to millworkers and the poor immigrants whom Ella helped throughout her short life.

"As for Reese, he never remarried. Ella was the love of his life. He and Esther and Auntie Bess raised Jonathon, who grew into a fine young man and a very competent civil rights attorney who married and fathered eleven children, from which you are a direct descendent."

Ari felt as if she was wrapped so tightly in the arms of destiny just then she was almost too enchanted to breathe.

"Ella had been born into a life of suffering and yet, she spent most of it fighting for others," Jacqui mused. "But in the last six years of her life, someone finally gave back to her. The years she spent with Reese were the happiest of her life. Auntie Bess said she would always love Reese for the joy he brought to the gentle soul of Ella Ward.

"But the most remarkable thing about her story is who she was and what she was able to accomplish. She never finished school, made five dollars a week at a clothing mill, and yet was instrumental in the movement that led to the formation of the Church's social justice teaching. Her idea to organize the poor parishioners to put pressure on the local churches spread to New York and Fr. McGlynn and then to Cardinal Gibbons, who went to the Vatican where he argued the same point Ella made at the Knights of Labor meeting. Whether the Church liked it or not, they were a church of poor immigrants and if they didn't embrace the injustices being perpetrated against this demographic, they were on the verge of losing souls either to Protestantism or to Christianity in general. This is what set the stage for the issuing of *Rerum Novarum* six years later.

"What Ella Ward-Marsden proved is that all it takes is one person with faith and fire in the heart to move mountains and make great things happen."

"Yes, but why did she have to die so young, Gram? And of diabetes! Just like I did, only they were able to bring me back."

"Ari, in those days, the life expectancy was only about forty-eight years, so dying young was not at all uncommon," Jacqui comforted. "But in Ella's case, it was particularly tragic because she died only thirty years shy of the discovery of insulin. It was discovered in 1922 by two scientists named Sir Frederick Banting and Charles Best at the University of Toronto. They tried it on a fourteen-year-old boy who was dying of ketoacidosis. He was already in a coma at the time. But the impurities in it caused an allergic reaction. Another scientist named James Collip worked on purifying it for the next twelve days and injected a second dose. This time it was completely successful."

"Thirty years too late," Ari sighed with sincere regret. "What a beautiful person. So giving and committed to her work, so in love with her husband, and he with her."

"Reese spent the rest of his life using his wealth to improve the conditions of workers. I guess, in a way, this story has a happy ending.

Even though she wasn't here to see it, Ella left a real mark on the world. She was truly a lioness of God."

Just then, Priscilla's words sounded in Ari's memory. "*You are a chosen soul, Ariella. You have a very special heritage that goes back to ancient times. . .maybe even a past life. It's all about to culminate into something. . .You are a woman of destiny destined to do great things for this world. You were created for this work, and you will accomplish it.*"

A chill ran down her spine. How uncanny!

"Can I tell you something, Gram?"

"Certainly."

"But it might upset you a little."

"Tell me anyway."

"I went to see my psychic friend, Priscilla, last week." Her grandmother's face fell the way it always did when Ari talked about her spiritual beliefs. "I know how you feel about it, but just hear me out."

"Alright. Go on."

She repeated exactly what Priscilla had said, then waited for Jacqui to look as surprised as she was.

It didn't happen. "Ari, love, I have no doubt that Priscilla might have made such a prediction that now seems to have been surprisingly accurate, but there are ways that she could know this information that are not from God."

"How else would she know it, if not from God?"

Jacqui looked at her over the top of her glasses. "I thought you didn't believe in God."

"I never said that. I think there probably is a God, but I don't think He's the one you worship."

Jacqui took a breath, sat back, and folded her arms over her chest. "Can I make a suggestion?"

"Sure."

"Would you talk to Fr. Luke about what Priscilla told you?"

Ari looked away, back at the computer screen and the mirror image of herself that was staring back at her. It was surprising to both of them that Ari was actually hesitating. Normally, she would have just said no outright, and the subject would be closed for another year.

"I do kind of like that priest," Ari admitted and glanced back at her grandmother, whose face was shrouded in the 1:00 a.m. shadows. "I've already talked to him about a few things."

"And?"

"He was a seeker too. Did you know that?"

"I did. He had quite a journey. The two of you probably have a lot in common."

"He's smart. And he backs up what he says. I like that."

Jacqui smiled, yawned, stretched her arms up high. "Just think about it, love. Maybe he can help you to find your way."

"Is that what I'm doing?"

"I think so, don't you?"

Ari thought about Marty just then, about the little boy whose parents left him on the doorstep of an orphanage and never came back for him. The mere thought brought a wave of that overwhelming, almost choking sorrow out of the depths of her being, from what seemed like the center of her very soul, the place where she was who she was—an unwanted child.

"I just want to heal, Gram," she whispered and swallowed hard. "I'm so tired of hurting inside, of hating myself, of feeling like it was all my fault and that I'll never be good enough."

This admission was so unusual, so out of character for Ari, that Jacqui knew something very momentous was going on inside of her granddaughter right then. And it all seemed to have started with

Marty's death, as if his story had scratched open every one of those childhood wounds that left her so uncertain and vulnerable and lost.

Jacqui shut the laptop, came to the sofa and wrapped her arms around her granddaughter. For a long time, Ari clung to her rock, her lifeline, and cried as she hadn't done in a long, long time.

"I'm sorry, Gram."

"Shh. . ."

"I don't know what's come over me."

"It's Marty death; you haven't been yourself since."

"He was so much like me. I just can't get his story out of my head, and it makes me feel so bad inside all over again."

"I know."

Ari sat up then, trying to get control of herself while she wiped at her wet face with a tiny shred of tissue she found in her pocket.

The sight of her upset made her grandmother wonder about the day to come, when Ari's parents would make their annual appearances. She wasn't sure Ari's emotional state was strong enough to handle it.

"I'll think about Ella and her beautiful story instead," Ari said and exhaled deeply.

"Did you like it, Ari? I so want to share all this with you to help you heal, to prove that you really are someone very special in spite of it all. You don't have to let your parents or anyone else ruin your life."

A smile broke across her quivering lips. "You're right, Gram. I'll try."

"Are you up for tomorrow?"

"Of course!" she said, and the old Ari was back, feigning courage, confidence, and control. "I'll just keep my focus on you and Chloe and the kittens."

"And maybe someone tall and handsome and obviously very interested in you. . ."

"Gram!"

Jacqui smiled and decided not to tease her about the very uncharacteristic flush of color that crept over her face just then.

"It's late. Let's go to bed."

Even though Ari felt emotionally drained, it took a long time to fall asleep. Ella's story made her suddenly, acutely aware of how little effort she made to reach out to others less fortunate than herself. Perhaps it was because of her woundedness, but it seemed as if she was stuck in a paradigm of perpetual self-help that left her near-sighted and self-absorbed, overly focused on herself, her need to heal, or at least to escape the pain with whatever she could find—drugs, mystical experiences, partying. What a myopic existence!

"Ella left a real mark on the world," Jacqui's voice rang in her mind. "She was truly a lioness of God. . ."

So, what does that make me?

A lioness lost.

Restless, Ari opened the curtains, looked up at the stars, and tried to connect with the vast universe beyond. She thought about Ella and Reese and Auntie Bess, whose blood ran in her own veins. About dear Marty with his pocketful of M&Ms. Where were they now?

Her eyes searched the stars for some sign of their life force, their energy, so that she could let it infiltrate her, soothe her, set her free from the broken, frightened, hurting little girl who was still very much alive within her.

I can't go on like this. Something has to change.

TWENTY-EIGHT

"CHRISTMAS IS ALL ABOUT LOVE," Fr. Luke was saying in his homily on Christmas morning.

Even though she woke up feeling exhausted, drained, and physically weak, Ari forced herself to get dressed and come along to Christmas morning Mass, but her mind was hardly on the service. It kept drifting from thought to thought—laying in Gram's arms and crying so hard she could barely breathe, the moving story of Ella Ward-Marsden, and having to face her parents today. There was only one thought that lifted her spirits that Christmas morning.

Jesse.

"Because I don't want you to get hurt, for more than one reason," he had said so quietly and yet so boldly the other night, his gaze as direct as the intention in his voice.

The mere memory made her heart skip a beat and made her vaguely wonder if she should be thinking about such things in a Catholic Church.

"If you think about it, Easter is the ultimate expression of the love God has for us, when He resurrected His Son, but there's sorrow attached to those events because of how Jesus died," Fr. Luke was saying. "There's none of that today. Now we see a little baby laying in a manger and only faith tells us that this baby is actually God— the God who created the universe, the Architect of time, the Giver of life—right there in that manger."

He pointed at the manger on the stage, and everyone looked at it. Even Ari.

Where is he going with this? It's so hot in here I can hardly concentrate. My sugar's low. . .I can't keep my eyes open.

Father was clearly laying it on thick now because he knew he had a church full of nonpracticing "Chreasters," the Catholics who only came to church on Christmas and Easter—like her.

"This is what real love looks like. Like this baby, who is God incarnate, who put Himself and all His power aside to assume a human form just so that we could relate to Him, be redeemed by Him. It's the prime example of selfless, agape love. The willingness to put oneself aside for another."

Who does that anymore?

"So today is a day for love, a day to celebrate love, the love that makes us family and Church. Okay, I know a lot of you out there have family problems. Maybe things just aren't that easy, but why not make this a day to start? And the perfect place to start is with forgiveness."

Seriously?

"Keep in mind, you don't have to feel it to forgive someone. Forgiveness is something that you *will yourself* to do. And why do you will it? Because unforgiveness is a prison, and you're the prisoner. Not the one who hurt you. *You* are the prisoner, because as long as you don't forgive, you're letting yourself be controlled by the one who hurt you. You're holding on to the pain, to the disappointment, to the *whatever*. You have to let go."

How many times have I heard this? Let me count the counselors.

"But in some cases, this is impossible. The wounds are just too deep. This is where the will comes in. You will yourself to forgive them because that's the right thing to do for yourself, not just because God asks this of us, but because you ask this of *yourself*. You ask yourself to forgive this or that family member who hurt you so that you can find healing for the wounds they've caused and get on with your life. If they want to wallow in it, in whatever behavior caused them to act this way toward you. let them. But let them wallow without you. That's the best Christmas present you could give yourself and your family this year."

Is he talking to me?

* * * * *

Two hours later, Ari was sitting across the dining room table from her mother and Ed, the chubby, unsuccessful country singer who played at every seedy bar in Philadelphia and whom her mother referred to as "your stepfather."

"This is so delicious, Jacqui. Thank you so much for having us," her mother was saying for the third time while sampling her plate full of the egg bake casserole that Ari had actually made but Jacqui was now getting all the credit for.

"It's our pleasure, Donna. How have you been?" Jacqui was so gracious, so in control of herself at all times. This was especially admirable on Christmas Day when she had to put up with her immature son and former daughter-in-law who insisted on visiting at different times—making twice the work for Ari and Jacqui—just so they could avoid the discomfort of having to see one another.

Ari was struggling to remain patient with her mother. She was growing angry just by the sight of her. The minute her mother had come into her presence, she'd reverted back to the rebellious teen who had nothing nice to say—or think—about her mother.

"We're still trying to find a house," Donna was saying. "Everything is so expensive in York these days and mortgage rates are soaring, as you know."

"Mommy, can I check on the kittens?" Chloe was restless having to sit at the table when all she wanted was to be with her new pets.

"Not now, sweetie," Ari whispered. "Finish your brunch first, then you can go."

"Aren't you going to show us the kittens?" Donna arched an eyebrow at her granddaughter.

"Mommy said they have to stay in my room until they're older."

"Well, I can come see them in your room, can't I?"

"I guess so."

They ate in silence for a few more minutes.

"How's the night life, Ed?" Ari tried for civility.

He just shrugged. "I get gigs here and there, keeps me busy." He looked her up and down in that vaguely inappropriate way that never ceased to make her feel uncomfortable, like he might try something if he was ever alone with her.

"Is country music that big around here?" she wondered aloud just to keep the conversation going.

"It is in the suburbs more than the city. It's all hip-hop and rap down there."

"I'm done, Mommy." Chloe was so desperate to get away she had cleaned her plate in three gulps.

Ari fought with herself not to laugh. "Okay, go get your room ready so Mom-Mom can come see the kittens."

Beep. Beep. Beep.

She checked her meter. "Sorry, my sugar's been off today." It was because she'd hardly slept last night and what she did manage was fitful.

"Poor girl," Donna cooed as if she cared, but her blue eyes, a mirror image of Ari's, were devoid of all feeling. "This diabetes is so persistent."

"It's incurable, Mom."

"Oh, that's right."

She watched as Ari gave herself a dose of insulin. "So, is there anyone special in your life yet?"

"Not really."

Donna went back to eating. "Well, I certainly understand why you might hesitate after what happened with Chloe."

"Chloe? I'm not following you."

"Well, you nearly. . ." she looked toward Chloe's room and smiled, "you got so sick. I mean, would you ever want to try again to have a family?"

"Certainly!" Ari said just for spite. "I couldn't think of anything better to die for."

Donna looked shocked.

"More coffee anyone?" Jacqui suddenly pushed her chair back and stood up.

By the time her mother and "stepfather" left, Ari was so relieved that she leaned against the door, took a deep breath, and announced, "One down, one to go."

"Oh, honey," Gram said and motioned her back into the kitchen. "Let's clean up before your father arrives."

"Maybe they'll cross paths in the parking lot and kill each other."

"Ari!"

"You're right. They're too selfish for that. They might end up in jail and that would be so uncomfortable for them."

Just then her phone beeped, and she was surprised to see a text message from Jesse along with a picture of his mother, sitting next to him and weeping.

"She loved it," was all he said.

"Oh, look Gram! Mrs. Sandoval loved it!"

Jacqui gave her a knowing look. "I can't decide what I like better, Mrs. Sandoval in happy tears or how suddenly your expression just brightened."

Ari laughed off her grandmother's comment, rushing into Chloe's room to take a selfie of the two of them with the kittens.

"Tell Eleana the kittens are having fun and getting lots of attention," she texted back to Jesse.

They had a few hours of peace and quiet, enough time to spend with Chloe who was glued to the kittens and entertaining ideas about what to name them.

"So far, my favorites are Ben and Jerry, just like the ice cream," Chloe announced.

"I like it!" Ari smiled and fixed the girl's ponytail for the third time that day. "Your grandad will be here any minute."

"Is he bringing the bimbo with him?"

"Chloe!"

"That's what MK calls her."

"She shouldn't have taught you that."

"Well, why does she dress like that? Her boobs are always showing!"

Ari choked on a laugh, which made Chloe giggle at herself. She loved to entertain her mother.

"I'm glad you're laughing, Mommy. You're always so sad when Mom-Mom is here. Why does she make you sad?"

"It's a long story and not a story for Christmas Day. Let's make the best of it and then we'll play with the kittens together."

* * * * *

Ari's father, Robert "Robbie" Dalton, arrived at half past four with Beverly on his arm. She was half his age, a bleached blonde who was always heavily made up and sporting the most provocative outfit she could find. Today, it was stretch pants and a red and green striped top that revealed a sizeable amount of both bosom and belly.

"Merry, merry Christmas everyone!" she gushed as she flung herself into the room and started hugging them. "We've got presents!" she said to Chloe and handed her a Macy's bag. "These are some pretty little things for you, you pretty little thing."

"Thanks Beverly," Chloe murmured.

"Hi, Dad." Ari kissed her father stiffly on the cheek. "Merry Christmas."

"Same to you, Ari."

He didn't irritate her the way her mother did. At least he acknowledged his failure as a father, unlike Donna. She still thought she was a good mother.

Their visit was much more pleasant as Jacqui and Ari served a full course turkey dinner, and even Chloe seemed to enjoy herself as she unwrapped some of her grandparents' gifts. One of the tops they'd bought her was a bit too low-cut but was tame by Beverly's standards.

But what would Beverly know? Ari mused. She'd never had children of her own.

When the house was finally quiet for the night, Ari spent some time with Chloe and the kittens and watched a Hallmark Christmas movie. It was during a commercial that Jacqui got up and rushed over to the tree.

"I almost forgot! I have one more present for you, Ari."

She handed Ari a small, neatly wrapped package the size of her hand. Within was a very unusual Christmas ornament. It was a tiny pair of Victorian button boots that dangled within a porcelain frame that read, "*In Memory of Ariella Ward-Marsden, 1864-1892.*"

Just to remember Ella's story, so romantic and awe-inspiring, brought a flood of emotions into her heart. "Oh Gram, it's beautiful! I love it." She had tears in her eyes as she looked at her grandmother and admitted, "Her story was the most moving Christmas gift I've ever received. Thank you so much!"

"Who is it, Mommy?"

"We're related to this woman, Chloe. She was very courageous. One day, I'll tell you her story. But let's get back to the movie now. . ."

They all went to bed early and for the longest time, Ari lay face down on the pillow the way she used to do as a child, as if wanting to blot out the world, and tried to be grateful that this most difficult day of the year was finally over.

As sleep slowly invaded her weary spirit, Fr. Luke's words whispered from the back of her mind, "*If they want to wallow in it, in whatever behavior caused them to act this way toward you, let them. But let them wallow without you. That's the best Christmas present you could give yourself and your family this year.*"

"Amen," she whispered into the pillow just before falling into a deep, sound sleep.

TWENTY-NINE

THE ENERGY INSIDE the modest Sandoval residence on Maple Avenue in Farmington was boisterous, joyful, and instantly infectious. Ari felt swept up into it the minute the door opened and exposed a room full of people, all of whom were delighted to meet the famous Jacqui Dalton and her family.

"I am honored to welcome you to my home, Mrs. Dalton," said a handsome man, about sixty-five years of age, who introduced himself as Javier Sandoval, the patriarch of the family.

He was a big, strapping man, like his son, and had the same commanding air about him that Jesse had, a kind of quiet confidence that suggested he was totally in control of the commotion that surrounded him.

And it was quite a commotion. Two little boys chased each other and snaked through the room while a pretty Latina woman kept trying to catch them and hush them to no avail. All the while, a girl about the age of eleven clung shyly to her waist. Ari instantly recognized them as Isabella and her daughter Eleana.

Mr. Sandoval's sons were standing in the living room poking fun at one another until their names were called and they dutifully came forward to greet their guests.

"You know my first born, Jesse. He is followed by Lorenzo, who we call Renzo, who is newly ordained."

"Congratulations!" Jacqui said brightly and clasped the hand of a dark-haired man in his early thirties whose clerical collar was sticking out the top of a tan tweed sweater. "This is my granddaughter, Ariella, and my great-granddaughter, Chloe."

"Pleased to meet you."

"You'll give us your blessing before we leave tonight?"

"Of course," he said.

"Next is Ricardo. We call him Ricci," Mr. Sandoval continued. Ricardo looked the most like Jesse. Tall and well-built, he wore his hair long and swept back off his face. His smile was like Jesse's, very broad and genuine and just a tad rakish. He shook their hands politely and gave Chloe's head a tickle that made her giggle shyly.

Next in line was Eduardo, known as Eddie for short, who was not quite as tall as the others, but had the same dark, handsome looks.

"The pleasure's all mine," he said to Jacqui even while his eyes were planted firmly on Ari's face.

Jesse, who was now standing behind Ari, chuckled and muttered something in Spanish under his breath.

"I told you no Spanish, Jesse!" Mr. Sandoval warned. "Our guests are *Inglese*, and it would be rude."

"Yes sir," he said and one of his brothers snickered at him.

Ari was beginning to like this family. A lot.

"And of course, there's our beautiful daughter, Isabella. . .who we call Bella."

Isabella was a true Latina beauty with dark olive skin and long pitch-black hair that fell around her face in thick, glossy waves. "We are so excited about this, Mrs. Dalton!" she exclaimed.

"Please, call me Jacqui."

"Mama has wanted this for years!" Bella said while motioning to the only children in the room, two little dark-haired boys. "These are my children. My husband Raul is working today. Look, Eleana!

Chloe is here!" she said to the little girl whose arms were still wrapped tightly around her waist.

Chloe was playing shy and holding on to Ari's arm, half hiding her face in her mother's side. "Say hello, Chloe," Ari urged.

"Hi."

"She's only shy for a few minutes," she assured Bella, who winked at her with understanding.

"And now, you must meet my bride," Javier said. "Maria? They're here!"

A short, slightly rounded woman rushed into the room, wiping her hands in her apron. She had the same thick head of black hair as her daughter, only hers was shoulder length and held out of her face with a pair of bobby pins.

The first thing Ari noticed about her were her eyes. They were Jesse's eyes. Big and round and brown and full of feeling. Maria's puddled with tears now as she clasped Jacqui's hand and breathed, "I cannot describe the joy this brings me, Mrs. Dalton."

"Oh, call me Jacqui."

"My whole family, everyone here and everyone in Mexico, is thrilled beyond words to finally trace the lineage of the Castillo family," Maria said, blinking away her tears.

"Especially Jesse, her favorite child," Ricci joked while his brothers chortled among themselves. "Oh, Jesse! You're my favorite!" Ricci mimicked Maria's voice in a way that made Chloe giggle.

"No, no, I have no favorites, Ricci," Maria corrected. "I love all my babies equally!"

"Except for Jesse," Ricci insisted.

Jesse threw his coat at him. "You're just jealous."

"Boys!" Maria clucked with a roll of her eyes that made Ari giggle. "They just tease, it's all affection. And you must be Ariella." Maria took hold of Ari's hands and fixed those tender eyes upon her in way that made her feel instantly welcomed. "You are even more beautiful than Jesse described. How can I thank you for arranging this for me?"

"I was happy to do it, Mrs. Sandoval," Ari reassured and smiled warmly into the woman's sweet, round face. "As Gram always says, we understand much more about our present when we understand our past."

"That is very true!" Bella piped up.

"I'm sure Gram will take you on a very interesting journey."

Maria's face lit with excitement. "I can hardly wait! And you, little cherub," she said, giving Chloe's head a pat. "Are you the keeper of the kittens?"

Chloe nodded.

"Eleana wants to know all about it. Did you bring pictures?"

Chloe nodded again.

"Eleana, take Chloe to the playroom and you can look at the pictures."

"Go ahead, sweetie," Ari said, pushing Chloe toward Eleana, who obediently put out her hand. Chloe took it, still a bit shy, and reluctantly followed her down the hall.

Jesse was finally able to take off her coat and she hoped her outfit was the right choice. She'd chosen to wear the sweater Gram got her for Christmas, bright red with a touch of glitter, which she tucked into a pair of high-waisted black slacks cinched with a wide fabric belt to hide her glucose meter. A pair of high-heeled boots completed the look.

Jesse tossed her coat at Eddie, who was gawking at her as if he had never seen a woman before. "Be careful what you say around her," Jesse teased, "She's a reporter. And a very good one, I must admit."

"But today, everything is off the record," she announced brightly, and everyone laughed.

"Come, come!" Maria said and took hold of their hands. "I made something special for you, Ariella. Jesse said you like your Mexican food so hot it makes your eyes water and your nose run so I—"

"What?" Ari turned around just in time to see Jesse put up his hands in feigned self-defense. "You told her that?"

"She asked me what you like." He had that *what-did-I-do* look on his face that made her want to laugh out loud.

"You are unbelievable," she feigned a deep sigh.

"That's telling him!" Eddie chuckled.

"He's worse than that," Ricci chimed.

Jesse growled. "Look who's talking."

Maria ignored them and hustled her and Jacqui into the kitchen where they sat around an enormous table set for fourteen people. Only when they were out of earshot from the men did she lean close, give Ari's back a comforting pat, and say, "Jesse told me about your diabetes, but not to embarrass you," she hurried in defense of her son.

"I know," Ari said. "I was just teasing him."

"He deserves a taste of his own medicine," Bella smirked.

"Just tell me if there's something you can't eat," Maria insisted, her eyes full of genuine concern. "He didn't know this, but my sister-in-law has Type 2 diabetes, and I know she has to watch certain things, so I made *pozole* and *chiles en nogada*, which is just chicken."

"That's fine, Mrs. Sandoval, thank you."

"Maria."

"Technology has come a long way with Type 1 diabetes," Jacqui informed the women. "She has a smart meter that's attached to an insulin pump, and it's all connected to her cell phone. It tells her exactly where her sugar is and delivers what she needs when she needs it."

"Really?" Bella looked genuinely surprised. "I'll bet that's a relief."

"It sure beats pricking your finger ten times a day and using needles," Ari grimaced. "Really, I'm fine, Maria, but I appreciate it." She patted her hand.

Thankfully, she had come prepared and had already given herself extra insulin to avoid the embarrassment of her meter going off during dinner.

"In that case, let's have some Sangria?"

By the time dinner was ready, Chloe and Eleana had become fast friends and apparently spent the hour before dinner indulging in Eleana's new makeup kit. They showed up at the table heavily made up and giggling naughtily. Their eyebrows were painted much too dark, their eyeshadow too heavy, their mascara slightly running, and their lips much too red.

"Look, Mommy!" Chloe said. "We used a YouTube video!"

"I see," Ari said, trying to suppress a laugh at the gawdy sight of them. She knew better than to tell them they looked like a pair of creepy clowns.

"Well. . .it's a start!" Bella shrugged. A beautician by trade, she gently turned the girls around and led them down the hall. "Girls, let's just go into the bathroom and I'll show you how we put makeup on the ladies in the salon." She motioned for Ari to follow.

The two of them could barely keep from laughing as they gave the girls some gentle instructions on how to apply makeup so that it looked more natural. When they returned to the table, which was now full of family, the girls were somewhat more presentable.

Ari was seated next to Jesse, with Chloe sitting between her and Jacqui.

Mr. Sandoval clinked a fork against his glass and said simply, "Renzo."

Everyone joined hands and bowed their heads.

"Let us pray," Renzo began. "Father, it is with deep gratitude that we come before You today, filled with joy and gladness that, in the midst of this holy season of Christmas, You have chosen to bless us yet again with the gift of these distinguished guests. We ask for Your blessing upon them, upon all of us, upon the food and the love that we will share during this meal. And we ask all this in the name of Your Son, Jesus Christ."

"Amen!" the two boys shouted loudly.

A moment later, food bowls were passing from hand to hand, children were laughing, elders were all talking at once, and Ari let herself be consumed by the jovial energy in the room.

"This food is as good as the company," Gram was saying, and Ari could see that the ever-studious Jacqui Dalton was truly enjoying herself. She and Maria and Javier were already discussing the lineage project, trying to make themselves heard overtop the noise of their rambunctious family.

"So, is your nose running yet?" Jesse leaned close to whisper in Ari's ear.

"Ha ha, very funny," she sneered.

He chuckled and she liked the way his eyes danced with humor when they looked at her. "You're not mad at me, are you?"

"I should be."

"Yes, you should," he winked at her.

Just then, Maria brought out the *chiles en nogada* and everyone cheered at the delicious sight of the steaming dishes.

"I only bake this on special occasions," Maria announced.

"Because it's Jesse's favorite!" Ricci crowed. "Oh, Jesse, what can I make you for dinner to thank you for your wonderful gift?" he mimicked, and Chloe burst out laughing.

"You're funny!" she said, and Ricci grinned, smug with himself for amusing her.

"At least I didn't get her a popcorn popper," Jesse said, looked at Eddie and Renzo for a moment before the three of them burst out laughing.

"She said she wanted it!" Ricci defended himself.

Ari could feel Jesse's shoulders shaking with laughter. "She was only kidding, you fool." He laughed so hard he had to stop eating.

"Ricci, when have we ever had popcorn in this house?" Renzo demanded as he wiped the tears out of his eyes.

"Stop teasing Ricci. I like the popper!" their mother scolded.

This made the three of them howl all over again. But Ari could see by the look on his face that Ricci thought it was just as funny.

"At least he picked out his own gifts!" Eddie teased Jesse.

"What?" Jesse demanded. "Ari offered to help me, didn't you?" he winked at her.

"I did because he was wandering around the store looking so helpless," Ari explained with a wry smile. "I took pity on him!"

"Well, they were the best gifts he ever gave us!" Bella announced. "You did a nice job, Ari!"

"She did," Jesse applauded. "And we walked right past the popcorn poppers because we knew better."

"Ha!" Renzo laughed playfully. "Let's have popcorn tonight! We might as well use the stupid thing."

"Boys! Be kind to each other," Javier said, then looked at Ari who was red-faced from laughing. "Forgive them. They know not what they do."

"Yes, we do!" Renzo roared back into laughter.

"Renzo! You're a priest now!" Maria chided. She looked at Ari as if to apologize but her eyes were shining with laughter. "It's all affection, they love each other."

"Yes, but they're still uncivilized, all of them," Bella rolled her eyes at the ceiling. "Especially Jesse. He starts everything."

"She speaks the truth," Javier gave Ari a playful wink from across the table. "Jesse starts it, then walks away and leaves his brothers to fight it out."

"I do it on purpose to spare them from having to fight me and get their butts whooped," Jesse bragged shamelessly.

"Ha!" Ricci scoffed. "I got you good the last time."

"You mean the time my arm was in a cast?"

Ricci hurried to explain to Ari, "He always taunts us about being able to beat us with one arm behind his back!"

"I can! Just not with one *broken* arm behind my back."

"How did you break your arm?" Chloe wanted to know.

"Uh, well, let's just say I fell down the steps," Jesse said, but Ari could tell there was a lot more to that story.

By the time dinner was over, Ari had laughed so hard her sides ached. The adults cleared the kitchen and then left Jacqui to sit with Maria and Javier to begin their work together. Bella led Ari downstairs to where the men were playing Wii bowling.

"Let me warn you," Bella said as they headed down into the basement. "The beasts are very competitive."

"I cannot imagine what you went through growing up with these four men for brothers."

"I am the baby in the family and the only girl, so I was truly treated like a queen by Papa. He would not allow the boys to lay a hand on me or speak to me disrespectfully, which means I could do or say anything I wanted to them, but they could not retaliate in anyway. Thanks to Papa, it was a very level playing field," Bella said with a naughty wink that made Ari laugh out loud.

The basement was nicely refinished and very spacious, running the full length of the house. While the girls played karaoke in a far corner of the room, Ari and Bella sat on a black leather sectional sofa sipping their coffee.

"I haven't laughed this hard in ages," Ari admitted and decided this was one of the best Christmas gatherings she had ever attended.

"Jesse? It's snowing outside," Maria called down the stairs. "And it's starting to stick."

"I have the Rover," Jesse called up to her.

"That means you have to go buy us some popcorn," Renzo said. "Besides, you're blocking the driveway."

"It might be slippery!" Maria called.

"Alright, just a minute," he called back to his mother. But as he strolled over to the sofa, sitting down next to Ari, he confessed, "I'm not getting popcorn."

She giggled at his antics. "Be serious for a minute and tell me, how did you break your arm?"

"You really want to know?"

"I do."

"Tell me it's because you care about me," he said, his eyes twinkling.

"Will you stop it? You're a relentless tease!"

"Among other things." He grinned down into her upturned face. "Okay, I'll tell you the truth. It was either that or get shot."

She looked shocked. "Oh! Good thing you didn't tell Chloe that. She's having nightmares about the bad people."

The humor momentarily fled his face. "Yeah, we've got to get those guys. . ."

"Jesse!" Maria called down the staircase. "It's snowing very hard! What about the Daltons?"

"*Mi madre me vuelvo loco,*" Jesse sighed, then remembered his manners and whispered in translation, "My mother drives me crazy."

Ari laughed at him. "She's sweet."

"Jesse Javier!" Maria called more forcefully.

He rolled his eyes. "I'm coming! I'm coming!"

"Hurry up, Jesse!" Ricci mimicked his mother. "You're the big, strong FBI agent who keeps us all safe!"

Jesse threw a remote at him, but his eyes were still laughing when he picked up Ari's hand and kissed it in a way that sent a little shiver racing down her spine. "Perhaps we should get going, *mi belleza.*"

"Perhaps."

"Why don't you bring Chloe for a play date?" Bella suggested. "Maybe you could also bring the kittens. Eleana would love that."

"That's a great idea! I'll be in touch!"

They exchanged phone numbers while Jesse went outside to warm up the car and clean the windshield. Just before they said their goodbyes, Renzo gave them all his blessing.

Chloe sat up front and talked Jesse's ear off the whole way home, babbling about school, her friends, and how many Twizzlers were stuffed in her Christmas stocking this year.

"Why do you have a rosary on your mirror?" she suddenly asked.

"Because it reminds me to pray it."

"Do you pray it?"

"I do," he said and looked over at her. "Do you?"

"Sometimes. It's kind of boring."

He chuckled, carefully navigating the snowy roads.

"Why does your mom call you 'Yesse' instead of 'Jesse'?"

"Because that's the way it's pronounced in Spanish."

"Oh. Are you really an FBI agent?"

"I am."

"Do you have a badge?"

"I do."

"Can I see it?"

"Wait 'til we get to the light, and I'll show it to you."

Five minutes later, she was holding the badge in her hands and reading aloud, "Department of Justice. Federal Bureau of Investigation. Wow! This is so cool!"

Jesse smiled in amusement.

"Do you have a gun?" she asked.

"I do."

"Can I see it?"

"No *mi hija*. You shouldn't be curious about guns."

"But I've never seen one!"

"Consider yourself lucky."

"Did you ever shoot anyone with it?"

"Chloe, let Jesse drive," Ari interjected. Jacqui just looked out the window and shook her head, smiling to herself.

"I enjoy her conversation," Jesse said and caught Ari's eye in the rearview mirror. "She is very bright, like her mother and her grandmother."

He winked at her, and she smiled out the window. There was something about this man that she found enormously appealing. He seemed to exude strength, from his confidence and self-control to his manly stature and dark, good looks. But there wasn't a trace of arrogance about him. Instead, as she saw tonight when he was around his family, he was down-to-earth, genuine, and friendly. The combination was as charming as it was irresistible to her—for some strange reason that she had yet to figure out.

"What does *mi hija* mean?" Chloe was asking.

"It means 'my child.'"

"Oh."

When they arrived at their parking lot, he pulled up to the front and opened the door for them. Jacqui and Chloe rushed into the building, but he caught Ari's elbow and held her back. She looked up at him, at the way the faint light played upon the angular bones of his face. The joviality of the evening disappeared as his attention focused wholly upon her, his eyes roaming over her face as if he secretly wished he could be touching it right now instead of just looking at it.

When he was sure that he had her full attention, he whispered, "So what you do you want to do with this, Ari?"

"With what?"

He frowned, pulled her a step closer, close enough to make the attraction spark between them. "With this. . .what is between us."

Her knees felt suddenly weak.

He sensed it and touched her face ever so lightly. "Do you deny it?"

"No," she admitted, "but you don't want to date me, Jesse."

"Why not?"

"Because I only date losers."

Did I really just say that?

Jesse looked at her for a moment to be sure she was serious, then let out one of those hearty, full-throated laughs of his that made his head toss and his hair dance around his collar. "I swear, I'll never figure out what you're going to say next."

She giggled at him. "I'm not trying to be funny!"

"Well, you are," he said, and his voice dropped a few notes lower as he added, "and I like it. I like you, everything about you. The way you look, the way you talk, the way you are who you are."

It was the most romantic thing anyone had ever said to her. For a moment, Ari was too overwhelmed to speak and stood there watching the snow fall all around him, settling in his hair, on his collar.

"I feel the same," she whispered when she finally found a voice, "as pathetic as you are sometimes."

He grinned. "So, you'll let me know when you're ready to end your losing streak?"

I should at least try to resist him.

Well, maybe not. . .

She reached up, brushed the snow off his shoulder and whispered, "You'll be the first to know."

EPILOGUE

ARI LAY AWAKE THAT NIGHT, reliving the conversation with Jesse over and over in her mind, hearing his voice, watching his brown eyes gleam as he whispered, *"So what do you want to do with this, Ari. . .with this, what is between us?"*

"You don't want to date me, Jesse," she remembered saying. *"I only date losers."* She felt so silly now for saying that, and yet it had only made him toss his head in that confident way of his and laugh out loud. Even after embarrassing herself, he was still interested!

Life suddenly seemed so good, so promising, so full of hope.

And yet, at the same time, a mere twenty miles away, a man stood staring out of the window of his apartment feeling like his life was falling apart before his very eyes.

Kyle desperately wanted out of Hades Hood. Before anyone else was killed. Before it was too late.

He wracked his brain for some way out. True, he was never formally initiated into the gang, didn't sport the tattoo, or hang around with other "Hooders," but he was one of their main heroin dealers. Although he wasn't stupid enough to handle the stuff himself, not after doing time for the same crime, he served as a middleman between the users and the dealers. If Hooders wanted smack, they always knew where to find him. Initiated or not, that made him a Hooder by default.

As he stood in the dark room, watching the headlights below cast eerie patterns across the dingy white walls, he realized with a sinking feeling that Yuri wasn't done yet. The inhuman bloodlust in the man would never be satisfied with killing one little old man on his way to church. No. Yuri was not just possessed by Satan, he was obsessed with him, with pleasing "the Beast" because he wanted more power.

In the short time that he knew him, Kyle had seen Yuri exhibit several of these superhuman capabilities. Besides being inhumanly strong at times, Kyle had seen him levitate more than once. While Yuri sat cross-legged on the floor in a trance state, his short, stocky body would slowly rise off the ground, hover in the air for a minute, then slowly sink back to the floor.

The mere sight of the phenomenon was enough to make every hair on Kyle's body stand up. What kind of power could do that to a man? Not even the Satanists who conducted "services" in prison could pull off feats like that.

Another time, when Yuri was "praying" to Satan before a meeting, Kyle watched his face distort until the very bone structure seemed to change. What was once a round face became thin and elongated with hollow, chiseled cheeks and a brow that hung so low over his eyes he could barely see them. He looked like a completely different person.

Just tonight, when Kyle had delivered some smack to Jamahl and his girlfriend, Shakira, he brought up the killing again, and Jamahl had laughed off his concerns. "I told you Yuri was possessed. You said you didn't care."

"Because I didn't know what that meant."

"Well, now you do."

"I don't like the way this is going, Jamahl."

"Why do you keep carping about that? So, he bumped off an old man. What's the big deal?"

"It's murder, Jamahl! We never agreed to this."

"Sue me. Look, Yuri's got the taste of blood in his mouth now, but it'll wear off in time. Just let him get it out of his system. He'll go after a few more churches and then he'll get tired of it."

"Is that what he said? That he's going after a few more churches?"

"Yeah. That old church on Menlo Avenue is next."

"Are you sure about that?"

"Positive.

Kyle was so shocked by this announcement that he seriously considered packing up and leaving town. "Is he going to kill someone again?"

"How should I know? He gives himself over to the Beast and lets it have its way with him."

"Aren't you afraid of getting sent up again?"

Jamahl sighed. "Yeah. I already told him I don't like it that the FBI is involved now. I don't want to tangle with the Aztec. That dude is good. He doesn't mess around."

"What did Yuri say?" Kyle wrung his hands.

"He swears he's going to take out the Aztec."

"You know that will never happen."

"Yeah, but he doesn't. Look, when you talk like this, it makes me nervous, man, like you're going to turn on us."

"No!" Kyle said quickly, firmly. The last thing he wanted was for Yuri to think he might fink on the Hood. Yuri personally offed any man whom he even suspected was turning on the gang. "You know I would never do that!"

"Yeah? Well, sometimes I wonder about you, Kyle."

"Well, don't. I'm a lot of things, but I'm not a fink."

Kyle recalled parting ways with Jamahl and walking toward his car while mentally calculating how he might be able to put a stop to this.

As if reading his mind, Jamahl called after him. "Just remember, Kyle, the only way out is in a body bag."

He paused midstride but didn't turn around. What was the point? Instead, he drove home and stood in his living room, staring out at the city lights, wondering if he should send an anonymous warning to the pastor of the church on Menlo so that the Hood was unable to carry out the attack. Maybe that would be enough to stifle some of Yuri's bloodlust.

No, an anonymous tip would surely come out in the news and Yuri might suspect him and take him out just to be sure. Or, if the note was turned over to the FBI, they might somehow be able to trace it and he'd end up in prison again.

Kyle let out a long, nervous breath, feeling like a man who suddenly found himself locked in a room with no door, no windows, no way out. Whatever was about to happen, he was powerless to stop it.

AUTHOR BIO

SUSAN BRINKMANN, OCDS, is a Secular Carmelite, award-winning journalist, and author of seventeen books on the New Age and the occult, Catholic apologetics and Carmelite spirituality. She currently serves as the Director of New Age Research for Women of Grace® which houses the largest library of research on the New Age and the occult in the world. In addition to educating the public on the dangers of the New Age and counterfeit Christianity, Susan's work will also open hearts to the glory of Christianity, the critical role of women in the Church, and the Truth that sets us free. Contact Susan at www.susanbrinkmann.com.

SUSAN BRINKMANN
LIONESS LOST
A CHRONICLES OF ARIELLA NOVEL

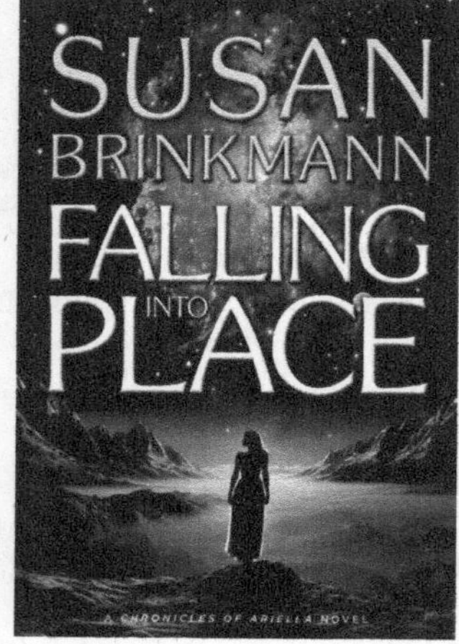

SUSAN BRINKMANN
FALLING INTO PLACE
A CHRONICLES OF ARIELLA NOVEL

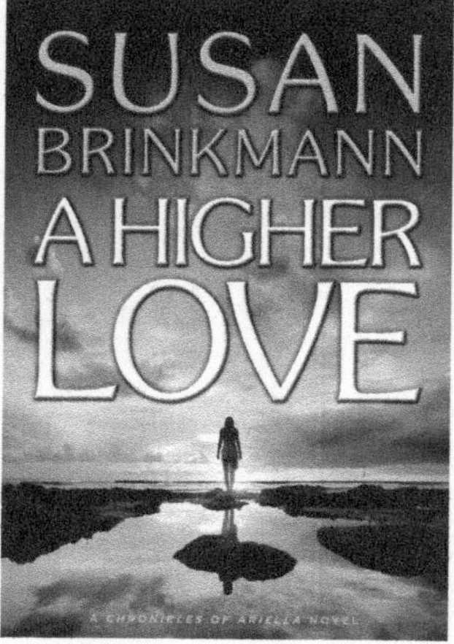

SUSAN BRINKMANN
A HIGHER LOVE
A CHRONICLES OF ARIELLA NOVEL

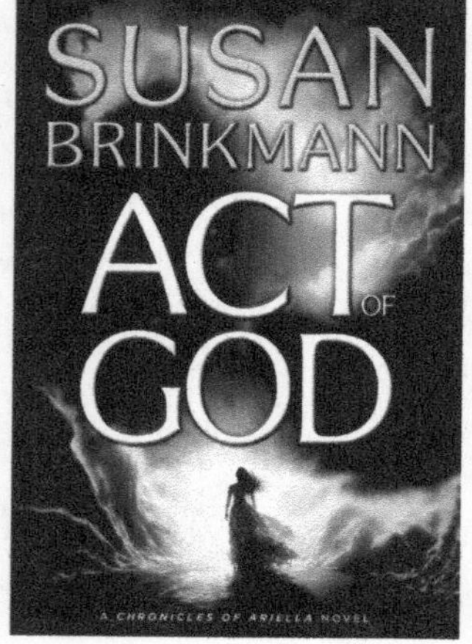

SUSAN BRINKMANN
ACT OF GOD
A CHRONICLES OF ARIELLA NOVEL

SUSAN BRINKMANN
MOMENT OF TRUTH
A CHRONICLES OF ARIELLA NOVEL

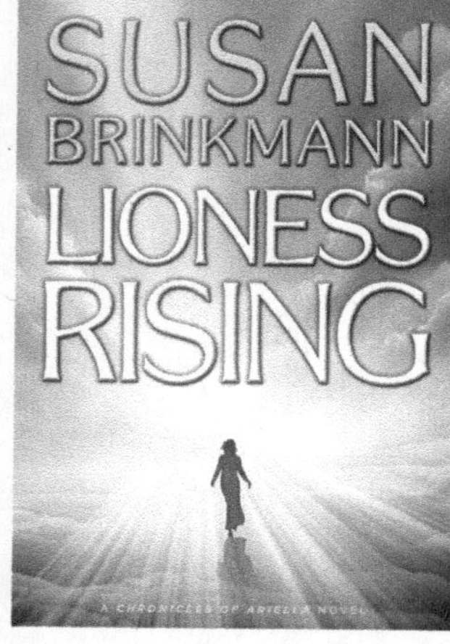

SUSAN BRINKMANN
LIONESS RISING
A CHRONICLES OF ARIELLA NOVEL